TO THE END OF THE LINE

SAGE GREER

First published in the United States by Contrarian Publishing

www.contrarianpublishing.com

Summary: A grad student must confront old wounds and new truths when his older brother's insufferable best friend, who he had a falling out with years ago, moves in and upends everything he thought he knew.

Library of Congress Control Number: 2024927034
ISBN: 978-1-965422-02-1
ISBN (ebook): 978-1-965422-03-8

First Edition

Cover photo and design © Charles Krause

Book design by Jamie Ryu

TO THE END OF THE LINE

A Novel

SAGE GREER

CONTRARIAN PUBLISHING

Brooklyn, NY | Est. 2024

To my sister, like everything else.

CONTENT CONSIDERATIONS

While not graphic, this novel does contain discussion of subject matter that may be distressing to some readers, including grooming of a college student and child death. Reader discretion is advised.

CHAPTER 1

NICHOLAS LIKED TO take the long way home.

Admittedly, taking the bus over any of its alternatives meant either spending hours stuck in traffic or enduring a much more reasonable forty-five minutes being tossed around unyielding seats and fearing for his safety. While most of his journeys provided a happy medium of both, he liked that something always went wrong. Reliability always beat perfection.

His friends tended to be oddly sympathetic when they heard about his commute on the 129, one of the city's oldest bus lines. Perhaps that had something to do with the weekly stories of multiple-vehicle near-misses he liked to entertain them with. Between the constant diversions and regular engine failures that only seemed to plague vehicles on this specific route, it was like the city itself wanted the line off the roads. But Sloane and Ajay failed to consider Nicholas's contrarian tendency to adopt unlovable things as his personal favorites.

He was certainly not the only one with an impractical, if not unhealthy, attachment to the 129. Nicholas was often met with a familiar face or two when he got on at his usual stop, making the bus something of a haven for burnt-out urbanites, despite its sticky corners and discarded empty bottles. Its regulars were consistently grumpy, although he could not remember the last time he'd had to make eye contact with any of them. Still, the rattling familiarity made him feel safer than any state-of-the-art, upside-down tramway car ever would. So did the passengers' propensities to follow a very stringent social code, which ultimately boiled down to one cardinal rule: *whatever happens, avoid talking to one another at all costs.*

The mid-August weather was pleasant enough to make the ride home almost bearable today. Nicholas loved this time of the year, when the constant oppressive heat started making way for a faint crispness in the mornings as the city woke up from its summery stupor. Hints of the focused pep of new beginnings finally pierced through the endless and sweltering afternoons, making him nostalgic for something that hadn't ended yet.

After a record thirty-seven minutes, the bus got to the stop across from the apartment he shared with his brother unencumbered, which could only happen in the middle of a Tuesday afternoon. At least Nicholas no longer had to dwell on the meeting with his advisor he'd just escaped. Last year, he'd made the mistake of confiding in her about his hopes to forego his program's teaching requirements by taking on additional research. She'd given him the summer to reconsider and insisted on seeing him before classes resumed—ostensibly to discuss his plan but really, as it turned out, to ask if he'd changed his mind and inform him that no credit adjustments were possible for any students.

The general understanding in his department was that English PhDs became English professors. Despite his nonchalant attitude to his brother's constant badgering about his professional aspirations, this worried him deeply. Teaching was the last thing he wanted to do. He had no patience, no talent for softening the truth, and was overall the last person anyone would trust to take care of a room full of students.

Seeing that he hadn't magically changed his mind over the summer, Dr. Green—who'd shown little interest in his choices in the year she'd been his advisor—had decided that today was a good time to engage in what she must have thought was a constructive conversation. She wanted to understand, she'd said, why he couldn't just "give it a try."

Trying to shake off the memory of the faux concern in her voice, Nicholas shook his head as he stepped out onto the increasingly busy street.

Day cares would be out soon, turning the sidewalk into a rotary of exhausted parents brushing shoulders against suits who were eager to head home and teenagers who didn't want to.

Their brick apartment building had clearly seen better days. Even with every unit being slowly bought out and remodeled, no one bothered taking care of the common areas with their sticky floors and groaning staircases. Still, it wasn't all bad, especially since Nicholas had yet to exchange a single word with any of his neighbors.

Once inside, Nicholas practiced putting a smile on his face as he climbed the stairs to his apartment two by two, remembering that his older brother was working from home that day. He'd been particularly unpleasant to Will as of late, which he always regretted yet couldn't prevent from happening again and again. Ignoring whatever was making his shoes stick to the half-rotten wooden floor outside their door, he told himself in too-familiar words that today would be different. He would come in, say hello, and head to his room without making any disagreeable remarks or rolling his eyes at Will.

As usual, Nicholas struggled with the rusty lock before entering the freshly renovated apartment. He stopped dead in his tracks in the middle of the living room. Though neither of them were prone to living in squalor, the room was spotless, which was definitely not how he had left it that morning.

"Did you clean?" he asked Will without bothering with the greeting he'd planned.

Will looked uncharacteristically frazzled. His dark blond hair was messier than usual and the top buttons of his shirt were open. He sat on the couch surrounded by construction plans and paperwork even though a perfectly good desk sat in his room.

"Hey, Nick. I was waiting for you."

Nicholas dropped his backpack on the not-quite-hardwood floor and finally closed the door behind him, unsure how to proceed—they were not the kind of roommates who waited patiently for the other to get home for… well, anything.

"Is this my eviction meeting?" he asked tentatively.

As much as he hated living with his successful and somewhat soulless older brother, Will had recently let Nicholas move into his spare bedroom for free. As a second-year PhD student who enjoyed sleeping every now and then, he had been in no position to refuse the offer or resent the pity that had clung to it.

"No, of course not. I told you, the room is yours for as long as you need it."

"What's this about then?" he asked with the tone of someone who had anywhere else to be. He took a few careful steps inside, stopping a safe distance away from the couch. Despite being only three years younger than his brother, talking to Will still made Nicholas feel like an over-eager little boy, always looking for something interesting enough to say and choosing to be mean when he couldn't come up with anything.

"Do you remember Matías?"

Uneasiness pooled at the bottom of Nicholas's stomach. He swallowed, tried to hold onto his voice tightly, and asked as nonchalantly as possible, "Soccer Matías?"

"My best friend Matías, yes."

He felt like sitting down, but the couch was taken by Will and his blueprints, so Nicholas remained firmly stood in the middle of the room. He stared intently at the tasteful rug his brother had recently bought, trying not to wonder why Will had a sudden desire to discuss his college best friend after they'd spent years carefully avoiding any mention of him. The man was everything Nicholas despised wrapped in a loud, obnoxious package and shipped straight from a Texan hometown where he'd been something of a local prince. Nicholas had done his very best to avoid him since the two older boys had graduated college. "What about him?"

"You know how he was in California for a while, working in the community and such?"

"How could I forget?" Nicholas couldn't help the mocking edge of his tone. He had a nagging suspicion that coddled prep school boys whose net impact on the world was only positive thanks to collegiate sports weren't the kind of people "the community" had anything to gain from.

"Right, well, he's starting law school this year. Here."

This put a halt to any self-righteous monologue Nicholas had been lining up regarding the state of the world and rich boys' ineluctable role in making it worse. "Here, as in… Chicago?" he asked, his voice sounding unnatural to his own ears.

"Yes. It was always the plan, except you know how… well, things happened."

Nicholas didn't bother pointing out that he did not, in fact, know. This ignorance had been carefully orchestrated by all parties involved and was entirely how he preferred it.

"Long story short, the decision is quite recent." William paused, looking at his little brother like he might want to say something to that. Unfortunately, Nicholas was too busy trying to remind his body that it wasn't falling from the top of a cliff to add anything to the conversation.

William continued with a sigh. "What I mean to say is that it's all rather spur-of-the-moment, and you know what the housing market is like this time of the year, so I thought—"

"No."

Nicholas's tone was unequivocal, but there was no surprise on Will's face, just blank composure. The silence that settled between them felt heavy with the anticipation of a fight.

"I know you're not his biggest fan, but I can't just leave him—"

"What makes you think I'd be any better at dealing with the housing market this time of the year when I have a tenth of the money he does?"

"Nick, I already told you, that room is yours," his brother replied dismissively. "I just said he could crash here until he finds a place."

Nicholas knew then that he wasn't winning this fight, not against Will's favorite person. The two of them hadn't lived in the same state in years but still called each other twice a week. If Matías Romero needed a place to stay, he would get one, even if it meant Will had to relocate to purgatory to free up his own bed.

He knew he had no say in the matter and had enough pride not to bargain with inevitability. Instead of the venom Will had probably been expecting, Nicholas released a sigh. "I'm not giving up my room."

"Of course not. He can take the couch." There was a pause, as if both of them were unsure what to do in the absence of an argument. "He should get here sometime next week."

"Great." Nicholas grabbed the bag he'd dropped on the floor and headed back toward the door, opening it with a sharp pull.

He really did try not to slam it behind him, but someone had once assured him that growth wasn't linear.

Outside, the warm afternoon air had once again become suffocating, and a fine layer of sweat settled on Nicholas's spine as he crossed the busy street in a hurry and climbed into the first bus to make it through the mid-afternoon traffic.

It wasn't the 129, but looking at the dirty route map plastered above a scratched window, he realized it stopped only a few blocks away from Sloane's house. On any other day, he would have spent the entire ride contemplating just how inappropriate it was to show up at someone's house unannounced, even if they were your best friend and had told you to feel free to do so dozens of times. Now though, all he could do was sit down quietly and close his eyes while he tried to force his heart to beat at a normal rhythm. Even the Wright biography at the bottom of his backpack wouldn't be enough to distract him from the turn his afternoon had taken.

It wasn't like he and Matías Romero were enemies. They weren't anything anymore, not since their failed attempt at friendship during Nicholas's first year of college. Matías and Will had been seniors then, and the stars of the school's soccer team. Instead of ignoring or treating him like the annoyingly shy little brother who stood in the way, they'd decided to welcome Nicholas into their ranks and show him the ropes of college life.

Maybe the Texan had always been interested in charitable work, after all.

The two older boys liked to drag Nicholas to parties that overwhelmed him, introducing him to people who all looked the same and invading his dorm room to ask what he thought of them the next morning. For much of the year, Matías got into the habit of coming over unannounced when Nicholas was trying to study, fiddling with his pens and waxing lyrical about things the freshman never had the slightest interest in, all of which Nicholas had taken to mean Matías cared about him.

They had spent almost an entire school year role-playing friends—just long enough for Nicholas's teenage crush on Matías to evolve into a real appreciation for his friendship. As he settled into college life, Nicholas had gone from blushing at dinner and hiding in his room whenever Matías visited Will over the summer, to considering him one of his own friends.

Yet all it had taken was one mistake, one single show of vulnerability, for Matías to humiliate Nicholas and betray his trust, making it obvious that the older boy had never actually seen him as a friend.

That had been almost six years ago.

Will, who had never gotten the full story of what happened between them, had chosen Matías over Nicholas when he'd realized he couldn't keep them both. This hadn't been a surprise—the two had met on the first day of college and Nicholas had come second ever since. Will and Matías were so similar, it was sometimes dizzying, their double act loud and captivating enough that no one ever wondered why they were both so incapable of being alone.

Nicholas already knew how the upcoming months would go. He knew the space the two friends took up when they were together. It went further than the physical delineation of their bodies; their love for each other would engulf everything around them, inexorably pushing Nicholas to the side until he left of his own accord.

Accepting that slowly breathing in and out wouldn't help him today, Nicholas looked up at the rolling cityscape and caught sight of his reflection staring back at him through the dirty window. He looked different from the frail fifteen-year-old he'd been when Will had first brought his loud, obnoxious, handsome new best friend home the summer after freshman year. Sure, the light brown hair he'd never learned how to tame, the nondescript clothes, and the typically Fisher hazel eyes—indistinguishable from Will's except for the dark shadows under his—remained unchanged. But he had filled out since his teenage years, and his voice had deepened enough that it hadn't been a source of embarrassment in years. More importantly, he wasn't desperate for Will's approval or dizzyingly jealous of how easily Matías Romero had gotten it anymore.

Nicholas looked up at the sound of someone coughing exaggeratedly, startling him out of his reverie.

"Can I sit here?" a pink-faced woman asked. Despite his objection to the atrociously green coat she wore, Nicholas surprised himself by nodding, only sighing lightly at how much he missed his inhospitable bus line.

CHAPTER 2

"HIS BEST FRIEND being here won't make him forget he has a brother, you know."

Nicholas grimaced. Sloane was the more reasonable of his two best friends, and he wondered why he had thought reason was what he needed right now. "If I was looking for your disturbing brand of armchair psychoanalysis, I would've asked for the invoice before showing up."

"That's all right, I take cash too." Sloane's steaming cup of tea hid the lower half of her face, but her impudent smile was made obvious by the way it shaped her words to sound even more British than usual.

Ignoring her comment, Nicholas grabbed the cup she'd made for him and headed toward her bedroom.

"This looks different," he noted approvingly when he reached the biggest bedroom of the apartment she shared with three other people.

He made a beeline for the dark green couch in the corner, which he was certain was a new addition to the jam-packed room. It somehow managed to match the other miscellaneous pieces of furniture just fine and had the benefit of providing at least one surface that wasn't buried under books, records, trinket bowls full of jewelry, or ridiculously small potted plants.

As he looked around, trying to avoid Sloane's gaze for a few more seconds, he noticed that one of her walls was uncharacteristically bare. Glancing at her unusual choice of sportswear attire and the assortment of art prints, drawings, and photos spread out on her bed, he realized that he'd interrupted her in the middle of redecorating yet again. Sloane's constant effervescence and the new hobbies she developed on a weekly basis were among his favorite things about her; they reminded him of when Emma had started going to school, how she'd come home every night with a new best friend and dozens of stories bursting out of her little frame.

Sloane joined him on the couch, seemingly unbothered by the interruption. She folded her legs delicately under herself. Her many rings clinked as she gathered her fingers protectively around the mug, breathing in the steam.

"Why are you so upset anyway?"

Even though Nicholas had raced to her house unannounced and started venting to her about his afternoon, he thought calling him upset was a bit of an exaggeration.

"I'm not."

"You have been visibly vibrating since you knocked on the door. And you came to my house *on purpose*. Last year it took—"

"Right, right, okay," he cut her off. Nicholas tried to find the right words to explain his reaction but gave up, deciding instead to just say something and see if it rang true. "I was just hoping this year would be different. That I could focus on my research and live somewhere quiet, instead of a dump I'd have to share with more people than it was ever meant to fit."

"Surely living with your brother and his friend can't be worse than sharing a wall with that German couple who spent their days either fighting or making up," she answered indifferently. "You said you know the guy?"

"Yes, he's been around for years." After a pause, he continued. "I mean, we… we used to be friends too."

"And? What's he like?" He could feel the barely concealed interest in her voice, her whole body leaning toward his slightly as she put her mug down on a side table.

It was a well-known fact that Nicholas Fisher only had two friends: Sloane, bold and British and wonderful, and Ajay, the heart of their colorful trio. This was a perfectly appropriate number of friends to have in your mid-twenties, according to Nicholas— certainly as many as he could see himself putting up with. Sloane, who collected acquaintances like the frayed dresses she promised she would one day fix, seemed to find this endearing, if mildly worrying.

The revelation that there existed someone else out there who had once called themselves Nicholas's friend seemed to be exciting news.

"He's horrible."

She frowned. She did that a lot when it came to Nicholas, her round face creasing in the middle in a confusion he knew was just staving off disappointment. "You said that you hadn't seen him in years. Maybe he's changed?"

It suddenly dawned on Nicholas how important it was that Sloane understood he was not exaggerating Matías's awfulness before she laid eyes on the man.

"Oh, I've seen him—Will couldn't possibly stomach a summer without bringing him around, showing him off to Mom and Dad like he's Jason doing a victory tour with the golden fleece." He paused. "Will talks about him so much, anyway, it's like the guy never even left. And I can tell you he hasn't changed." Nicholas took Sloane's blank stare as encouragement to keep going. "You don't really need to know him to *know* him. He is more of a stereotype than a person. You know dozens of him—six-foot-one, athlete, big smile, treats the world like it's one big game that's already been rigged in his favor. Probably has been too."

"Six-foot-one, you said?"

He clumsily threw a pillow at Sloane's grinning face, but she caught it easily and laid it on her lap, possibly to keep him from doing it again when she continued to ignore the gravity of the situation. The look on her face did not bode well.

"Did something happen between you two?"

Nicholas was silent for a few seconds. "What do you mean? Of course not. He's straight as an arrow."

She rolled her eyes at him. "I didn't mean it like that. It just sounds more personal than some jock moving in with you. Like you guys have history."

Nicholas scoffed. "Yes, the history being I've had to deal with said jock walking all over my life for years, and I was just hoping that living with my brother was the worst thing I'd have to deal with this year."

She looked at him with such disbelief that Nicholas almost felt bad for pretending there wasn't more to the story.

"Well, I think you're either being incredibly dramatic and a little self-centered, or I'm not getting the full picture."

He decided not to point out that it could also be both, but she must have taken the guilty look on his face as answer enough.

"And I'm not asking for it if you don't want to tell me," she added in a softer voice. "But whether you like it or not, you'll have to cohabitate with him for a little while, which was an understandable thing for Will to offer his best friend." She looked at him pointedly, waiting for a riposte; he had none. "Being this angry about it will only make it worse for everyone, Nick. Plus, maybe he's not as bad as he once was. I've sure changed a lot since my undergrad days. I think you have too."

Nicholas nodded almost imperceptibly. His throat felt too tight to allow for a better answer. Her words would have to do, since he didn't think he'd ever be ready to tell her the whole story.

No matter what he tried to tell himself, only the burning shame he'd first felt about the whole thing had started to fade away. The anger at his own helplessness and Matías's entitlement still shone brightly in his chest, which was hard to explain with a simple, "I don't like jocks."

Still, Sloane must have sensed that he'd reached his limit. Her countless bracelets tinkled together as she got up and extended her hand out to him, holding his thin fingers in hers like they were breakable.

"Come on, let's go steal the couch before my flatmates come home. We can watch one of those horrid American adaptations you like so much," she said, doing a poor job of keeping the fondness out of her voice.

ಌ

Nicholas walked out of Sloane's house a few hours later as the sun was starting to set. He wasn't sure whether it was the company or the amount of chocolate she'd fed him, but he was feeling a lot calmer and—he could admit at least to himself—more reasonable. He decided to walk the half hour back home, wasting time on the way to look up at the cotton candy sky. Summer sunsets would become a distant memory soon enough.

Closing his eyes against the soft breeze that played with his hair, he could almost fool himself into thinking he was the only person in the city, and the quiet sense of peace that came over him made it easier to admit that walking out on Will had been an overreaction. After all, the first step to being five years older than the last time he'd had to deal with Matías Romero was to *act* five years older.

Of course, no quiet street or pretty sunset would ever pacify him enough to admit any of this out loud. The Fisher brothers hadn't apologized to each other since their mother had stopped forcing them to. Instead, he got home holding two plastic bags filled to the brim with groceries and headed straight for the stove. Will walked out of his room twenty minutes later, driven to the open-plan kitchen by the smell of his favorite seafood rigatoni recipe, gave Nicholas a short nod, and started clearing the living room to set the table. Still without exchanging a single word, Nicholas made two plates—his was bigger but Will's had more seafood—while his brother queued up *The Golden Girls*.

They had caught a rerun of the show in their parents' living room four years ago, on one of the rare afternoons in Wisconsin where it was too hot to be outside, and had accidentally found themselves stuck on the couch for hours. Their mom had brought them ice cream and let them eat in front of the TV, even sitting with them for an episode. It was probably the happiest Nicholas had ever felt visiting home.

The next day, Will had found a way to watch the show online, which had made that year's mandatory summer visit home almost bearable. The next time they'd seen each other was for Thanksgiving, when they had realized neither of them had watched any more episodes on their own and picked up where they left off. Now that they'd been living together for over a month, tradition had turned into habit, although it remained unspoken.

It probably wouldn't work for everyone, but it worked for them. Silence, seafood rigatoni, and a show was all the apology either of them needed.

⁊

As the date of Matías's arrival grew nearer, Will grew restless.

The architect could barely refrain from rearranging the living room every day and asked his younger brother—multiple times—if he had any thoughts on the best way to create a "laundry rotation." One day, Nicholas got home to Will holding an industrial-grade level, drawing thick lines on the living room wall.

"I thought it was time I got that gallery wall together," was all he had to say for himself.

Seeing his brother so involved in making sure Matías felt welcome awoke something green and bitter in Nicholas, so he spent most of his time outside, enjoying the last of the August sunshine.

Ajay was back in town, thankfully. It had been a lonely summer, with them gone and Sloane studying all the time. After a relentless summer of emails, she was still desperately trying to get her department to allow her to pursue a joint degree, even though the deadline to declare it had long passed. It was frustrating to witness how difficult the Chair was making it for her, because anyone who knew Sloane and her work ethic should have been begging her to join their department. Until they realized that, she spent her time reading, convinced that the only way they would let her take joint classes was to become so knowledgeable that she barely needed them anymore.

Nicholas exhaled in relief when he caught himself laughing out loud on the street, phone against his ear as he listened to Ajay's outrageous retelling of meeting their new neighbor. Finally, all—two—of his people were in one place.

Even Will, distracted as he was by the dimpled, curly-haired storm that was about to reenter their lives, had noticed the lightness in Nicholas since he'd been able to fill his afternoons with his friends again.

"You should invite them over," he'd proposed.

"Maybe."

They both knew he wouldn't. Nicholas understood his brother's curiosity, what with his near-chronic lack of friends growing up. But Ajay and Sloane felt delicate, not because their bond was fragile but because it was so important to him. There was no way he was letting his brother anywhere near them, even if it meant they couldn't come over now that Nicholas lived with him.

Nicholas had met Ajay the summer before graduate school, so early that the clothes on his back still bore the wrinkles of their journey to Chicago. From the moment he'd met them, they'd reminded him of a supernova, brighter and more powerful than anything the human eye could see. That was until Sloane had gently reminded him that supernovas were dying stars throwing one last hurrah, and he'd never thought that again.

Ajay was the most alive person Nicholas had ever met. They seemed to be from a completely different universe than the one he'd always known; it was like he and Ajay were two people meant to spend their lives running parallel to each other but never coming into contact. That was the excuse he gave whenever Ajay reminded him of his poor behavior on the day they had met, unable as he was to visualize a world where the two would ever have anything in common. Thankfully, he'd been wrong.

One August afternoon before the start of his first year, Nicholas had been standing in line at a coffee shop on the edge of campus. He still remembered the jacket Ajay wore, both brighter than any shade of blue had any right to be and warmer than anyone in their right mind would ever wear during one of Chicago's hottest months.

Halfway through getting their order in, they had turned around to Nicholas with a distracted expression on their face. "What do you think?"

Nicholas had stared straight at them without taking his headphones off, his brain short-circuiting at the impossibility that this loud, outspoken, colorful person was asking him… what exactly?

Undeterred, Ajay had continued in a voice devoid of any irritation. "Hello? Care to weigh in? I'm terribly uninformed on all things sweet—I've got more of a savory tooth myself—and am simply too hungry to play guessing games or line up somewhere else, so democracy it shall have to be."

"Huh… What?" Nicholas had answered eloquently. He remembered thinking about how long their eyelashes were, how intimidating the length made their deep-set brown eyes.

Still unbothered, Ajay had pointed at the pastries on the other side of the counter with a dark brown finger adorned with a large ring and red nail polish. "They're out of sandwiches," they'd explained with what looked like a pout. "And I've never had anything else. We've got two votes for the muffin and two votes for a donut," they'd continued, pointing at the people around them with a wave of their hand. "Therefore, I need you to be the deciding voice."

Looking around them, Nicholas had realized that almost everyone in the nearly empty coffee shop was looking at him expectantly. Wonderful.

"Croissant, if you're not used to sweet things," he'd concluded, pointing at the third pastry left on the counter. "Unless you're ready for the sugar rush."

Ajay had laughed, turned back to the barista, and ordered a croissant. "Smart."

After grabbing his own order, Nicholas had started looking around for a quiet spot to read, only to be met with the dark-skinned customer—who actually looked about his age—waving at him from where they were waiting at the end of the counter.

"Not as worried about your own health, then?" they'd asked with a smile when they saw the double-glazed donut and over-sweetened coffee Nicholas had chosen for himself.

He'd shrugged. "I'm used to it. You just need to work your way up to it."

"I'm Ajay."

"Nicholas."

After a slightly awkward beat, the soon-to-be first-year graduate student had nodded and headed to the empty spot by the window, not realizing that Ajay was following him. It was only once they'd sat down at the other end of the same table and taken off that horrendously bright jacket that they had looked up and asked, like an afterthought, "You don't mind me sitting here, do you?"

Pointing out the countless empty tables in the café did not seem like it would make a difference, so Nicholas had just shaken his head.

The unlikely pair had ended up sitting together in silence for a few hours. Nicholas, used to solitude, had watched with a certain fascination as half a dozen people came up to Ajay throughout the afternoon, eager to greet or catch up with them and demanding stories about their summer. He had gathered that the other student was in their third year of some sort of engineering PhD and was apparently more popular than anyone Nicholas had ever conversed with, except maybe Matías and Will at the peak of their college years.

But these interactions had remained short, Ajay always finding a subtle way to quickly dismiss the intruders before murmuring a "sorry" to Nicholas when they left. These were the only words they had exchanged all afternoon, so when Nicholas got up to leave, he was surprised to hear Ajay ask him if he'd want to study together one of these days. The rest was history. Again and again, the larger-than-life engineering student had made time for him, showing him the best coffee shops on campus and updating him on their action-packed dating life, even though Nicholas didn't ask.

One day, Nicholas had looked up and realized Ajay was his best friend.

He'd asked them multiple times why they'd unilaterally decided to befriend him so aggressively, but they always ignored the question. "Well, whatever it is that prompted me to be your friend, it certainly was incredibly short-sighted of me, because you sure are annoying," they had said once. Nicholas had stopped asking after that.

The two had met Sloane a few weeks later, at an English department presentation Nicholas had dragged Ajay to, and their future friendship had been evident from the first eyeroll the three of them had shared across the room. Suddenly, shy and solitary Nicholas found himself with two social butterflies as best friends, neither of whom seemed to mind his quiet nature.

No, he didn't want Will's tendency to destroy anything that brought Nicholas joy anywhere near them.

જી

Thankfully, his friends were as enamored with the sunshine as he was and had both been in Chicago long enough to know they need-ed to enjoy it before it was too late. On the last Sunday before the semester officially started, the three of them were laying on the grass of a downtown park few people seemed to know about, their bellies full and their feet sore.

Since Nicholas had admitted it was unlikely that he'd go out and explore the city on his own, these afternoons had become something of a tradition. They would pick a neighborhood at random, grab a sandwich from the deli, and waste entire Sundays strolling around. Sometimes, Sloane would drag them to go antique shopping or they'd follow Ajay into a thrift store. Once or twice, Nicholas had even convinced them to stop by whatever hole-in-the-wall bookstore he'd researched in advance.

The lounging in the park afterward was a nice summer-only bonus.

"Does putting hair removal cream inside someone's shampoo bottle actually work?" Nicholas found himself asking in the peaceful silence.

"I've never tried it," Sloane answered. "Wouldn't it be considered assault?"

Ajay looked at both of them, their heavy eyebrows drawn together. "It's not foolproof anyway. I like food coloring in toothpaste more, or taping off their computer mouse. Is this for your brother?" they asked distractedly. Nicholas's misadventures living with Will again after almost ten years apart had been a recurrent topic of conversation. "You could also replace Oreo filling with toothpaste, although that does take some time and effort. And I guess you're the one eating the most Oreos anyway."

Nicholas pulled out his phone to start taking notes.

"Wait, these are really good. What else do you have?"

❧

Nicholas came home with a certain pep in his step that night. By the time he reached his front door, his friends' bubbly personalities and helpful suggestions on how to prank his brother had renewed his motivation to start the academic year on the right foot. They'd almost managed to convince him that attending his department's welcome breakfast the next morning could be a good way to do that—almost.

Earbuds screwed into his ears, Nicholas scrolled through the email chain about it as he blindly opened the door to the apartment, mechanically closing it with one foot while he dropped his backpack on the floor.

"Hey there."

Nicholas stilled, one hand holding his phone and the other hovering above the new trinket bowl Will had just bought to "liven up their entryway." It hadn't really done much to counterbalance the white-furniture, fake-wooden-floor, generic-art-on-the-wall office feeling of the place, in Nicholas's opinion.

He finally dropped his keychain with a noisy clink. Turning off the music still playing in his ears, Nicholas slowly looked up at the two boys sitting on the couch, his eyes immediately drawn to the mountain of bags next to the large windows.

The dark-haired man spoke again, undeterred by Nicholas's silence. "It's been a while."

"Nick, I told you Matías was coming to stay for a little while, right?" The anxiety was so visible on Will's face that Nicholas wondered, not for the first time, how much Will knew about what had transpired between him and his best friend years ago.

"Right." His mind was oscillating between blank and extremely loud, which made trying to hold on to a single thought difficult. "Didn't realize that was today," Nicholas finished lamely.

At least it seemed like all three men were under the same paralyzing spell, glued to their spots by the volatility of the situation.

The Matías Romero sitting on the couch looked nothing like the twenty-one-year-old Texan heir he remembered. His branded polos and slicked-back hair had been replaced by unruly curls and a plain white t-shirt that complimented the California tan he was made for but had never been able to keep in the Michigan weather they'd had to endure during college. Only the pearly white, all-American grin remained unchanged.

His hair was short, but not the shortest Nicholas had ever seen it. That honor belonged to the first summer after the boys' graduation, when they'd come back from a road trip with matching buzzcuts. Nicholas had spent the week Matías had visited the Fishers locked in his bedroom, trying to avoid the sight of him.

Nicholas wrangled his face into one of his practiced smiles.

"Welcome," he managed in a clipped voice. He wanted to be angry and rude, but the fear on his brother's face made him settle for cold.

He was not prepared for the genuine smile he got in return.

He should have been; Nicholas remembered how good the soccer-star-turned-econ-major was at showing people what they wanted to see. His smiles were wide and plentiful, but they were rarely genuine, except perhaps for when he was with Will.

"Thanks, man. How have you been?" Matías's eyes sparkled like those of a man who had never had to face any of the hurt he'd caused. His body shifted forward as if he cared about the answer Nicholas would give him.

"Good, thanks."

Silence filled the living room.

"Have a good night," Nicholas continued, heading to his room, which was separated from what was about to become Matías's room by nothing but an ordinary door.

As he closed said door behind him, he could hear his brother's relief. "That went well, I think."

Nicholas winced at the hope in his voice.

CHAPTER 3

NOW THAT HE was entering his second year of graduate school, Nicholas was finally starting to feel like he wasn't constantly drowning. Living at his brother's had even allowed him to reduce his hours at the community library where he had been working since moving to Chicago. During his first year, he'd had to spend so much time there that he barely ever saw the room he worked so hard to afford.

Second year also meant a lighter load of classes, which had allowed him to pick more interesting ones. The one he was most looking forward to, which unfortunately happened to meet on Monday mornings, was run by Professor Michaelson, a cutting-edge researcher in biblical hermeneutics. Nicholas's obsession with the man's work was obvious to anyone who would listen—something his two best friends were clearly not doing. Sloane and Ajay seemed to be more interested in the contents of the breakfast they were enjoying outside the Humanities building than in his new professor's pioneering work.

"He sounds old," Sloane cut him off, even though he was only halfway through his summary of Michaelson's latest article on the anachronisms of applying lexical semantics to orally transmitted texts. "And did anyone ever tell him we've published other books since the Bible? *Please* tell me he's hot, at least."

He scoffed. "I wouldn't know. And studying the Bible isn't any weirder than any of the stuff you're always reading."

Sloane looked at him pointedly. She didn't need to tell him what she was thinking out loud. Thankfully, Ajay finally looked up from their phone and decided to participate in the conversation.

"I bet *he* knows all of Ovid's Metamorphoses, though," they said with a grin.

Nicholas scowled at the reminder of his disastrous date at the beginning of the summer. "That was different. He was the one who brought up Ovid. How was I supposed to know he didn't know the first thing about his work?" He paused. "And I wouldn't expect anyone to know all of them. You make me sound so tedious."

"Regardless, while it's definitely high time you found yourself a boyfriend, I'm not sure we should be pinning our hopes on some boring ancient linguistics professor. What happened to meeting someone at a party?" they lamented.

Nicholas rolled his eyes at his friend's dramatics. "I don't need a boyfriend. And I don't go to parties."

"Two things I'm determined to fix this year."

Although he was used to Ajay's complete inability to walk on eggshells around anyone, this conversation was starting to ruin the quiet happiness Nicholas always felt on the first day of classes.

"I was just trying to convey my excitement at the possibility of finally being taught something interesting in this place," he answered gruffly. "And anyway, his assistant is the hot one."

This got both of their attentions, as he knew it would. Ajay locked their phone before putting it down, while Sloane's bagel was left hovering in midair. Nicholas drawing his friends' attention to any sort of romantic or physical interest was nearly unheard of. They both looked like they wanted to squeal in excitement but were trying not to spook him.

He'd seen Michaelson's research assistant, a fourth-year classics student, at a department meeting the week before. He was handsome in a broody and academic way, with sharp cheekbones that were framed by a dark, jaw-length curtain of hair. More importantly, he was smart and ambitious enough to have gotten a coveted job on Michaelson's research team. Nicholas had found himself sneaking glances at him all meeting long, fascinated by the cool air about him. It was utterly ridiculous that Nicholas was still thinking about him a week later, but there he was.

But before either of his friends could pick which question they wanted to ask first about the mysterious research assistant, he stood up with a grin. "Anyway, I've got to run—don't want to miss out on a front-row seat."

Nicholas grabbed his bag, ignoring their protests, and headed to class twenty minutes early.

∾

Just like Nicholas had hoped, the largely-forgotten bathroom on the third floor of the classics wing was empty.

Looking at himself in the mirror, he couldn't deny that the bags previously sewn under his eyes had faded over the summer. Even the shaded lines of his cheekbones, which had once looked like they'd been drawn in charcoal, weren't as sharp now as they had been last year.

Despite his empty social calendar whenever Sloane and Ajay were busy, it hadn't taken long for the toll of combining a full-time job and a PhD straight out of college to start showing on his pale skin. In less than a year, sleepless nights had etched permanent marks under his eyes, thinned his wrists, and dulled the color on his cheeks.

Even though they'd both lived in Chicago for a year, it was only on the Fourth of July that Will had realized how much Nicholas was struggling. It was the one holiday his parents still used the sliver of authority they had over their sons to require both Fisher boys to come home. Will—whom he hadn't seen in over six months—had taken one look at him, and his face had immediately closed off in grim determination. It was a familiar look, and Nicholas hadn't been surprised when, a week later, his brother had instructed him to tell his landlord that he was moving out. Said landlord, a polo-wearing undergrad with a thick Boston accent who'd gotten the four-bedroom apartment as a present from his parents, had never bothered to say anything about a notice period when Nicholas had rented out the place, and by August, the dump he'd called home for a year was nothing but a memory.

Since then, Nicholas had moved in with his brother, decreased his hours at work, and started sleeping again. As always, William Fisher had saved the day, Nicholas thought with a grimace.

Snuffing out the hope that things might be different this year, he ran a hand through his light brown hair, giving up quickly when it just came out messier. The front bits were starting to reach his eyes, and he made a note to cut it soon. He fussed with the collar of his dark brown shirt, wondering if he should have made an effort to dress properly for once, before shaking his head at the thought. He had never paid attention to how he was dressed in his twenty-four years of life; surely, one attractive teaching assistant couldn't be enough to change that. Still, it had been a long time since he'd found anyone interesting enough to remember their face. He was rather enjoying this little rush of adrenaline sharpening the studious flow of another September.

His friends wanted him to loosen up after all, didn't they?

∽

Nicholas sighed in relief when he walked into the classroom and found out he wasn't the only one who was grossly early on the first Monday of class. The TA was already there, and one exchanged look reminded Nicholas that he actually had no idea how to even talk to the guy. His statuesque features were illuminated by the sunlight coming through the side window, and the intensity of his gaze made Nicholas's stomach twist. His nonchalance was back; he didn't even smile when their eyes met, so Nicholas walked to an empty table at the back of the room in silence. Loosening up would have to wait for another day. Kieran—who turned out to be Scottish, which ex-plained the lilting accent, obviously softened by years spent in the States—introduced himself as the course assistant, until Professor Michaelson walked into the room with the gait of someone who'd been chased there and the year started in earnest.

It felt nice to be busy again. Nicholas had missed the ever-growing to-do list of the school year and the comfort of having both of his friends close by—even if he was spending a lot more time with them compared to his usual hermit-like lifestyle. But any distraction from the anxiety he'd carried around in his gut since he'd spotted the new toothbrush on his bathroom sink and the piled-up sheets on the couch was good for him. Even listening to Ajay prattle on about life-cycle engineering while Sloane went on about her romance of the week was better than thinking about Matías Romero living in his apartment, or Nicholas's gripping fear that the man was here to destroy this new life he'd so carefully built.

Their starkly contrasting lifestyles had at least given Nicholas a few days' respite. Matías was one of those insufferable people who assigned a moral value to how early and active one's mornings were, while Nicholas was more likely to stay in bed until the last possible second on any given day. Matías was out of the house by first light, as if chased out by his own conscience, and Nicholas worked the closing shift every evening at the library. This clearly meant one thing: the apartment was his in the mornings and Matías's in the evenings. With a bit of effort and conscious choreographing, it took three whole days for Nicholas's fragile sense of peace to come to a crashing end.

It was an otherwise gentle morning, rays of sunshine falling on Nicholas's face. He hadn't closed his curtains the night before, he noticed with indifference, and woke up before the shrill whistle of his old radio clock for once. He only had an hour until he had to leave anyway, so he got up and made a beeline for the kitchen, needing a cup of tea before he could welcome any thoughts.

Nicholas was opening a cupboard when a pointed cough made him nearly jump out of his skin and send the cup he'd grabbed flying out of his hand. He wilted around to face the IKEA catalog living room from his side of the kitchen counter, ready to tell his brother exactly what he thought of his little stunts.

"I swear—" Nicholas stopped in his tracks at the sight of a rumpled Matías Romero smiling sleepily, even though the clock clearly showed that it was ten in the morning. He'd grown so sure that Matías was putting just as much effort into avoiding him as he was that it took his brain a few seconds to understand what was happening. Nicholas felt underdressed in his old flannel pants and band tee, which immediately annoyed him.

"Sorry," was all he said in the ensuing silence, running a hand through his brown curls awkwardly.

Nicholas glanced at him, the clock on the wall, and the cup in his hand.

"I figured you hadn't seen me, but I wasn't sure what else to do. Didn't mean to scare you." The Southern drawl he remembered had dwindled to a mere hint of otherness in Matías's voice. How much time had he spent away from home?

"That's fine," Nicholas answered coldly.

Matías was still sitting on the couch he'd been sleeping on, wearing nothing but gray sweatpants. Nowhere in the room seemed safe to look at, so Nicholas turned back toward the kitchen counter, desperately looking for the teabags as if he wasn't the one who had decided where they went.

"Didn't take you for a tea man," Matías continued from behind him while the kettle finished boiling.

He hadn't been until he had met Slone. "It's a new development."

Nicholas wanted so badly to be mean and dismissive, but neither his wit nor his anger seemed to be answering his call now that he needed them. All he was left with was the truth and the hope that this conversation would end as quickly as possible.

"Would you mind making me one? I never know how long to leave the teabag in for."

Nicholas grimaced, something he seemed to be doing a lot this week. "Tea really doesn't go with soy milk, you're better off having something else," he said over his shoulder, remembering the assortment of plant-based products he'd noticed slowly invading their kitchen over the last few days. He wasn't sure if that was true, but he thought it sounded reasonable enough.

"Oh," was all the response he got, which made him feel petty and stupid.

Nicholas finally turned around, leaning against the kitchen counter as he discreetly started blowing on his hot drink, only to be met with the sight of the taller man getting up and stretching while he looked out the grotesquely large windows of their living room.

"Any plans for today?" Matías asked, in the tone of someone who was still pretending they were old friends.

"Same as every other day."

"Grad school, right? How's that going?"

"Well. How's apartment hunting going?"

"*Not* well." Matías sighed before sitting back on the couch, as if he was gearing up to tell Nicholas more. "I was hoping to be here for a couple of weeks max, and I really am trying, but it's like this whole city is on gridlock. It's an investor's paradise, but God forbid you're just trying to live half-decently. Thankfully, Will's helping. And you, of course, letting me stay here," he added like an afterthought. "Thanks for that, by the way."

Nicholas was waiting for the arrogance that had always defined Matías Romero to make its appearance, a well-placed barb or perhaps a casual insult to everyone he'd met thus far in the city. When it didn't come, he decided to reply rather than think about why.

"Isn't your family helping you?"

"Not really."

Nicholas couldn't help the look of surprise that must have made its way onto his face. They'd never talked much about Matías's family, even when they'd been on good terms. Everything he had learned about, from his father's political career to his mother sacrificing her own life so the Romero boys could have everything they wanted, had been against his will. Still, he wondered why Matías's proud and wealthy family wasn't helping him find a place while he attended law school.

He waited for more, but when Matías didn't offer any details, Nicholas remembered he didn't actually care.

"Well. Don't rush on my account. Plenty of space around here." He had to force the words out, but he thought they sounded genuine.

Matías's laugh, quick and full, told a different story.

"Right. Thanks, man," he continued, his eyes lighting up in quiet amusement before he got up and headed to the bathroom.

Nicholas's gaze followed him out of the living room. Until he burnt his tongue on the hot liquid when he distractedly brought the cup of tea to his mouth.

At least Matías didn't turn around when Nicholas choked.

∽

"Haven't we taught you anything at all in the year we've been friends?" Ajay asked with a hint of despair. The three of them were having lunch the next day, tucked away in a forgotten corridor in a basement that delightfully combined stone alcoves and central heating, a luxury they all agreed was wasted on the business school.

"I didn't think joining the horde of already confused students queuing at the TA's door was the best way to get a date," Nicholas said sarcastically.

Both of his friends stared at him impassively, probably refusing to admit he was right, before grabbing a forkful of their respective lunches.

"Right," Sloane continued once she was done. "Do we know anything about this guy, other than the fact that the entirety of the English department wants to shag him?"

She was right—this morning had only been Nicholas's second class with Kieran, and already students he'd never bothered to talk to were wriggling their eyebrows conspiratorially at him while whispering about the hot assistant.

"All I know is that he's from Scotland. And that everyone wants him."

"That's pretty thin."

Nicholas sighed heavily. "It's really not important. I don't have time for a distraction."

Ajay put down their salad bowl with a sigh. "Everyone has time for love, Nick."

Sloane spoke up before Nicholas could try switching the conversation to her newly-dyed red wine hair. It was a pity because it looked particularly beautiful, contrasting with her pale skin and making her almond eyes look darker, and he wasn't sure why he hadn't taken the time to tell her that.

"If you like him, you should go for it. Who cares about all the others? You're a catch, Nick. I bet there are quite a few people around campus who'd be ready to pounce on that mysterious Sontag-ian thing you have going on. You just never look up from your books long enough to give them a chance," she commented around a mouthful of couscous, as if she was stating a fact so universally known that repeating it didn't warrant her to stop eating.

The three sat in silence for a little while, Nicholas's appetite quickly disappearing.

"Can we move on now?" He hated how vulnerable his voice sounded.

After giving his shin an affectionate kick, Sloane put him out of his misery and changed the topic.

"One of my housemates never showed up, so we're looking for someone to fill his room." She looked at him pointedly.

"No," he said, realization hitting him at once.

"I thought you wanted to get rid of the athlete as soon as possible?"

This caught Ajay's attention. "What's this?"

"Nothing," Nicholas answered quickly, while Sloane finally felt it was appropriate to stop chewing long enough to speak clearly.

"Nicholas has a new housemate who's apparently his sworn enemy from years back," she unhelpfully summarized for Ajay, who looked as delighted by this turn of events as he'd expected.

"Tell me more," they said excitedly, leaning closer.

"There's nothing to tell," Nicholas added sternly. "It's just Will's best friend from college. He decided to attend law school last minute, as people do, so he's crashing in his—*our* living room until he finds a place. He's an insufferable snob, which is not particularly surprising considering we're talking about a friend of Will's."

"Did you know him well?" Ajay asked.

Nicholas shrugged. "He was always around, so, yeah. They were roommates and teammates. That's a lot to have in common when playing college soccer is your only personality trait."

"I didn't know your brother played *football*," Sloane corrected him. "Terrible guys, footballers. Very magnetic, though."

Nicholas snorted. "I know." She looked up, a question in her eyes. "I used to play too."

He chuckled at the shock painted on both Sloane and Ajay's features.

"It was a long time ago. But terrible is right. Which is why, as much as I want him out of my living room, I won't dump him on you." It was only half a lie. Nicholas could easily picture Matías, all charm and confidence, sweeping Sloane off her feet the way he did everyone else. "Look, there's nothing to talk about, let's move on. I'm sure you'll find a roommate in no time."

"Quite a lot of things we're not allowed to talk about today, aren't there?" concluded Ajay. Their tone was soft, however, and when Nicholas looked up, he found that their eyes were too.

From: Elizabeth R. Green
Cc: Jasmine Miller-Reed
To: Nicholas Fisher
Subject: Checking in
August 30, 11:21 AM

Dear Nicholas,

I hope this email finds you well and that the start of the semester has been both productive and engaging.

I wanted to follow up regarding our meeting last week. After giving your case further consideration and consulting with colleagues, I must reiterate that substantial teaching commitments are a required component of the PhD program. While there is flexibility in how you fulfill these teaching credits, research-related projects cannot be substituted to meet this requirement.

As I mentioned last Tuesday, there are several options available within the department, including interning, tutoring, mentorship, and course assistantships, particularly for third-year students. Additionally, I encourage you to explore the resources offered by the Education department, which supports graduate students in meeting their teaching obligations through various projects.

I have also reached out to Dr. Jasmine Miller-Reed, who oversees a mentoring program between the undergraduate and graduate schools. She may be able to provide additional pathways or suggestions that align with your goals. I encourage you to contact her directly to discuss potential opportunities. Once you've had a chance to explore these options, feel free to share any updates or progress with me.

Please don't hesitate to reach out if you have further questions or need additional guidance.

Best regards,

Dr. Green

CHAPTER 4

BY THE SECOND Thursday of classes, Nicholas was standing out-side the door of an office he'd never visited before, wiping his sweaty palms on his jeans in vain. It had taken him months to warm up to Professor Green when she'd first become his advisor, and now there he was, having to introduce himself to someone entirely new because she hadn't known what to do with him. He hated feeling like a problem she'd handed off to someone else. The sterile, hospital-like corridor he found himself in was not helping his discomfort.

"Yes?" came a warm voice from inside the office after his shaky knock. He walked in to find an older woman, perhaps in her fifties or sixties, with dark skin and earrings so large they threatened to wrap around her neck. The room was surprisingly inviting, with slanted yellow walls and packed bookshelves that looked oddly familiar. He couldn't help but twist his neck around, hungrily trying to memorize as many titles as he could from the messy piles awaiting shelving. It seemed like the kind of place where be glad to spend Chicago's long gray afternoons.

"Hi. My name is Nicholas Fisher, I emailed you about stopping by?"

"Ah, yes. Please sit down." She gestured toward the comfortable chairs in front of him and turned to a small cabinet on the right side of her desk, making two cups of tea and handing him one wordlessly.

"Professor Green told me about your situation," she said distractedly. Nicholas winced. "Do you want to tell me about what you've been working on?" she asked when he remained silent.

With a sigh of relief at being asked a question he knew the answer to, Nicholas drew up the story of his research interest. He talked about reading *The Land Beyond the Forest* and the ensuing decision to spend half a decade studying traveling narratives further. When Nicholas looked up mid-sentence and caught her staring straight at him, he wondered if she was even listening to a word he was saying.

"This all sounds brilliant," she did say when he finished. "So why don't you want to teach anyone about it?"

He made a small sound of surprise. That wasn't quite how he'd put it to Professor Green.

"I just don't think I'd be any good at it," he said, shocked into telling the truth.

It tasted bitter on his tongue. Nicholas had always claimed he simply had no interest in teaching, no attraction to the idea of spending his days telling privileged kids things they couldn't care less about, losing track of his own interests in favor of a numbing routine of grading bad papers written by students who had, at best, watched the movie.

"I see."

He wasn't sure what it was that she saw—was his conviction that he couldn't be trusted to take care of anyone visible on his features?

The professor sat unmoving, her wide shoulders and curly hair reminding him of an engraving of Cassandra he'd seen at the museum this summer, especially with her knowing gaze trained on him. After a while, she spoke again, seeming to have come to a decision.

"I won't do you the offense of offering a pamphlet on the joys of educating young minds. Whatever this is about"—she waved a dismissive hand in his general direction—"I'm sure it won't be solved that easily."

Nicholas raised a brow, ready to feel offended, but all that came was relief.

"You don't have to become a teacher, but you do have to get teaching accreditations in order to obtain your degree. It's part of the program. Now," she continued after a breath, "if you truly think course assistantship isn't for you, there are other options, but they won't cover all the pedagogy credits you require." She took a sip of tea, and Nicholas mirrored her. "So you'll need to show a real appetence for trying your best, if you want a chance at bending the rules."

Nicholas nodded, trying hard not to let hope bloom in his chest.

"I will," was all he said.

"Here's my proposal. I have been trying to set up something of a mentorship program for undergraduate students. We don't have any credited mentor spots left, so I suppose the amount of effort you'd like to put in is yours to decide. But if you wanted to help now, you'd be at the top of the list for the credited spots next semester. It won't cover all that you need, but it would be a start."

His confusion mixed headily with apprehension.

"Help how?" he asked after he realized the silence had gone on a bit longer than was comfortable.

"I have this group of undergraduates, very eager to get their hands on everything. They're doing a little research project for me this semester. Obviously, I've asked for slightly more than they can chew on, but we all have to learn one day." Her laugh was warm and fond. "They could definitely use some guidance."

"Guidance?" He couldn't hide the worry in his voice.

She hummed. "You said you liked research, right? This would be a project-based mentorship, so you'd be closer to that than with tutoring. Be the person they turn to when they're lost, give them a nudge in the right direction when they start getting overwhelmed. Someone to read the early drafts. All the qualification you need is to have been where they are right now and gotten through it unscathed."

Nicholas let out a breath. Working with undergraduates would look good with the department and get everyone off his back for a few months. But he wasn't sure it was enough—even with the promise of a credited spot next semester, it was clear that the department wasn't going to let him get away with no teaching at all. And he didn't have time to waste running an over-eager undergraduates' support group, especially if it wasn't going to count toward his degree.

He didn't think said undergraduates had anything to gain from it either.

"How much of a time commitment is this supposed to be?"

"However much time you want to commit to them." The professor let another silence hang between them, apparently as fond of them as Nicholas was. "They'll get it done, with or without you, but I did say I would find them someone to help. I'll pass your email along, yes?"

Something about her tone and the politeness of her smile made it clear the conversation was over. He was surprised at all the questions she hadn't bothered asking him. Advisors usually loved questions.

"Let's meet again next month, shall we? I'll let you make your way out, if that's all right," she said, drawing his attention to the cane propped against the side of her desk with an unreadable smile.

Nicholas walked out of her office in a daze. He had no idea whether things were better or worse than they had been when he'd walked in. All he knew was that he would have to find a way to shake off the discomfort crawling under his skin before he ruined these kids' chances of getting a decent grade.

es

It was a Thursday, which had quickly become Nicholas's favorite day of the week. The first thing Matías had done after moving in was join a local soccer league, committing to spending every Thursday evening at practice despite the cold weather and biting wind that would soon be invading the city. A strange choice, considering the league was average at best, something Nicholas knew because he'd checked it out on his first week in the city. But he wasn't about to complain about regaining ownership of his living room for one evening a week.

He decided to make curry the way Sloane had taught him, which was a clear improvement from the diet of cold wraps and overpriced bagels he'd been surviving on for the past two weeks, busy as he'd been pretending he wasn't avoiding his own kitchen.

Nicholas hadn't talked to his brother in a few days, which was a perk of avoiding Matías, who seemed to be glued to Will at all times; still, he made enough food for two. He didn't dare wonder if William would remember that this was the only evening they could spend together.

When William walked through the door with a bottle of his favorite red wine and an expectant glint in his eyes, Nicholas had to hide his relief with a cough. He might not get the loud, back-slapping, ride-or-die kind of brotherhood that Matías got from Will, but as he served dinner and they settled on the couch, he thought he preferred the silent TV shows and homemade meals anyway. William was apparently in a conciliatory mood, since he refrained from starting a fight and carefully avoided the subject of whose bed they were sitting on.

It was the best night he'd had since Matías's arrival.

❧

It was almost worth waking up with a wine-induced headache the next morning, that particular kind of half-hungover craving for sugar driving him out of bed and to the kitchen hours before his usual wake-up time. Except that when he got there, he stumbled upon the sight of a very shirtless Matías holding the bottle of oat milk Nicholas had left on his shelf last week, a focused frown on his face as he looked to be attempting to make a cup of tea.

"Yo, Fisher," he said without looking up.

Nicholas nodded, but all he could think about was the lack of tan lines on the man's ridiculously defined caramel chest, which made him wonder just how much time he spent shirtless. After a few seconds of still silence, Matías looked up at him from under that mess of curls, and the sight of his curious dark eyes spurred Nicholas into answering, forgetting to be rude in the process. "Good morning."

As he put some frozen waffles in the microwave, Nicholas resisted the temptation to look behind him where the Texan was or to awkwardly check his reflection in the oven door. Thankfully, he was wearing newish pajama bottoms and an oversized band tee which was probably cool since it was Sloane's and he'd never heard of them.

Not that it mattered.

"How have you been? It feels like I've barely seen you since I got here," Matías said after a few seconds, an easy smile obvious in his voice.

Nicholas couldn't tell if he was being sarcastic or purposefully glossing over the fact that their lack of interaction had been carefully orchestrated. Either way, it was too early to give himself a headache over it—or make his current one worse, he thought with a wince as he caught sight of the empty bottle of wine next to the trash can.

When he turned around, only the kitchen island separated him from Matías.

"I've been busy with classes and work. And research."

"Oh, is that this year? I thought you had more time."

Nicholas frowned. He wasn't sure how Matías could've known that. "I do. It's something on the side, I'm trying to—" Nicholas cut himself off, feeling his cheeks flame up. "How's law school?"

He wasn't sure why they were acting like two old acquaintances caught catching up at the coffee machine, but he wasn't in any state to start a fight now. With a chuckle, Matías took this change of topic in stride. "It's all right. A lot of snobby people, but that was to be expected, wasn't it? It's fine otherwise."

"Anyone could have told you that. Chicago law schools aren't really known for their Southern charm and kindness."

"I bet you think I fit right in."

He did, but in a prowess of maturity, Nicholas did not nod in agreement. Instead, he took pity on the tepid-looking mixture sitting in front of Matías. "Do you want some tea?"

The grateful look Matías sent him felt like a trap. "Yes, I'd love some. Thanks, Nicholas."

He'd already turned back toward the counter, so Matías couldn't see on his face how strange it felt to hear his name in a voice that hadn't said it in years, and never so carefully.

He knew he couldn't let his guard down, though. That had always been his problem when it came to Matías.

"While I've got you here, I wanted to ask you something. Will and I are thinking of having people over tomorrow night before we head out." Placing a tea bag in each of the mugs in front of him,

Nicholas nodded distractedly. He wondered if Will's friends from work would be in attendance—he wouldn't mind seeing some of them again. But Matías continued before he could find out. "I just wanted to let you know, so you'd be gone in time. We've told people to come over around seven, and the coast should be clear by eleven for you to come back."

A burning warmth invaded his neck, inexorably making its way over his whole face. He'd thought this was an invitation; as it turned out, Matías was just clearing the house. The bitter taste of déjà vu flooded him. All he could do was stir his tea until he was sure that not a single grain of sugar was left undissolved.

"Right," he finally said when he thought he could trust his voice. "I'll make sure to stay out of sight," he added coldly before grabbing his mug and heading back to his bedroom, leaving the other one on the counter.

He heard his name coming from Matías's lips, once, but it remained unanswered in the quiet apartment.

Alternating between berating himself for behaving like a child and feeling like one, Nicholas sat at his desk, fruitlessly attempting to get some work done before he had to head to campus. He'd been a fool to hope that an explosive falling out and five years of silence would be enough to change the fact that Matías would only ever see him as William's little brother, always in the way.

He heard a light knock on his bedroom door half an hour later.

"Come in." The words sounded more like a question than an invitation.

The door opened to reveal Matías, somehow about as wide as the doorframe, which Nicholas found incredibly irritating. He was freshly showered, his brown curls still wet and a lot tamer than usual. His smile was reserved, almost polite.

"You left your waffles in the microwave," the man said, holding up the long-forgotten plate in his hands. When Nicholas didn't say anything, he continued. "I thought you might want them, so I heated them up again."

"Thank you," was all he could say, surprise evident in his voice.

Matías grinned, his eyes lighting up and giving Nicholas a glimpse of the boisterous twenty-year-old he remembered. He quickly took the plate and set it down on his desk, but the loud presence next to him didn't go away; instead, when Nicholas looked up, he found Matías distractedly standing in the middle of his room. He smelled like citrus and clean sheets.

Whatever he saw on the wall behind Nicholas seemed to open a floodgate of curiosity. He stared avidly at the room around him, his attention jumping from the album covers and poems on the walls to the homemade shelves and the piles of paperbacks on the floor. He looked and looked, unbothered by the stretching silence, his eyes dancing around the room. Nicholas gave him a few seconds, noticing the way Matías's hands kept trying to escape his pockets as if they wanted to touch everything, how he kept opening his mouth as if to speak every time his gaze fell on something new. But he didn't say anything, and Nicholas didn't know if he was thankful or disappointed. Not knowing what else to do, Nicholas let him stand there, turning back to *Fuenteovejuna*'s first act sitting on his desk.

In the end, the scrutiny became too much when he caught Matías smiling softly at a poster of one of Ajay's favorite bands.

"I take it you don't have class on Fridays, then?" he asked to slice through the silence.

Matías almost jumped at the sound of his voice but didn't lose his smile. "I just have the mornings off. Although I should be working. I'm heading to campus now. I just… wanted to make sure you… had your waffles."

The uncertainty in his tone was something else Nicholas was unfamiliar with. Matías was loud and proud and, above all, confident. He had never been able to resist filling a void with meaningless conversation and easy laughter. Nicholas didn't know what to do with this version of him. It went further than the newly golden tan and grown out hair; there was something less defiant about the man now standing in front of him, like he'd learned a thing or two about consequences while he was away.

"Thank you," was all Nicholas said.

Despite the definitive tone to his voice, Matías still hovered by his door.

"And, Nicholas," he said suddenly, the words resonating in the room, or maybe the echo was in Nicholas's ears. Matías's knuckles tapped against the frame in a rhythm only he knew. "I should have led with the fact that you're obviously invited tomorrow. It'll be the team and a few people from my law classes, some of Will's buddies too. I assumed you wouldn't be interested. I just told you so you wouldn't be caught by surprise." He waved a hand in the general direction of the living room, the meaning of which was unclear to Nicholas. "But we'd love to have you. You could invite some friends too."

When he caught Matías's eye, there was none of the pity he'd expected to find there.

With a mysterious nod, Matías left, closing the door behind him.

A small smile formed on Nicholas's lips, despite his best efforts to prevent it. Will would have left the door wide open, and probably turned the light on to make sure his little brother was as inconvenienced as possible. He certainly wouldn't have brought him his breakfast and an apologetic clarification.

Unlike his own brother, Matías had always been able to see him so clearly, to understand when he could push and when Nicholas needed space, like he was the most legible book Matías had ever opened.

Yet as far as he could remember, Nicholas was certain the Texan had never been so gentle with the knowledge.

From: Kieran Donne
Cc: Andrew Michaelson
To: CLAS 46903
Subject: Literature review schedule
Attachment: Literature review schedule
September 6, 5:57 PM

Dear all,

As was discussed during our last seminar, you'll find the schedule for your literature reviews for the semester attached to this email. Each of you has been assigned a week to post your review on the class discussion board. Please check the document carefully and note your deadlines.

A quick reminder that this assignment is not an exercise in summarizing what others have written. You are expected to select a thesis related to this class's topic of interest and build an extensive, methodical review of the existing literature surrounding it. The goal is to establish a foundation that could credibly serve as a springboard for original research. In short, treat this as practice for your dissertation.

While I will give actionable feedback on each review, you are encouraged to interact with and critique one another's work by responding to it directly on the discussion board. Feel free to evaluate the completeness, relevance, and overall quality of the work. Consider the perspectives presented (and perhaps more importantly, those left out), and assess whether the student has convincingly articulated the landscape of research. Think of this as a peer-review exercise—but one with teeth.

Remember that the quality of your work will not only shape your final grade but also your reputation in this program. Don't squander the opportunity to demonstrate the depth of your thinking.

I'm happy to answer questions about the assignment, but please check the syllabus and previous emails before asking—save us all some time.

Best of luck,
Kieran

CHAPTER 5

AFTER SPENDING TOO long debating it, Nicholas decided to stay out of the way of Will and Matías's little soirée. Even the resentment that Matías's initial assumption had been right wasn't enough to pretend it was wrong.

Sloane and Ajay's disbelief when he asked them if they wanted to go out with him that evening was, he thought, a bit of an exaggeration. Still, he let Sloane pick him up from the library as soon as his shift ended. Not wanting to "break whatever spell had been cast on their little hermit," Ajay gathered their supplies and materialized at Sloane's apartment with drinks and a make-up case within the hour.

They could probably count on one hand the number of times the three of them had gone out dancing together. Ajay was too much of an extrovert to understand the appeal of Nicholas's cherished nights in with only a book and a nice meal to keep him company. He suspected Sloane understood better, and even yearned for his quiet evenings, but she had her own reasons for overfilling her schedule.

"Let's get our party animal all dressed up!" Ajay squealed with delight.

They stood in front of Sloane's wardrobe, contemplating her endless collection of long skirts and eccentric tops, while she and Nicholas sat on her already littered floor. The first order of business was apparently to fix his "nerdy nineties dad look," which both of them agreed was charming if you were a virgin or a good thrifter, but not their first choice for Nicholas's first party of the school year.

After extensive negotiations, they landed on an elevated version of what he always wore: Sloane's baggy jeans and a white t-shirt of Ajay's so tight he only agreed to wear it after intense negotiations and two shots of tequila. Sloane managed to push a fitted dark-green jacket against his chest, daring him to argue, but he drew the line at Ajay's attempt to add some kohl to his eyelids. Instead, he agreed to wear cologne and rings, and to let Sloane do his hair. This was his version of a silent apology for not being everything they were, for needing to be handled so carefully. If Ajay's whistles and Sloane's soft smile were anything to go by, they knew and appreciated it just the same.

"You look like you just walked out of a pretentious double spread on *Hip Entrepreneurs*." Ajay sighed. "I'm not sure it's in my best interest to walk in next to you." Nicholas scoffed at his friend's exaggeration, but he couldn't fight off a small smile. "They're going to be falling over themselves trying to talk to you."

"There's no *they*. I just want to have fun with you guys and be out of the house for a few hours."

"You, out of the house?" Sloane chimed in.

"William and Matías are having a thing at the apartment, and I don't feel like being around for the ensuing beer pong and testosterone Olympics," he said with a grimace they instantly matched. "Anyway,

I'd like to be able not think about… that whole situation for at least a few hours, if you guys don't mind."

Ajay took pity on him and moved the conversation to the topic of Sloane's upcoming meetings with the English department, asking if she was any closer to being granted her joint degree.

She pouted in response. "Not really. They're still being twats, but I'm going to keep trying to convince them. Anyway," she continued dismissively, "are we planning on actually going out at some point, or do we need to move on to the hair-braiding portion of the evening?"

Apprehension started pooling at the bottom of Nicholas's stomach when he remembered that going out involved more than just drinking tequila on the floor of his best friend's room. Instead of thinking about it any longer, he took another shot, enjoying the warmth the liquid left behind on its way down his throat. Nicholas took a minute to compose himself, looking around Sloane's cluttered room while Ajay ranted about something promoter-related. He smiled at the number of dirty mugs and tangled jewelry pieces precariously balancing on every available surface. Nicholas wasn't sure why he hadn't spent more time here last year, although an all-too-familiar voice in his head whispered that it might have something to do with being unsure Sloane had meant it when she'd said she wanted him here.

But that was enough of that. Tonight, he was going to be the fun best friend they both deserved.

Ajay pulled out their phone. "Right, since it's Saturday night, bars and clubs will be too full." The implied *'for Nicholas'* rang loudly in the small bedroom. "But there are a few parties happening. One of the theater kids we met last year said he was throwing a little something, then there's always the frats, or those sociology girls with the big house. Some people from my department also invited me to a little shindig, but I don't think a bunch of engineering nerds getting drunk on flavored vodka is the way to go for tonight."

"You're a nerd who tends to get drunk on flavored vodka," Nicholas said with a frown.

"Exactly. Why look for more when you already have me?"

Nicholas smiled. "I'll follow your lead. Wherever you think is best."

He wondered if it was too late to back out entirely when they announced, after a few minutes of deliberation, that they were headed to the suburbs.

☙

As it turned out, house parties weren't as close to Nicholas's worst nightmare when he was flanked by his two best friends. Sure, the music was too loud and too far from his own taste to make dancing even slightly tempting, but as they wandered around looking for cups and somewhere to leave the bottles they'd brought, they came across a large kitchen that didn't seem to have any speakers. The volume was lower, and most people were leaning against counters and chatting away at a reasonable volume—for now.

Sloane and Ajay stayed with him, delighting every acquaintance they bumped into with tales of their summer adventures. Their magnetism always made his own quiet more palatable. The two of them took the lead, one of them constantly keeping a shoulder to his or a hand on his elbow until Nicholas had enough drinks in him to find himself in a conversation he didn't want to leave just yet. Then someone poured more wine in his barely empty glass, and he was too busy talking to the host about her research to stop them in time.

Finally, he started having fun, so much so that when his friends dragged him to the front room, where the speakers were the loudest and the bodies most tightly packed, he followed them with a grin. The crowd seemed younger here, energetic, more drawn to the revolving chaos of a thumping bass than red wine and conversation. Egged on by Ajay's whistles and Sloane's hands on his hips, moving him along to a rhythm that didn't match the one currently blasting, Nicholas allowed himself to join the crowd, exhaling deeply and closing his eyes.

If only Matías could see him now, normal and happy and dancing— Nicholas shook his head to dispel the thought and grabbed the first plastic cup he could find. The crowd blurred into tan arms and brown curls every time he opened his eyes, so he left them closed and tried to enjoy the feel of bodies pressing against his.

The music changed to something slower, and Sloane grabbed his waist, dragging him into a sensual dance. The two friends grinned as they lost themselves to the music and the feeling of warm skin under warmer hands. He quickly noticed the hungry eyes of the men around them, the hesitation in their step as they glanced at his hands on Sloane's hips, which seemed to discourage and anger them proportionally.

Tilting his head, Nicholas let go of her. "I'm going to find the bathroom," he whisper-screamed in her ear.

She stared pointedly at him. "You don't have to, you know. I just want to dance with you."

"I guess you'll just have to get over me and under one of the hunks that have been staring at you all night, then," he answered playfully.

He walked backward from her, his arm extended and holding her hand until they both had to let go.

"Have fun," he mouthed with a wink.

While he wanted Sloane to have fun, Nicholas still didn't know how to escape the embarrassment of standing around on his own, so he headed outside to the front porch. The air was bitter, finally starting to feel like the Chicago he remembered, but he sighed in relief as the sounds of the party grew muffled. He grabbed an old pack of cigarettes from his pocket and drew one, letting it hang from his lips for a few seconds before lighting it. There was the usual moment of hesitation, thoughts turning to the years he'd spent using cigarettes as a lifeline. It was better now; he rarely carried a pack around, only smoked to take the edge off or when he was nervous. Still, the threat of sinking back into addiction never left.

Someone opened the front door, a pair of footsteps hovering behind him. Nicholas hoped not turning around would make it obvious he had no interest in making small talk.

"It *is* you."

Even through the alcohol-induced haze, Nicholas caught the familiar accent, almost American but not quite. *Kieran.*

"Sorry, have we met?"

With a grin, the Scot played along. "Not properly. I just recognized you from Michaelson's class. Sorry, this is probably inappropriate, but I've had quite a bit to drink, and you looked lonely out there," the handsome teaching assistant said, waving around a glass half full of what looked like whiskey.

Nicholas took a long drag of his cigarette, trying to cover a shaky breath. He'd been hoping to have a bit more time to prepare before he had to talk to him. A full semester, preferably.

"What's your name?" the Scot continued, coming up next to him to lean against the wooden balustrade surrounding the porch. All of a sudden, the air felt particularly warm.

"Nicholas." He cursed himself for having left his glass inside. The olive-green gaze trained on him was making him all too aware of his own skin.

"Nice to meet you, Nicholas. I'm Kieran." He finally stopped getting closer, just a few inches short of their arms brushing. Nicholas wondered if the amount he'd had to drink tonight had anything to do with the thrill of excitement he felt instead of the usual desire to run away.

"I know," Nicholas answered without any of the awkwardness he was used to. "Didn't really take you for the house party kind."

Kieran chuckled. "What, did you expect me to spend my Saturday nights archiving ancient texts in dark basements?"

"Something like that," Nicholas admitted, letting himself smile a little. He felt far braver than he had the last few times he'd been around the dark-haired man, brave enough to turn his head to look at him properly.

He'd had plenty of opportunities to watch him in class and around campus, but there was something different about the way the streetlights illuminated the sharp angles of his face, his loose fingers wrapped around his glass distractedly. Kieran had long, dark eyelashes and a preppy-meets-Gainsbourg way about him, his heavy leather jacket looking weightless on his shoulders.

"Well, I won't pretend that it hasn't happened before. But I think I made the right choice for tonight, don't you?"

Nicholas smiled again, turning around so he was now facing the house, Kieran's heavy gaze still staring at his profile. There was condensation on the windows, so he couldn't see into the living room. "I suppose, if sweating bodies and warm beer are your idea of a perfect night."

"Is that why you're outside?"

"I thought so, but now I'm cold and wine-less."

Kieran laughed at that, although Nicholas hadn't been making a joke. "Well, I thought you were the quiet type."

"And me standing out here alone is disproving your theory?" Nicholas asked, looking at Kieran with what he hoped was a casual and humorous glint.

"I like it. It makes you stand out."

Nicholas gave him an easy smile. He knew many before him had probably heard that line, but it still sent a thrill surging through his veins. Instead of shaking his head, he grabbed Kieran's elbow.

"I really need another drink," he added, not wanting the feeling to go away. "Are you coming?"

They headed back inside together, Nicholas leading the way to the kitchen and savoring the opportunity to get a break from his face being scrutinized for a few seconds as Kieran followed. Perhaps they had been keeping an eye out for him, because as soon as he crossed the hallway to the kitchen, both of his friends appeared in his periphery. He saw the surprise on their faces, quickly followed by conspiratorial grins when they caught sight of Kieran's hand wrapped around his forearm as Nicholas led them through the crowd.

"Want some?" Nicholas offered when he found the bottle of wine he'd started earlier, hoping he sounded casual. He had no idea where to go from there and hoped that more alcohol would light the way.

"Sure," Kieran answered with a smirk.

He looked almost dangerous in this light, watching Nicholas pour as carefully as he could manage. Their fingers grazed when Kieran grabbed his glass, and Nicholas shivered at the cold touch.

"Do you want to dance?" the Scot asked in a low voice, saving Nicholas from having to figure out what to do next. With a nod, Nicholas let Kieran grab his hand.

Around them, the music had grown even more suggestive, which seemed to have emboldened everyone. As he let his body sway to the rhythm, Kieran's hands were quick to find the small of his back. His hands made Nicholas think of other hands, hands that had never touched him like that. Nicholas took a deep breath, dismissing the thought and grabbing the neck of the attractive man who was very much not making him feel like an afterthought.

He tasted like whiskey.

From: Brianna Ann Nelson

To: Nicholas Fisher

Subject: Hello!

September 7, 5:17 PM

Dear Nicholas,

Jasmine gave me your email yesterday and told me that you would be happy to give us some pointers on our research project. Thank you for agreeing to help us. I know you must be really busy with post-graduate life, and I hope we can work together as efficiently as possible.

I would love to find a time for us to meet, maybe next week?

I have attached the brief of our assignment to this email, as well as the bibliography I have gathered so far. I will start working on it, so we have something to discuss when we meet. Don't worry too much if you don't have time to get to it yourself. I just wanted to give you a heads up.

I am not sure when the other students working on this with me will be available, but I will try to talk to them during our next class together, and I have CC'ed them to this email.

Thanks again for your help!

Brianna

CHAPTER 6

NICHOLAS GOT BACK to the apartment the next morning, prepared to be welcomed by the usual post-party still-life of discarded glasses, pizza boxes, passed out bodies, and unidentifiable puddles.

Instead, he was met with two visibly full trash bags waiting by the front door, clean countertops, and the dishwasher running loudly. Their white and gray living room was back to its soulless, pseudo-modern glory. He was also, more critically, met with the sight of Matías Romero reading a book on the couch, wearing his usual sweatpants and white t-shirt and looking freshly showered. Even more distressingly, he was wearing round, wire-frame reading glasses.

Nicholas was too tired to think about whether he'd ever seen Matías wear glasses and accidentally let the front door slam behind him. Instead of apologizing when it made Matías jump, he looked at the open windows around the room with a scowl.

The surprise was clear on Matías's face. He looked in the general direction of Nicholas's bedroom then at Nicholas, who was obviously coming from outside in yesterday's clothes, and then back at his closed bedroom door. When they finally made eye contact, the shock was quick to turn into a mischievous smile.

"Hey, Nicholas. Just getting in?"

Nicholas met Matías's playful tone with what he hoped was a stern and unimpressed face, trying to convey to the older boy that no questions or comments about his recent whereabouts would be tolerated. It didn't seem to work, so Nicholas begged his foggy brain to find something to say before Matías got a chance to make whatever joke he had in mind.

"I didn't know you could read," was apparently the only thing he managed to put together.

He blamed the early hour and the current water-to-tequila ratio inside his body. Yet his remark was met with a grin wider than any human should be capable of. Wanting to get away from it, Nicholas threw his keys on the kitchen counter and put the kettle on.

"I thought I'd give it a go for once," he heard above his shoulder.

Nicholas couldn't help but turn around, trying to catch a glimpse of the battered title the man was reading.

"Actually… this is yours, I believe," Matías said almost shyly, holding up an old copy of *To the Lighthouse* when he noticed Nicholas's gaze. "I just found it on the shelf and remembered you saying it was good, thought I'd try it."

Nicholas grabbed two mugs from the cupboard.

"Whatever," he muttered, suddenly embarrassed as he tried to remember how heavily he'd annotated the book. The edition Matías was holding was from his undergraduate years, which doubtlessly meant the margins were full of embarrassing notes and musings he'd rather not share with the world. That would teach him to leave his things in the living room. At William's insistence, he'd started to fill up the half-empty shelves with his old books to make the place feel like his too. He would not be doing that again.

"So… fun night?" Matías asked again hesitantly.

"We don't have to do that," Nicholas assured him, his tone kinder than he'd intended. He knew very well Matías had no interest in polite small talk and forced conversation with him, and neither did Nicholas. He was nauseous and tired enough as it was.

Matías nodded, and Nicholas could have sworn it was relief he saw on his face.

He made two cups of tea, wordlessly dropping the one with oat milk on the coffee table before heading to his room with the other one.

"Thanks for the tea," Matías said to his back.

"Thanks for cleaning up," he answered reluctantly.

☙

Fueled by Nicholas's very out-of-character display of affection at the party, Kieran quickly became his friends' favorite subject of conversation. Even though Nicholas hadn't gone home with him, deciding to sleep on Sloane's new couch instead, he had never seen them as enthusiastic as they were for this budding romance.

By Wednesday, Ajay was still listing all the reasons Nicholas should already have asked Kieran out on a real date. They were walking across campus together, looking for somewhere to eat their lunch while Nicholas tried to deflect his friend's questions—again.

"Playing hard to get, I see. I like it. We'll think of something, don't worry."

"Maybe I don't want to think of something."

Ajay, as usual, did not even pretend to humor him. "You don't want to, or you're too scared to?"

Nicholas picked up the pace. Maybe if he started walking really fast, his friend would give up on speaking to him entirely.

"He's running the seminar tomorrow. I will… try. To give him my number."

"And?" Ajay asked, still unimpressed.

"And I will let you know everything that happens in detail."

Ajay hummed in satisfaction and went back to discussing their own post-party developments. Nicholas was listening to his friend distractedly, his gaze on their two pairs of feet walking side by side, their contrasting taste in footwear and the browning leaves starting to fall all over the south lawn painting a dizzying picture.

If home was a sound, it would be that of Ajay recounting one of their wild tales, with Nicholas's noises of assent in the background.

Unfortunately, the familiar melody was interrupted when Ajay suddenly grabbed Nicholas's elbow.

"Don't look up, but there is a human Poseidon staring at you like he wants to eat you for dinner. Or perhaps more of an Apollo," they added with the tone of someone genuinely wondering which Greek god Nicholas proceeded to accidentally lock eyes with.

"I think you mean Dolos," he said bitterly.

"You know him?"

Nicholas turned to his friend. "Never mind, it was just a joke. That's Matías."

Of course, he was standing directly in their path, just a few yards away. Although Nicholas's heart was now all the way up in his throat, they walked on, getting closer to Matías and the two—beautiful— girls he was standing with. They were laughing at something he had just said, one of them pushing his shoulder playfully.

For two people who lived together and attended the same university, they'd barely seen each other on campus in the two and a half weeks since the semester had started, accidentally locking eyes across a crowd only a few times. Nicholas was not one to seek out the popular spots around town unless his friends asked him to, and he might have purposefully avoided the law school buildings a few times for his own peace of mind.

This meant that he had no idea how he was supposed to act now. The air around him felt brittle, and he could barely hear whatever Ajay was saying through the sound of blood pumping in his ears. Seeing his roommate surrounded by people who seemed to adore him was like hearing an echo of earlier years. Back then, their interactions always had an audience, Matías on the way to somewhere else, too busy to look at him while he spoke.

Inevitably, the two boys' silent recognition drew the attention of their friends, making it impossible to skillfully ignore each other. At least Ajay was there, and Nicholas discreetly slid closer to them. They were the one to break the silence with a smile as they came up to the group, Nicholas's own world blurring between past and present.

"Hey, man, you're Will's friend, right? I'm Ajay," they said enthusiastically, extending their hand firmly like this was not the first diplomatic meeting they were attending today.

"That's me. Nice to meet you," Matías answered without missing a beat. "This is Gabi and Leila," he continued pointing at his own friends. The girls' smiles came with a warmth Nicholas had rarely seen in the people Matías tended to surround himself with.

For a few seconds, he seriously considered making an effort to try and dispel the awkwardness; he might never have been one for small talk, but after years of college and grad school, he had learned to navigate it, his early shyness having morphed into a general annoyance at the charade. But something about the dimples invading Matías's face as he gave them his usual, probably fake smile, irritated him. He remained silent.

"And who's this?" one of the girls, Gabi, finally asked.

Matías caught his eye then, a question in his. Nicholas knew what he meant: *are you going to talk, or should I do it for you?* He'd gotten that look a lot in the first few months of their pseudo-friendship.

"That's Will's brother, Nicholas," Matías informed them with a small smile.

Both of their faces lit up.

"Oh," Gabi said. "You guys live together, right? We didn't see you on Saturday."

"Yes, sorry about that, I already had plans." His tone came out genuinely apologetic, and he could almost feel Ajay buzzing with pride next to him.

With introductions out of the way, Nicholas thought they might be allowed to continue on with their day. But his friend did not seem to agree. "That was my fault, sorry, I had no idea you guys were doing a thing, so I dragged him to this party." A blatant lie delivered with perfect sincerity. Nicholas admired them. "But next time, for sure. You're at the law school, right?"

Matías's other friend wrinkled her nose, but didn't say anything. She was wearing a hijab and dressed in all black, and Nicholas couldn't figure out whether she was shy or deeply uninterested in him.

Matías just laughed. "No, no, they're from the team. Soccer."

"Oh, wow. I don't think I've heard it called soccer in months," Ajay marveled. "Maybe I *do* need to get out more." It was true that between Sloane's insistence on keeping her British slang and Ajay's native Hindi, even Nicholas hardly bothered calling it soccer in front of them anymore. Everyone laughed.

It seemed to come so easy to Ajay.

Matías's trio exchanged knowing glances. It reminded Nicholas of what it was to have a team, to share secrets and handshakes and a bond that went further than friendship. The way they stood close together, their bodies angled toward one another, made him wish Sloane was here so she could stand on the other side of him.

"Don't worry, when you guys come over, we'll ban the word entirely."

Matías inviting Nicholas's own friends to Nicholas's own apartment was so typical that it almost made him smile.

"We probably need to ban Will from the house altogether, then," Nicholas heard himself say without thinking. His brother was known to be a staunch supporter of doing anything he knew annoyed the people around him.

Matías smirked. "That could be arranged. Or just lock him in the bathroom."

"What if they need the bathroom?" Nicholas asked, waving in the direction of their friends.

"The washing machine, then."

"He wouldn't fit."

"Well, not with all the sugar you keep stuffing him with, he won't."

Outraged at the remark, Nicholas looked for Ajay's support. "Can you believe this?"

Unfortunately, the guilty look in Ajay's eyes told Nicholas he wouldn't like what came next. "Well… you do bake a lot. Remember my last breakup?"

"I'm sorry, did I hear something about baked goods?" Leila asked.

Matías was the one to answer. "Oh, you sure did. Give that guy twenty minutes and two eggs, and he'll make you a three-layered cake for no other reason than he felt like it," he continued. This was quite the statement for a man whose presence in the living room meant that Nicholas hadn't baked anything in weeks. Did he just remember that from the summers him and Will would come home from college? "I'm sure they can attest to it," Matías continued, pointing to Ajay.

Warmth bloomed in his chest.

"It's decided, then. You take care of the verbiage, and we'll handle the baked goods," Ajay said with a smile, and everyone but Nicholas nodded with decided hums.

Before another awkward silence could settle over the group, Ajay started exchanging goodbye nods and Nicholas sighed in relief. Their jewelry clinked together as they wrapped an arm around his.

"It was nice meeting you," Nicholas couldn't help but throw over his shoulder, catching the eyes of one of the girls. They seemed nice despite their poor taste in friends.

He waited until he was sure the group was out of earshot before even drawing a breath. He could feel Ajay charging up next to him, trying to control the flow of questions begging to escape their lips.

"Go on," Nicholas said with a defeated exhale.

"What the hell?"

"You're going to have to be more specific."

"Remind me why we hate him, again? And it better be outrageous, because he's making it quite difficult right now."

Nicholas sighed. He had known this was coming, which was also why he'd made such efforts to hide the man from his friends. "It's all right. You don't have to hate him. No one does. Even I still struggle sometimes, even after all the shi—you know, he's good at getting people to like him." Nicholas paused, his next words coming out of their own accord. "It would be like hating the sun just because your friend got burned. I get it."

Ajay looked at him curiously, probably waiting for him to expand. But nothing else came.

"Nick, stop with the cryptic nonsense, would you? I'm on your side. My point is," they continued, their voice sounding alarmed, "that I had no idea your nemesis was a tall, dark, gender-affirming sex god with dimples and friends that look straight out of the university brochure. I'm surprised there wasn't a photographer hiding in a bush somewhere." Nicholas laughed at that. Ajay had a point. "When you were talking about him, I was picturing a questionable tan with boat shoes and a rich but absent dad who makes everyone else's life miserable and treats women like garbage. Or, like, Satan reincarnate."

Nicholas shrugged. "That's who he was when I knew him, if that helps. I mean, at least the whole... arrogance and chinos and preppy friends part. The tan was always natural. And anyway," Nicholas rushed to add, "there is a reason Satan is so popular."

Ajay hummed suspiciously. "Are you calling Satan attractive?"

Nicholas scowled. "I'm not calling either of them attractive."

"Whatever we hate him for, do you think there's a chance it went away in the last few years? Maybe at the same time that the Hamptons wardrobe did?"

Nicholas barely had the energy to be frustrated by his friend's insistence that he must be mistaken. He was used to it: everyone always loved Matías. Wherever the man went, he took the people Nicholas thought loved him the most and made them his own.

"Look, Aj, of course you're free to like him. I get it, I really do. He's charming and confident and he can make you feel indestructible by just looking at you. But I've known him a long time, and whatever he is now, I can promise you it's just the new and improved version of the same selfish and destructive person he always was. He has as much genuine kindness in him as lab glassware."

Ajay raised a perfectly plucked eyebrow, but they were smiling. "Are you thinking more beaker or cylinder?"

Nicholas rolled his eyes. "Just make sure not to get your hopes up, okay? He's not a good friend."

Ajay, surprisingly solemn, shrugged. "I have enough friends, anyway."

❧

That evening, Nicholas almost missed his stop on the way home from work. He was on the phone, trying to negotiate bypassing a third round of edits on the article he'd finished over the summer, when he looked up to the sight of his building flying past the window. He got up in a panic, stumbling through a group of teenagers standing in the middle of the bus, and threw himself outside before the doors closed on him.

By the time the phone call finally ended—only half-successfully, since he'd need to sit through another one in the next few days—Nicholas was walking into his apartment. Instinctively, he headed to his bedroom, his head bent over his phone as he went through the few emails he'd received during his shift at the library. He was about to close the door behind him when he heard a low chuckle, which was his first indication that the house wasn't empty as he'd assumed. Matías stood against the kitchen island, his back turned away from both doors. He was wearing his soccer clothes, a sports bag sprawled over the couch. Matías laughed again, louder this time, which was when Nicholas noticed the phone in his hands and the tangled earbuds disappearing under the mass of brown curls.

Nicholas wondered if he should make his presence known. The other man obviously hadn't heard him come in, and it looked like he was on the phone. But when Matías still didn't turn around, he decided to silently go to his room instead. As he was closing the door, he heard soft Spanish, which was enough to make him freeze in place for a few seconds. Matías rarely ever spoke Spanish. The language was reserved for his family, and he always seemed to use it with reverence—Nicholas could still remember being sixteen and deciding that was a good enough reason to learn it. *Maybe he'll see me as family too*, he'd stupidly thought.

Nicholas tried to be discreet as he moved around his room, unsure if he was trying not to bother Matías or to hide his presence. He felt something of a forbidden thrill at the thought that Matías still didn't know he was in the apartment. But the murmurs went on for long minutes, so many that Nicholas finally gave up on eavesdropping and settled in with a book.

He'd been hiding for long enough that he'd resigned himself to doing so until Matías went out or morning came, when the sound of something clattering loudly made him jump. It was followed by Matías's raised voice, spitting out venomous words Nicholas's extensive Spanish classes hadn't covered. He tensed immediately, thrown back to the only other time in his life he'd heard Matías this angry, when everything between them had finally exploded. Not a memory he liked to dwell on, especially because Matías so rarely let his temper get away from him.

But the muffled sounds coming through the wall reminded him that said temper did exist, even though his façade of constant happiness and easygoing attitude made it easy to forget.

Nicholas should have stopped listening, should never even have started. But then Matías called the person he was talking to "dad" with a vulnerability in his voice that Nicholas had never heard before.

"*I don't care that you warned me,*" he caught, Matías's voice raw. "*You're just going to have to accept it.*"

The long silence that followed made Nicholas wonder if he'd hung up.

"*Leave Mom out of this. Don't talk about her.*" The sentences kept starting angry, but they always seemed to deflate into hurt before

Matías got to the end of them. "*This isn't one of your situations, I'm not some problem you can fix.*" Another short silence. Something thudded against a piece of furniture. "*So that's it, then?*"

Nicholas scrambled to the other side of his bed, grabbing his headphones, turning on his music as quickly as possible.

He was almost fast enough to miss the pained, incredibly human noises coming from the living room.

From: Brianna Ann Nelson

To: Nicholas Fisher

Subject: Thank you

September 11, 6:25 PM

Dear Nicholas,

Thank you so much for your prompt response. I would love to meet on Friday morning, thank you for being so available.

I will have a look at all the publications you have suggested so we can discuss them then.

And if you want to send me a copy of the article you mentioned on adaptive translation & ancient languages, I'd be really grateful, even if it's still in editing! It sounds really interesting.

Looking forward to working together!

Brianna

CHAPTER 7

AS HE'D PROMISED his friends, Nicholas went up to Kieran after class the next day. He had been so busy trying to figure out what he would say that he had barely been able to listen to the two-hour long seminar. He tried, and failed, not to feel too embarrassed about the five other students who'd found excuses to go bat their eyelashes at the assistant before him and waited his turn, trying not to be too obvious while he observed the Scot interacting with them. He looked different from last weekend; clearly more controlled and less disheveled, even though the leather jacket and long eyelashes were still there.

"Now I definitely think you were lying about not spending your Saturday nights in the archives," he said when his turn came, referring to the extensive personal research Kieran had told the class about.

"I was starting to wonder if this weekend had only happened in my imagination," was Kieran's response when he looked up. Nicholas was having trouble making sense of his tone. Did he expect an apology from Nicholas for ignoring him on Monday?

"It was real. Sorry, I've just been busy."

"Yes, I remember what it's like. You're in your second year, right?"

Somehow, Nicholas felt uneasy at the reminder and simply nodded.

"This was great," he tried, pointing at the board behind him and hoping to distract the TA by talking about the discussion he'd just led on foundational Persian texts. "You're a good teacher."

Kieran just shrugged as he finished putting a stack of papers in his bag before shouldering it. "It's not my favorite part of the job, but it's the price to pay to be in on Michaelson's research."

"How is he?" Nicholas asked, unable to keep the admiration out of his voice.

"He's all right. A bit messy, but I suppose you're allowed to be when you're as smart as he is."

Kieran started toward the now empty corridor, Nicholas falling into step next to him.

"Does he let you do any real research?"

"He does, or the tedious parts at least. He's the only person for whom I'd spend entire weekends in the archives, that's for sure," he said, finally smiling.

Nicholas was still looking for the next thing to say when Kieran came to a stop. They'd reached the heavy double doors that led outside, and although it was obvious that they were both going that way, the older boy was hovering in front of them. "Look, I have friends waiting for me to join them, but how about we grab a drink sometime?"

"I'd like that."

Kieran handed him his phone so Nicholas could input his number.

"I'll call you," he called out distractedly before heading outside.

Nicholas was left standing there, wondering why he felt like a nagging child begging for attention.

❦

Will insisted on cooking that night while Matías was at practice, which rarely ever happened and should have tipped Nicholas off right away. But the younger Fisher didn't think anything was wrong until Will pressed the pause button halfway through the second *Golden Girls* episode of the night. They'd barely just finished eating, and the wine bottle was still half full. It really was awful timing to pick a fight, Nicholas thought bitterly.

"I don't know if I mentioned it," William started with the tone of someone who knew very well he had not, in fact, mentioned "it." "I have an event with work. A retreat thing. It slipped my mind until today. It's just for the weekend. Most of the team is going tomorrow afternoon, but I could join them on Saturday and be back the next day."

Nicholas was so perplexed, he even forgot to act as irritated as he usually did whenever William spoke to him. Did his brother think he would miss him too much if he left for more than forty-eight hours? The two had spent years of their lives not even talking to each other. Surely one weekend away didn't call for fancy cooking and a sit-down conversation.

"You know I'm an adult, right?"

"Look, I'm just trying to be cour—"

Nicholas cut him off. "Where are you going, anyway? The weather isn't going to hold much longer," he said with a grimace. He looked out the window mechanically, although the dark night sky seen from inside the apartment made it almost easy to ignore the cold wave that had settled over the city in the last few days.

"Countryside." William paused. "There'll be fishing. And bonding."

Nicholas wrinkled his nose. "Well, I guess that's punishment enough for leaving me alone with Tim Riggins all weekend."

Will looked at him for a long time, but he seemed to know this was the best response he was going to get at the news that Nicholas would have to spend almost three days alone with Matías.

He wondered what would happen once they didn't have to pretend they could stand each other for William's sake anymore.

There was also the small matter of the phone call he'd overheard, which had obviously shaken Matías, but not enough for him to let the mask of cool nonchalance slip the next day. Nicholas wondered if William knew anything about that before remembering he didn't care. He tried his best to shake off the memory. It wasn't for him to have, anyway.

His phone chimed in his pocket, interrupting his doomsday scenarizing.

About that drink. Are you free on Saturday?

Kieran must have known that no one else was inviting Nicholas out for drinks on a Saturday night, because he didn't bother signing the text. Still, the younger man couldn't help but smile at the opportune timing of having plans outside of the house this weekend.

Yes, I just have work until four-thirty.

"Do you need me to pause?" Will's gaze was on him, and Nicholas could sense the tense air of expectation around his brother. He'd probably never seen Nicholas smile at his own phone.

Nicholas put his phone away. "No, I'm all right."

He could feel Will's searching gaze. He was probably waiting for his little brother to tell him who he was texting late at night, but Nicholas carefully avoided his eyes. He had never in his life talked about boys with his older brother, and he wasn't about to start now.

Let's meet at seven, then.

❦

One of the only downsides of William being away for the weekend was that his best friend seemed to be at a loss as to what he was supposed to do now that the Asterix to his Obelix wasn't there to share every breath he took. Matías barely left the house on Friday, snacking his way through the cupboards instead. Will was usually the one to take care of buying adult things like produce and condiments, so Saturday morning found Nicholas cursing in the kitchen, unable to find anything that could pass as breakfast.

Matías was up already, although he was smartly remaining silent. He sat at the kitchen island scrolling on his phone while Nicholas opened every cabinet he could find. The younger man let another frustrated noise escape when even the dishwasher did not yield any hidden treats.

When Matías finally spoke up, his voice was careful, like he was about to ask a ticking bomb what its thoughts were on not blowing up. Unfortunately, as long as Nicholas's stomach remained empty, the odds were not looking great. "I was planning on going to the store today. Do you want me to get you some things?"

"No," Nicholas answered curtly without sparing him a glance. "You wouldn't know what to get."

He felt rather than saw, since his back was turned, Matías's skepticism. Nicholas was a creature of habit, had a sweet tooth, and had eaten the same exact breakfast every morning for a decade: something sweet—like a muffin or a donut, a waffle if there was nothing else—and a coffee. That had only changed once, last year, when he'd replaced coffee with tea at Sloane's insistence.

Chances were, Matías would know exactly what to get.

"You could come with me. You'd know better than me what Will wants, as well."

Nicholas snorted at that. It was true, because those were the kinds of things that he paid attention to, but he was surprised at the admission that there was anything in this world Nicholas would know better than Matías, especially about Will.

"I've got work," he replied coolly.

"We could go after."

"Fine."

He decided to stop talking until he found something to eat, because he liked to keep his rude comments for when they were well thought-out and uttered with intention. Right now, his empty stomach was just throwing blind punches at anything it could get its grabby hands on. Not that Matías didn't deserve them, as a general rule.

Matías quirked an eyebrow over his cup of tea, but he didn't look annoyed or offended. He almost seemed… amused.

Resigned, Nicholas grabbed the bowl of sugar and added three large teaspoons to his cup of tea, before slamming it back on the counter. It seemed like this was the only nutrition he was going to get this morning. When he turned around, Matías was hard at work trying not to laugh at him, staring intently at the phone in his hand and hiding half of his face behind his own cup.

"I can be back at four, we can go then."

"I can wait until four-thirty."

Nicholas was about to ask him why, but he realized this worked out great for him since it meant he didn't have to sneak out of work early. He wondered if Matías knew that.

"Fine. Four-thirty, then."

❧

All the work in the world wouldn't have been enough to distract Nicholas from the things he was trying not to think about. It wasn't just the looming dread of a grocery run with Matías Romero that was throwing him off balance; it was the fact that, right after, he'd be heading to his first real date in months. Since moving to Chicago, his few attempts at dating had all turned into horror stories shared with his friends around bunch the next day.

To call his shift a test of Nicholas's strength and patience would have been an understatement. He was snappy and short-fused and ended up buying a pack of cigarettes during his break in the hopes that it would make him less irritable. Even his supervisor Marge's cheery mood and exaggerated winks when a queue of moms started forming next to him after story time weren't enough to get a smile out of him.

At least it was Saturday, which meant high traffic and an all-hands-on-deck afternoon. He could ignore parents and coworkers in favor of the kids, helping out on the floor and volunteering for story time instead of standing around, shelving and thinking. Preschoolers had a restless energy that was perfect if you were trying to ignore everything else that was going on in your life.

"Do you think ghosts can read?" a young girl asked him after he was done reading. "Or should I read to the one in my closet a story, in case he's bored?"

The look of genuine concern on her face made him think of Emma at that age, worried that a haunting spirit might feel lonely. A wave of remembrance hit him. At least, he wasn't thinking about tonight anymore.

Despite his repeated attempts to either stop time entirely or fast forward it until the next day, four o'clock did come. After spending the whole way home telling himself that all he had to do was buy his groceries and ignore the other man, Nicholas walked in to find Matías sitting on the couch, schoolbooks lying open on the coffee table as he frowned down at his phone. The jiggle of the keys in the rusty lock seemed to have just snapped him out of something, and he got up quickly. He looked so guilty that Nicholas wondered if he'd just caught him watching pay-per-view in the middle of his living room on a Saturday afternoon.

"Ready?"

Matías nodded.

Thankfully, after three weeks of living in each other's peripheries with minimal contact, the silence as they walked to the bus stop and started waiting wasn't uncomfortable anymore. What made Nicholas squirm, rather, was that Matías wasn't trying to break it. It was in the dark-haired man's nature to talk ceaselessly, to fill the silence with jokes and words of no consequence, while it was in Nicholas's to roll his eyes and beg for peace and quiet. But when Nicholas accidentally caught Matías's eye, he seemed too lost in thought to even notice.

When they boarded the bus, Matías settled in beside him, put on his headphones, and closed his eyes, apparently happy to relax during the short ride instead of drowning his companion in his usual stream of half-formed thoughts. For once, Nicholas thought, he'd be spared. But then Matías shifted slightly, and Nicholas's palms began to sweat. Suddenly, he forgot what he usually did with his hands when he rode the bus, every nerve ending in his body migrating to the thigh that was pressed against Matías's. He adjusted again, and now their arms were also flushed together. Nicholas was sixteen again, unable to eat at the same dinner table as Will's best friend without choking on his food.

He could already feel the fight bleeding out of him. He wanted so dearly to be able to hold on to the rage that he'd cloaked himself in during all the years Matías had been away; but the closer he was, the harder it was to remember that Matías Romero was the worst person he'd ever met. It had only been three weeks since he'd come back into his life, and already Matías's constant smile and uncharacteristic discretion were tugging at the part of him that would have once forgiven the older boy for anything.

Except he had never even bothered asking for forgiveness.

It was the bright colors of the store they were going to, as they passed it, that threw Nicholas out of his reverie. When he turned around, he saw the same realization in Matías's eyes. He grabbed Nicholas's wrist unceremoniously as they ran up the aisle, dragging him out of the bus before the doors closed on them.

"Shit," Nicholas exhaled as they made it onto the sidewalk.

"Sorry, I almost missed that." Matías replied with a smile. "Let's do this?"

"Let's."

ↃↃ

Shopping was laborious, to say the least. Every time Nicholas sent Matías off to grab something from their list, he would come back with the wrong kind, a glint in his eyes daring Nicholas to be rude about it. Not wanting to give him the satisfaction, Nicholas took a lot of deep breaths, falsely dipping his voice in honey as he sent Matías to aisles he knew were on the other side of the store while he rushed to get as much done as possible in his absence.

It wasn't long before Matías started getting distracted by shiny packaging and acting out every tagline he caught sight of. Nicholas was used to Matías garnering all of his attention without having to try, but this was different, somehow. It was like the other man wanted his attention, his silly comments and playful back-and-forths reminiscent of a child wanting to be seen.

Matías's open playfulness was unfamiliar territory, at least when it was aimed at Nicholas. The three years that separated them had always come with a clear code of conduct. They had been almost sixteen and freshly nineteen when they'd first met, galaxies and doors slammed in Nicholas's face separating them. Then there was college, and even if Matías had grown closer to treating him as an equal, his popularity and the hierarchy of athletics had been an inescapable reminder that they would never really exist in the same realities. But now they were both adults, real adults, and the boundaries had to be redrawn. It was a surprise to find out that Matías was clearly the more childish of the two.

So childish, in fact, that it quickly became obvious that everything Matías was doing seemed to be with the goal of making Nicholas laugh.

He wouldn't give him the satisfaction.

When Matías got distracted by the ingredients list of a ready-made meal long enough that Nicholas lost track of him again, the younger man was ready to give up.

"You know I don't actually need you, right? You can just wait for me somewhere. Maybe they have a playground area," Nicholas said neutrally when Matías caught back up with him. "Just tell me what kind of beer you want."

Matías waved him off. "What, and abandon you when I was the one to drag you out here in the first place? How will I ever learn what kind of cereal the Fisher household prefers?"

"Neither of us eats cereals."

"See? I definitely need to stick around."

Nicholas rolled his eyes. He was doing a lot of that today. "Stop talking and pay attention, then."

Matías followed him around the store in semi-silence after that, hovering behind him and picking up items they didn't need only to put them back down when he realized Nicholas had kept walking ahead. When they reached the miserably small books section after going through every other aisle in the store, Nicholas spoke up.

"There's a café by the checkout, if you'd like to wait for me there. I won't be long."

"But what about…" Matías hesitated. "Why?"

Already distracted by the titles on display, Nicholas said simply, "I want to look at these for a minute." He turned to Matías, challenging him to object.

"Maybe I want to look at them too."

Nicholas shrugged, gesturing at him to go ahead. Matías grinned as if he'd just been handed the keys to Disneyland and immediately started perusing, picking up every book that caught his attention before putting it back down with a grimace. As usual, his presence was too big to ignore, and Nicholas gave up on being able to focus on anything but the warm body and the hums and the smell of citrus next to him with a heavy sigh.

"All right, let's go."

"What? No, man, take your time, I'm having a blast," he answered, waving his hand at the shelf directly next to him. "Don't worry about me."

Nicholas looked at him dubiously. "Good to know you've expanded your repertoire. I always wondered what kind of people bought their raunchy romances directly from the grocery store," he said with a calm voice.

"What?" The panic in Matías's voice was almost enough to break Nicholas's resolve not to give him the satisfaction of laughing this afternoon, so he nodded toward the banner next to Matías. It read "Adult Novels" in bold pink letters, the words surrounded by flowers that reminded him of an Easter display.

"Oh, that—no," he spluttered. "I wasn't looking at that. No, no, I was looking at"—Matías looked around himself frantically—"foreign literature," he finished with relief as he caught sight of the sign on the next shelf over.

Nicholas smiled. He couldn't help it. "Nice. My personal favorite."

"Russian, right?" Matías rushed to ask, clearly eager to change the subject.

"Among others." He realized just in time that perhaps it wasn't necessary to explain how his teenage fascination with broody Russian writers had morphed into a passion for Latin American literature around age eighteen.

"I remember how obsessed you were with the Russians. Did you ever get through *Crime and Punishment* in the end?"

"I did. I was right, it was worth it," Nicholas said proudly.

"Of course, you would be a Dostoyevsky fan."

Nicholas felt like he should have been offended, but he could detect no unkindness in Matías's smile. "There's nothing wrong with appreciating the classics. Let me guess, you're more of a Strugatsky guy yourself?"

There was a long pause, during which Matías's smile slowly faded.

"I've read *Lolita*," he answered, although it sounded more like a question.

Nicholas laughed at that, surprising them both.

"What did you think about it?" he asked, his tone kinder than he'd planned.

Matías grimaced. "Kind of gross, honestly."

Stupidly, Nicholas caught his eyes then, and was immediately transported back to the last time he'd heard him say that word. Except back then, it hadn't been aimed at a book.

"Yeah, it's supposed to be," Nicholas finished in a weary tone. They headed toward the checkouts in silence.

❧

On the way back home, Matías decided he wanted the window seat, and sat down clumsily while trying to keep the heavy bags upright. Once he was settled, he didn't take his headphones out of his pocket, and Nicholas spent most of the ride wondering if that meant he wasn't supposed to listen to music either.

"Do you never drink coffee anymore, then?"

He almost jumped in surprise when Matías's deep and honeyed voice broke their comfortable silence. Matías had always done that.

He asked questions related to nothing they'd been discussing with no preamble, as if he was speaking up halfway through a conversation he'd started in his head.

"I do, sometimes. I've just switched to tea in the morning."

Nicholas waited for more, but looking at Matías's serene expression, it seemed like that was all the answer he'd been looking for. With a sigh, Nicholas settled in and got lost looking out the window, too tired to search for his phone buried at the bottom of his bag.

"You're not the only one who's changed, you know."

Matías had spoken softly, staring out into the distance and avoiding his gaze. Nicholas tried not to get distracted by the dark curls falling into his eyes, or the way the dimming light outside cast shadows on his face. With the dirty bus window behind him and the grey sky above, it was like a painter's brush had spent hours illuminating his figure against a background that paled in comparison to his subject.

Nicholas tried hard to muster the anger he wanted to feel at the sight of him, but there was only a familiar ache.

While a small part of Nicholas wanted to believe that was true, it didn't really matter whether the man sitting next to him was the same one who'd betrayed and hurt him years ago. If he let himself be honest, he could admit that he might be sitting next to a stranger. But as long as the past couldn't be magically erased, it would never be enough.

After a long silence, Nicholas admitted, "I don't know how to answer that."

Matías sighed. "I know."

From: Brianna Ann Nelson

To: Nicholas Fisher

Subject: Thank you Pt. 2

September 14, 6:17 PM

Nicholas,

Thank you SO MUCH for your help yesterday. I'm so sorry the others didn't show up. I think it may just be me working on this in the end, so I'm even more grateful for all your help!

I'm sorry I kept you for so long. I feel like I have so much to work on (and read) after all that we discussed, so it should be a while before I need to pick your brain again.

I'll email you when I've got a rough outline as discussed and read up some more on the topic. Don't hesitate to reach out if you think of anything else that could help, or if you suddenly wake up with a marvelous idea on how to organize the project!!

Thank you again,

Bri

CHAPTER 8

AS IT TURNED out, planning his first date in months for right after his shopping escapade with Matías hadn't been the worst idea. They got home later than he would have thought, which meant Nicholas didn't have time to pace anxiously around his room until it was time to go, wondering how long it would take Kieran to realize there was nothing interesting about him when he wasn't drowning in tequila. He got ready in a clean version of the same clothes he always wore, and by the time he'd taken a few deep breaths, it was time to head out.

He had no idea what Matías would get up to on a Saturday evening with Will gone, and almost felt sorry for him, but then he realized it wasn't his problem. Spending two hours together without jumping at each other's throats was no declaration of friendship, and it was high time Nicholas stopped wondering what Matías meant when he said he had changed.

He let out a breath when he walked into the living room and saw Matías quietly leaning against the kitchen counter while a pot of boiling water stood forgotten on the stove. He was wearing his sweatpants again.

"Night in?" he couldn't help but ask, like they were regular roommates. Like he cared.

Matías put down his phone and turned to him, taking in Nicholas's outfit change with an unreadable expression. His eyebrows rose, and Nicholas could have sworn he looked him up and down for just a beat too long before breaking the now-awkward silence.

"Yes. What about you?"

Nicholas looked down at his dark-green shirt self-consciously, wondering if he'd put too much cologne on.

"Just going for a drink." He wasn't sure if he was supposed to volunteer any information, but then realized he didn't want to give Matías a chance to ruin that too. "I'll see you tomorrow?"

Matías nodded, avoiding his gaze entirely.

☙

The bar Kieran had chosen looked like the kind of place that didn't want to be a sports or college bar while being mostly frequented by sports fans and college students. It wasn't full when Nicholas got there, but it looked like it would get there quickly enough, if the frantic rhythm with which bus boys were gathering up empty bottles was anything to go by.

Kieran was standing by the counter with the open smile that Nicholas hadn't seen since the party. He was dressed entirely in black, his collarbones visible under the half-buttoned shirt and his signature vintage leather jacket. The monochromatic look made it clear that Kieran was careful about his appearance, and Nicholas immediately felt inadequate.

"Hey, handsome," Kieran said, with an accent thicker than Nicholas remembered. In fact, his whole demeanor had nothing in common with the course assistant he'd tried to talk to on Thursday.

"Hi," Nicholas replied, barely loud enough to be heard.

Their hug was stilted and awkward, but Kieran had the decency to pretend it wasn't. He ordered a whiskey, and Nicholas almost did the same to impress him. But he knew there'd be nothing impressive about him being drunk after one glass, so he settled on a beer. Nicholas sighed in relief when Kieran grabbed his elbow and took him to a table in the corner. When he sat down and looked back at the man in front of him, the dim lights hit the sharp angles of the Scot's face like they'd been adjusted with him in mind.

"Have you been here before?" Nicholas asked.

Kieran chuckled at his rehearsed question. "I have. I've been in the city eight years, so—"

"Eight? How old are you?" Realizing how rude he sounded, Nicholas caught himself. "I mean, I'm sorry, I just meant—were you here for undergraduate too?" he asked hopefully.

"I was. Moved here at eighteen. Don't worry, I'm not some old creep." Nicholas didn't manage to laugh. "So, I was saying, I've been here before, but it has changed a lot. Just like the rest of the city, for that matter. It seems like every other week I want to visit an old restaurant I used to love, only to find it boarded up or worse. And that's without even talking about the declining standards at the university—"

While Kieran talked, Nicholas allowed himself to enjoy how his accent oscillated between Scottish and almost American depending on the words he was saying. Admittedly, he also got slightly distracted by Kieran's deep, almost-black eyes and the dark, jaw-length hair he kept having to comb back with a careless hand. He looked less like the tortured scholar he was used to seeing on campus tonight and more like he'd squeezed in a drink with Nicholas before the underground rock concert he had to attend after this. Even his ringed hands contrasted against Nicholas's bare ones on the table between them.

Perhaps he'd picked up on Nicholas's discomfort with being the center of attention, because it was a while before Kieran asked him about what he was doing in the city.

"I just moved to Chicago last year, for the PhD program. I didn't really know what else to do with an English degree, and I heard there were great professors here, so. Also, it was time for a change of scenery."

He was relieved when Kieran didn't ask why. "Yes, I can't argue enough in favor of seeing what the rest of the world has to offer, instead of sticking around the same places your whole life. Leaving Scotland so young definitely taught me a thing or two about life." He chuckled.

Nicholas was about to ask him about his home country when a loud group of college boys entered the bar. They were clearly not on their first stop of the night and headed for the counter without realizing the attention they'd garnered. There was a familiar exuberance about them, slapping one another on the back and extending their arms eagerly at the secrets the evening still held. Mechanically, Nicholas's eyes looked for familiar brown curls among them.

"Sorry, maybe I should shut up for a while?" Kieran asked, a bit louder, which made Nicholas's head whip around as he crashed back into the conversation, embarrassed at having been caught staring. Kieran's hand had settled on his wrist.

"Sorry. They just got me distracted. I'm listening," Nicholas assured him, locking his eyes on Kieran in apology.

The Scot laughed it off. "Tell me about yourself, then."

Nicholas frowned. "I just did."

"Oh, come on." The low, deep chuckle came out again. It was a rich and attractive sound, except, Nicholas suspected, when it was used at your expense. "I want to know the real you, not just the headlines."

Nicholas's palms were starting to feel clammy.

"I—I'm afraid that's about it, as far as the real me goes. All I do is go to class, study, maybe see my friends, try to make it to work on time…"

"Where do you work?"

"The community library in my old neighborhood. It's small and grossly underfunded, but the work is easy and the woman who's in charge is actually—"

"I bet it's nice being around books all the time, isn't it?"

"Yeah, it is." Nicholas stopped there, assuming Kieran had more questions.

He did.

"What's your favorite one, then?"

"Book?" Nicholas frowned, his tone accidentally coming out more dubious than he'd intended. The question felt like a trap. Kieran just nodded, the corner of his lips drawing a challenge. "I guess… The easy answer is always going to be anything by Hurston. *Tell My Horse* had an incredible impact on me. Although I'll always have a weakness for *Mrs. Dalloway*. I can't really tell you why, but I find myself going back to—"

"Have you read any of her other stuff?"

"I have, but *Mrs. Dalloway* was my first, and I never really managed to get that feeling again. Like everything suddenly fell into place, when you close the page and feel this… relief. Like finally, you've caught a glimpse of the grand design. Which qualifies it as a favorite book, I suppose."

Kieran hummed. "Of course, that's what literature is all about, isn't it?"

"What's yours?"

"I can't say that I could pick just one."

Nicholas smiled. A memory flashed into his mind—Matías, when Nicholas was a freshman and considering majoring in English, stubbornly maintaining that Brandon Sanderson was the only writer in the world worth reading.

"Spoken like a true academic."

Kieran looked pleased at his remark.

With every round of drinks the Scot ordered for them, the conversation became smoother, and soon enough Nicholas lost track of time. Everything Kieran said seemed to be perfectly crafted to tick the invisible boxes his friends always called unreasonable. He wondered if this was what they meant when they said dating was supposed to be fun, when they insisted he give it a try every time someone looked at him twice.

Nicholas could feel himself getting dangerously drunk, but every time Kieran asked if he wanted another drink, there was a hint of challenge in his tone that made him nod in response, even though he wasn't done with the last one yet. He shook his head, trying to focus on what Kieran was saying.

"Sorry, what was that?" The music around them was slowly growing louder, and Kieran stood up. "I can barely hear you from over there," he explained as he walked around the table and threw himself on the seat next to Nicholas. There wasn't really enough space with Nicholas sitting in the middle of the booth, but he didn't seem to mind.

From up close, Nicholas could see the way Kieran's eyes kept coming in and out of focus, like they had last weekend on the dancefloor. Maybe the drinks were starting to get to him too.

"So, did you have anything planned after this?" Kieran asked, lazily wrapping an arm around Nicholas's shoulder.

He might not have much dating experience, but he knew what the question meant. He looked at the mysterious man next to him, who'd told him a lot of things in the few hours they'd been sitting there, yet not enough for Nicholas to feel like he knew him at all. Although Nicholas supposed he'd done the same thing.

Kieran was smart, there was no doubt about that. And there was something thrilling about holding a conversation with him, with the accent and the sharp features and the challenge in every question. But he'd also been drinking all night—both of them had—and Nicholas was developing a headache. He'd have to pay for a cab to get him home if he didn't head back soon.

"I don't," he said, still unsure as to which words would come next. He wanted Kieran to ask him for more, to feel desired the way he had at the party. He'd been so drunk by the end of the night that he'd said no when Kieran had mentioned they go home together, but Nicholas thought he might say yes if he were asked again.

Kieran was staring at him, his lips stretched into a daring smile. But nothing came.

"I like to take things slow, though," Nicholas let out in an exhale when he understood it was his turn to ask, disappointing himself with his lack of bravery.

He glanced up at Kieran, an apology on his tongue. For a second, he thought he'd blown it. Kieran looked at him before unhooking his arm from across Nicholas's shoulder and downing the rest of his whiskey with a wince.

"Of course," he finally answered after a few seconds. And as suddenly as Kieran had sat down next to him, he got up. His smile was back, and he touched Nicholas's fingers gently. "You'll be okay to get home, yes?"

"Of course."

They both stood up to put their coats back on. Kieran looked flushed in the now-full bar, but he still exuded his usual confidence, the polar opposite of Nicholas, who was wondering if there was a wall that could absorb him.

"I really enjoyed tonight," he said in a rushed voice, worried he'd ruined his chances of seeing the other man again.

He didn't have to worry for long. Kieran grabbed his elbow and dragged him flush against his body, his other hand settling on his cheek as he kissed him.

Nicholas let himself be pulled in, but he had trouble keeping his mind off the crowd around them. He'd never been the kind of person who liked to have an audience, not even if it was people he knew. He tried to relax, knowing that the last time they had kissed had also been in a room full of people. It had felt different, though. More anonymous, safely tucked away in a college house amid people who all had only one thing in mind.

Nicholas shook it off. He was tired of being the boring friend, the one who wouldn't kiss another man in the middle of a crowded bar. So he did just that, putting a hand on Kieran's waist. His lips were cold from the ice in his drink, and he tasted like whiskey, which Nicholas's brain was starting to associate with the man himself.

Kieran knew what he was doing. As Nicholas relaxed, the other man's hand moved from his cheek to his neck. He soon melted into the Scot's strong hold, shutting his eyes and his thoughts. It had been a long time since he'd been kissed like that—hungrily. Like he was wanted.

"I'll see you soon," Kieran said when they parted. He didn't move from where he stood next to the table, though, and Nicholas realized he wasn't planning on following him outside.

"Text me," Nicholas breathed out, a little hot. He could feel his cheeks remain flushed as he walked through the crowd, trying to make himself as small as possible. He was still light-headed from the kiss and tense from how public it had been; he felt like a block of cement walking through the room trying to pretend he had four working limbs. But there were only a few looks sent his way, and by the time he noticed them, he was out in the fresh air.

Taking a deep breath to settle himself, Nicholas pulled out his phone and noticed he had a text from Ajay.

How did it go???

Come over tomorrow? Will's out of town.

Yes!!! was Ajay's only reply.

Nicholas tried not to wonder how disappointed his friend would be when they learned he'd chickened out of going home with Kieran.

༄

Matías was still out running his daily marathon—or so Nicholas assumed—by the time Ajay came over the next day. Nicholas opened the door to find his friend carrying a bag big enough for a normal person to live on for an entire semester. The two of them hugged in the entryway, Nicholas's pale figure and forgettable clothes fading into the background against Ajay's lime-green tunic, their golden jewelry shimmering against their dark skin.

Two freshly poured cocktails were already waiting, and Ajay sighed in satisfaction. It only took Ajay five minutes to stop pretending they had any other reason for being there than hearing about Nicholas's date. Somehow, however, the words remained stuck in his throat. Nicholas didn't know why he couldn't find the words to talk about what had been, crippling anxiety and sweaty palms aside, a really good date, but thankfully Ajay didn't push.

They were on the couch when Matías came home, sweaty and flushed and unbearably smiley. He said hello to Ajay with a wave, only staying long enough not to be impolite. As soon as the bathroom door closed behind him, Nicholas turned to find Ajay with their mouth wide open. He understood. He suspected everyone remembered the first time they'd seen Matías post-exercising, and no one could be held responsible for how long it took them to recover.

"I do apologize, but that is one fine specimen," Ajay concluded longingly.

Nicholas rolled his eyes. The two of them, at least, were not in the habit of fighting over men. Where Ajay's interest was usually overwhelming and short-lived, Nicholas tended to spend months pining in silence. He knew it was better to let this predictable crush on Matías run its course rather than waste energy trying to prove to his best friend that Matías wasn't worth their attention.

He wasn't even sure that was true anymore.

So, he just wrinkled his nose and hummed distractedly. Soon enough, Ajay's attention was on something else, rattling off stray thoughts like they were racing to an imaginary finish line. Ajay rarely talked about themself in any real way, instead preferring to get lost in anecdotes and loud debates. Perhaps because they had no choice but to wear so much of their identity outwardly, available to everyone for the taking, they tended to shroud everything else that made them who they were in secrecy.

Matías was still in the bathroom when Ajay sat Nicholas down on a stool in the middle of the living room, getting an impressive range of tools out of their bag and claiming that two cocktails in was the perfect moment to deal with Nicholas's overgrown haircut. Nicholas diligently closed his eyes while Ajay was tutting and huffing in disapproval at what they were working with.

"Where did you learn how to do this again?" Nicholas asked, worry in his voice.

"High school. Don't worry about it," Ajay answered, their tone clipped.

They never talked about anything that had happened before college. All Nicholas knew was that their family hadn't been supportive, and they'd spent those years hiding who they were, tucking pieces of themself away until they finally left for college. But Ajay had always done their best to make it work at home because of their younger siblings. They rarely volunteered any information about them, but when they did, Ajay's voice always softened and their eyes lit up. It reminded Nicholas of how very human his best friend was. They felt so much and loved so hard; the loud careless words and easily dismissed acquaintances only served to balance out the deep loyalty they were capable of once they deemed you worthy of it.

"I'm going to make you so handsome, that TA of yours won't know Plato from Socrates when he sees you," Ajay let out when they were almost done.

"If I'd known the only thing standing between me and complete memory loss was a few inches off my hair, I would've booked an appointment earlier."

They both laughed. When Ajay didn't say anything else, Nicholas knew this was his best chance at talking about last night. He took a large sip of his drink before finally breaking the silence, quickly telling his friend about the nice conversation, the drinks that had helped him lose track of time. The kiss at the end.

When they realized he was done, Ajay chimed in, surprisingly gentle. "He sounds great."

Nicholas smiled. "He is. He's the whole package." He paused.

"Why the long face, then?" Ajay asked distractedly as they shook the wet hair on top of Nicholas's head.

Nicholas was going to deny it, but he crossed Ajay's eyes in the mirror, warning him against it.

He sighed. "I just… I felt so on edge the whole evening. Like the whole thing was a test. I was trying so hard to be my best self, it was exhausting. I know—I know it's the point of a date, but I felt like I was holding my breath for hours, and I don't know when it's going to stop feeling like this. Maybe I'm just not meant for dating."

Ajay's face made a series of contortions, which made Nicholas laugh. It was obvious they had quite a few things to say to that.

"One thing at a time," Nicholas said, trying to be helpful.

Ajay took a second to organize their thoughts.

"Firstly, I do want to say that I am proud of you for actually going out with this guy instead of taking years of planning to even ask his name. Now," Nicholas winced in preparation for what was to come. "I know you don't have much experience, but being your best self is not the point of dating at all, and I'm slightly upset that in all our months of trying to get you to meet someone, we never mentioned that." They took a deep breath. "The point is to figure out if *their* best self is good enough for *you*. The nerves are normal, if you want to make a good impression, but you're trying to figure out if you want to be with them, not proving that you're good enough to be." There was something stuck in Nicholas's throat, and he couldn't talk. "Only if you decide that they are should you brush up on your ancient Greek, or whatever it is you guys do to impress one another."

Nicholas kept his head down, busying himself with his cuticles. Ajay's tone was as soft as Nicholas had ever heard it, but they must have known this was all Nicholas could handle for today, because they turned Nicholas around and started working on the back of his head. After a while, the easy banter and snipping remarks finally eased the weight on Nicholas's chest. They were still cleaning up the mess they'd made when Ajay stopped mid-laugh and looked up at Nicholas, catching his eyes.

"You deserve it, you know. The whole package." Nicholas kept sweeping the now-spotless floor, but his friend continued before he had time to disagree. "Seriously. Especially because *you're* the whole package too. Plus, now that I'm done with that bird's nest on your head, you're handsome as the devil."

It was definitely the cocktails making his best friend so effusive, Nicholas reminded himself.

"I don't think that's how the saying goes."

The words weren't Nicholas's, although they mirrored his own thoughts. When he looked up, he saw Matías coming out of the bathroom, wet-haired and grinning, a towel around his neck and sweatpants slouching dangerously low on his hips. Low enough that whenever Matías took a step, his tan drew an inviting line from one hip to the other. Nicholas coughed his embarrassment away, although he was grateful for the interruption. Ajay's psychoanalytic rants were few and far between, but they tended to cut deeper than he was ready to admit.

"Perhaps, but I'm not wrong," his friend replied unhelpfully.

The wide smile seemed to freeze on Matías's face when he caught Nicholas's eye. He was about to ask if he had something on his face when Matías said, in a single breath, "You cut your hair."

Nicholas ached to say something cutting about stating the obvious and dusting off the glasses he'd only seen Matías wear once.

Ajay must have known that, because they took over. "Actually, I cut his hair. The devil we'd be talking about would definitely not be of the handsome kind if we'd let Nicholas anywhere near that pair of scissors."

They chuckled, but Nicholas was still tense and ready to pounce, Matías's eyes stared somewhere between Nicholas's cheekbones and his eyebrows. Had Ajay missed a strand? He reached up a hand self-consciously but didn't find anything there.

Ajay, probably trying to extricate their little group from the blanket of awkwardness suddenly draped over the living room, clapped their hands enthusiastically. "We should bake something."

Before anyone could protest, Ajay had put a whisk in Matías's hands, and Nicholas was portioning out ingredients for chocolate chip cookies. He was too stunned by the sight of Matías silently obeying to do anything but get to work. There was no time to be rude, and the sharp warning in Ajay's eyes whenever they caught Nicholas's stopped him from even trying. Instead, he looked for sea salt while Ajay regaled Matías with a series of Chicago-themed stories about Sloane and Nicholas from the beginning of their friendship.

Nicholas tuned them out, his thoughts drifting back to the first time he'd baked with Ajay. It had been winter break, and they'd both been stuck in Chicago while Sloane had gone home. That was when Ajay had really started opening up to him. It was hard not to, with everyone they knew gone to be with family. Ajay had been there when Nicholas had rushed back to town two days after Christmas with bags under his eyes and a foul mood, and they'd been the one to make him smile again. Nicholas had slept over a lot, glad to escape his own roommates' holiday celebrations, and he'd spent most of the week baking, trying to distract Ajay from the phone calls home that had all seemed to dim their light.

Of course, those weren't the memories they picked to tell Matías about. They talked about Spring Break, which the three friends had spent lazing around watching Bake-Off and eating junk food, and all the times they had joined Sloane for her graveyard shifts at the campus radio. When they started swapping coffeeshop recommendations, Ajay sent a discreet look Nicholas's way, silently asking for permission to tell their favorite story.

A few months ago, their favorite café had hired a new guy who kept asking them both out, refusing to choose. Nicholas laughed to himself, remembering how offended Ajay had been.

"So, obviously, per Nick's suggestion, we decided to play Rock, Paper, Scissors to see who would get to take him on a date."

"And who won?" Matías asked. Nicholas wasn't looking at him, but he could hear the smile in his voice, the lack of awkwardness in his tone. Matías had never made it seem like he cared about Nicholas being gay, but it wasn't something they had ever talked about either. Girls—or in his case, boys—were the one topic Matías had never covered in all the months of trying to educate Nicholas on college life.

"I did, of course," Ajay said proudly.

Even though there was nowhere he'd rather be than baking with Ajay, Nicholas couldn't help being hyper-aware of Matías's presence. It was so different from anything he'd ever known, being the one who was part of a duo while Matías was the odd one out, struggling to understand all of their inside jokes. Yet Matías seemed to be dealing with it better than Nicholas ever had; he laughed when something was funny and only talked to ask follow-up questions, like he was trying to fill the gaps of Nicholas's life left by the years he'd spent away.

Nicholas wondered if the only reason Matías was being so attentive to the stories was so he had more material to hurt him with later.

Every now and then, like when he was busy splitting the dough—so focused that he later realized he'd been biting his lip in concentration—Nicholas felt Matías's gaze on him. It made him want to rub the back of his neck self-consciously, wondering if Ajay had cut his hair too short.

Neither Ajay nor Matías put up much of a fight when he asked them to leave him to do the dishes on his own. He needed a minute to himself after spending the whole afternoon surrounded. But wiping counters that were already clean while the two most extroverted people he knew talked each other's ears off in the living room, Nicholas couldn't ignore the fear in his chest that Ajay would be quick to realize they had picked the wrong person to be friends with.

When Nicholas finally brought the plate of warm cookies to the living room, Matías and Ajay were laughing comfortably on the couch. The sight made him pause in the middle of the room. Ajay was perhaps the only person in this world capable of taking up more space than Matías, able to dispel any tension around them and spark joy instead, dismissing the need for Nicholas to shape himself into something that was palatable to others. Matías was no exception to the pulling orbit of Ajay's kindness.

"Sorry, are we putting you out?" Ajay asked after dinner time had come and gone, seeming to realize that they were sitting on what was evidently Matías's bed.

"No, don't worry, I don't sleep much these days. Are you headed out tonight?"

"No, we need our beauty sleep," Nicholas heard Ajay answer. "I think we'll head to bed soon, actually."

Nicholas hummed at the thought. He was leaning against the back of the couch with his eyes closed, almost dozing off after the amount of sugar he'd ingested.

At least he didn't have to find the energy to fight to get Ajay to stay over like he used to when they'd started being friends. His friend lived on the other side of town, and Nicholas knew enough about the world outside these doors not to let them face it alone late at night. Ajay had fought him on it at first, insisting that they faced the world every day. Nicholas had nodded, put on his coat, and walked them all the way back to their front door.

Now whenever Ajay came over, they brought a bag.

"Oh."

When he opened an eye, Matías was standing in the middle of the room, staring at them with a frown. "Good night, then."

Nicholas was too tired to wonder about the sudden coldness in his voice. Instead, Ajay headed to the bathroom to take off their makeup, and he set up the projector in his room to play *Family Guy* on the wall so they could fall asleep to it.

Sometimes, even silence was too loud.

From: Jasmine Miller-Reed

To: Nicholas Fisher

Subject: ENGL 12307

September 16, 9:27 AM

Dear Nicholas,

Just a quick word about the research project I have assigned to my ENGL 12307 students. Brianna tells me you have been readily available and a great help to her, which I was happy to hear.

The rest of the group has officially dropped out of the project, so it will be just her—however, I am tempted to maintain the scope of the prompt as it is now; I think with your help, she can handle it.

Let me know if you deem this fair.

Best,
Jasmine Miller-Reed

CHAPTER 9

THEY WOKE UP to a text from Sloane telling them she was expecting them for lunch at their usual spot on campus. They had morning classes to get to first, so the two friends got up in silence, Nicholas opening the window to a bitingly cold morning even though October hadn't arrived yet.

Nicholas was famously not a morning person, so Ajay's habit of needing what seemed like hours to get ready in the morning worked out perfectly for them. Still not having exchanged anything more than hellos with his best friend, Nicholas headed to the kitchen to make himself tea and eat the leftover cookies. When he went back to the bedroom, Ajay was done with their shower and trying to decide on an outfit—because, of course, they had brought options. Their dance was a well-practiced one; Nicholas used the bathroom while Ajay packed up their things, sliding into a pair of jeans and a long-sleeved shirt before heading back to the room, where his friend was doing their makeup.

They still had a few minutes to spare before needing to leave, so Nicholas headed to the living room. He'd opened his phone and started reading an article he'd bookmarked for Brianna earlier in the week when he bumped straight into a hard chest, feeling a hand wrap around his bicep to keep him from stumbling while his whole body tensed.

"Shit, fu—sorry about that," he said in a single breath, feeling his neck heat up.

"It's fine," Matías answered abruptly before taking a large step away from him.

Nicholas frowned. Something about Matías's tone brought him right back to being the annoying little brother who was always in the way. It almost gave him whiplash, the steely edge in his voice making Nicholas look up at him. Matías wasn't looking back—his eyes were screwed on the window behind Nicholas, his jaw tense with effort. Nicholas stared for a second longer than was probably acceptable.

"Ready?" Ajay asked as they walked out of the room. "Sorry about the delay, I had an eyeshadow situation."

Nicholas looked up at his friend's eyelids, but any thoughts on the intricacy of the design they'd drawn on effortlessly were interrupted by the sound of Matías snorting derisively behind him, muttering something he couldn't catch.

A heavy silence settled over the apartment as the two friends turned toward Matías with a questioning glance. He had the decency to look embarrassed, a grimace drawing itself onto his features. Still, Nicholas felt cold all over.

After they'd all bumped into one another on the green, he'd thought it would be safe for Ajay to be around Matías. But he would know the mocking tone and avoidant eyes anywhere.

Perhaps last night hadn't gone as smoothly as he'd thought—Ajay tended to shield their friends from the amount of abuse they received. Perhaps Matías had already been cold and mocking, and Nicholas had been too stupidly distracted to even realize.

"Good morning," Ajay just said, shaking off Matías's contempt.

After another extended silence, they seemed to realize Matías wasn't planning to respond.

Nicholas hated himself for the feeling in his chest, the one that didn't want to believe it. That whispered to him that this was not the Matías he knew. Despite what he claimed about the man to ease the sting of what had happened between them, Matías wasn't unkind. Sure, he was entitled and full of himself, had clear favorites and realizing you didn't make the cut tended to hurt. But he got along with everyone, he said hello and goodbye and always asked about people with the look of someone who cared about the answer.

And he'd never been a bigot, which was why Nicholas had allowed him near Ajay at all.

Whatever mood Matías was in now, Ajay was the last person in the world who deserved to suffer for it. He remembered what it felt like to be on the receiving end of Matías's sharp judgement, and it made Nicholas's whole body flare up in anger. But Ajay minutely shook their head and started moving toward the door, grabbing his arm with the look of someone who wanted to be safe more than vindicated, so Nicholas had to let it go—for now.

Ajay didn't seem to want to discuss Matías's rudeness, and Nicholas didn't know how to bring it up without making everything worse.

"I'm sorry," he whispered as they were waiting for the bus, Nicholas's hands in his pockets while he was staring at his beat-up shoes.

Ajay looked up, their face neutral. "What for?"

Nicholas struggled to order his thoughts and find the words that matched them. "Well, I mean, Mat—sorry, he was a dick. I mean, I know I said he was, but I thought you'd be safe from it, I really did. I wouldn't have—"

"Don't worry about that," they answered genuinely. Nicholas opened his mouth and closed it again, unsure how to proceed. They did seem... all right, more all right than Nicholas was. But if habit was the reason for that, it was no comfort at all. "Seriously, Nick, I don't care. He was fine last night. He's probably as bad a morning person as you are."

Nicholas looked at them dubiously, then up at the living room windows they could see from the bus stop.

"All right," he finished lamely.

If there was one thing he knew about Matías Romero, it was how much he enjoyed early morning practices and blaring reggaeton in the shower before the sun was even up. But he kept that to himself. The only important thing was that Ajay was okay.

❧

As usual, Sloane looked beautiful, her long brown coat and black boots reminding him of a wealthy widow meeting her friends for lunch to tell them about her newest affair. Which turned out to be exactly what happened, minus the wealth and widowhood. She did look happy for a Monday, her cheeks slightly flushed as she told them how the man who worked at the antique shop next to her house had invited her to his cabin for the weekend.

"When you say he works at an antique shop," Ajay started asking, doubtful, "do you mean he's a rich and refined antique dealer or some lost, pretentious soul on minimum wage?"

The way Sloane bit her bottom lip told them everything they needed to know.

"Well, at least this one's not trying to make it as a promoter by hanging around strip clubs," Nicholas said positively, shuddering at the memory.

"He says that if he works at the shop long enough, there's a chance that the owner might show him the ropes of arts dealing. And he's a poet. He read me some Dumas," she added pointedly, obviously trying to impress her friends.

"Henry or Alexandre?" Nicholas asked.

Once again, her expression did not bode well.

"Please do not tell me you agreed to spend the weekend in a remote cabin with a stranger who still thinks the height of romance is serenading you with the unintelligible poetry of an exploitative aristocrat who didn't even write his own books."

"Well, if you guys don't want to hear about it, I suppose we can just talk about Nick's weekend with his new football lad of a best friend," she countered.

"Did you guys read his plays or poetry?" Nicholas asked without missing a beat.

He played along after that, asking the right questions and trying to find something to like about this stranger, although even Sloane herself seemed to struggle to come up with anything.

"Probably never," she clarified with a smile when Ajay asked when she was going to see him again. "The sex was great, and the cabin a nice change of pace if a bit rustic… But the weather is only getting colder, so that shouldn't be a factor. Perhaps I'll give him a call in the spring." She let out a heavy sigh. "I just don't think a poet is what I need." She finished her bagel, knowing that her audience was patiently waiting for the rest of this new insight. "Too interested in the sound of their own voice."

Nicholas faded into the background of his friends' animated conversation, distracted by what was going on outside the window they had their backs to. The rain that had taken over the city while they were eating cleared as quickly as it had come, although by the time Ajay had to rush out to the lab and Sloane to a meeting, the heavy clouds above them still shed a greyish glow on Chicago's decaying buildings.

"So, do I get to hear about your poet too?" Sloane asked as he was walking her to the English department.

Nicholas smiled. "He's not a poet."

"They're all poets if you give them half a chance," she said with a dismissive wave of her hand. But it wasn't enough to distract her from the topic, and she looked back at her best friend with an expectant glint in her eyes.

"It was great. He's really interesting and smart."

"And hot," she continued with a wiggle of her brows.

"And hot," Nicholas admitted with a chuckle. "I just don't know where to go from here."

She paused, forcing Nicholas to stop in his tracks. "Well, you see him again, obviously."

"I don't know if he'll be interested," Nicholas answered in a low voice, walking ahead after he caught Sloane's eyeroll.

"Did he say anything to indicate that to be the case?"

"No. But..." Nicholas sighed, remembering the tense look he'd gotten when he'd said he wanted to take things slow. "I don't know. Maybe nothing will come out of this."

Sloane looked like she wanted to respond, but nothing came. They'd had this conversation before. Whenever anyone expressed interest in Nicholas—asking for his number or holding his gaze a little too long—he'd start explaining why it would never work.

When the English department building appeared on the far end of the quad, Sloane wrapped a hand around his wrist. "Give him a chance. Or, actually, give yourself a chance on this. It could be amazing. Okay?"

Nicholas could only nod.

❧

For the rest of the afternoon, Nicholas did his best to hold onto the peace he always felt after being with his friends, all too aware that a fight was waiting for him at home if he caught Matías there. Cowardly, he decided to head to the library instead of facing it just then. He walked the long way across the green, sighing at the state of his flimsy shoes after he was done crossing the muddy grass. The soaking pairs of sneakers left in the hallway outside their apartment to dry were beginning to pile up, and he wondered how long it would be before William sat him down to have a conversation about season-appropriate footwear.

Nicholas had always liked to be surrounded by pretty things, but he decided to forego the old, beautiful rooms of the library in favor of a secluded corner on the upper floors that could provide him with complete isolation.

Perhaps he'd forgotten more than he thought about the throes of undergraduate life, because most of the rooms were busier than he had expected. Students sat in neat rows, their shoulders tenser and their faces paler than they had been a month ago.

Nicholas silenced his phone and got to work. He had received some feedback on a piece he'd submitted for review and was hoping to find more literature for Brianna's project. He knew there was more scholarship out there than they had managed to gather so far.

It wasn't long before the fluorescent lights and industrial heaters had to be turned on, bringing the old-fashioned carpets' moldy smell out of hiding. Feeling a headache coming on, Nicholas finished annotating the last few articles he'd hoped to get through and prayed the traffic wouldn't be too bad on the way back.

Hoping the delay wouldn't mean Will got home before him, Nicholas stopped by the poetry section on his way out. He roamed the shelves uncertainly, losing himself in titles he only knew of. He always regretted not reading enough poetry, but whenever the choice came to allocate some time to it, he felt a longing for everything else he was missing out on that was hard to ignore. Whenever he thought about poetry, he thought about all that he didn't know, all that he would never have enough time to read, and it was often easier to give up on the endeavor entirely than to laboriously begin to remedy the gap in his knowledge. He also felt like poetry had not been written for him. It took him days to make sense of his own feelings; he wasn't sure how a sentence or a word would ever be enough to capture entire truths, their meanings a comma away from its opposite.

In the end, he didn't borrow anything at all.

Remembering Sloane's words, he sent Kieran a text while he was on the bus home.

I had a great time on Saturday. Can I see you again soon?

The apartment was empty. Will was nowhere to be seen, and Nicholas was able to spend time cleaning the mess he'd left the previous evening. Most of it was already gone, which he could only assume was all the apology he was going to get for Matías's behavior that morning. Thinking about the cold tone with which he'd talked to Ajay riled him up again, and he used his outrage to scrub at the dishes with renewed energy.

Nicholas had always struggled with letting things go, especially where his loved ones were concerned. It had been the same after Emma's death. He had been the only one still throwing fits about it, asking where his sister was years after the accident, lashing out at Will and his mother.

Nicholas didn't know how to move on.

He was busy scraping the bottom of the oven tray, wondering if piercing a hole through it would lighten the weight on his chest, when the sound of the door opening made him look up.

Through it came a sweaty Matías clad in full soccer gear, although the bottom half was more mud and wet grass than anything else, Will's old ball under his arm. He must have been freezing, wearing nothing over his jersey, but his flushed cheeks seemed to be from exercise rather than the cold. Had he… run home?

Nicholas went back to his scrubbing, faster, the blue sponge slowly dematerializing between his reddening knuckles. He heard the squeak of Matías's muddy shoes as he started crossing the living room, not bothering to take them off.

"Any chance you could avoid making the whole place disgusting?" he bit.

"Don't start."

Nicholas looked up, stunned into silence. Matías's tone was weary rather than aggressive, but the words themselves were more confrontational than anything he'd uttered in the four weeks he'd lived with them.

"Don't—*excuse me?*"

"Whatever." Matías waved him off, heading to the bathroom, dirty cleats still on.

"I know you have no respect for anyone but yourself, but seriously, this—"

"You're talking to me about respect?" Matías whirled around. "When exactly have I disrespected you, since you're apparently such a pleasure to be around yourself?"

The angry cut to his voice was not one Nicholas had heard directed at him in years. Apparently, kicking a ball around town all afternoon had not assuaged the mood that had taken over Matías this morning. It seemed to have made it worse, if anything.

Great. Nicholas, too, was in the mood for a fight.

"Are we doing this, then?" he asked, dropping the tray he'd been holding and trying his best not to wince as it clanked against the bottom of the sink. He was glad to finally be facing the Matías he remembered, breathing heavily and bracing for a fight. The new and improved version was too soft to go for the jugular.

"Oh, I don't think you want that," Matías started. The younger man distractedly wondered if he was planning on getting any closer. "You've been rude and petty the entire time I've been here, man. I'm bending over backwards every day, trying to stay out of your way when you're in a mood and be available when there's a small chance you won't bite my head off. It's like you get to decide what kind of day everyone around you is allowed to have. I'm sick of it, and I'm sick of walking on eggshells around you, Nick. So, now I'm the one having a bad day, and it's your turn to deal with it!"

Nicholas's cold chuckle came out gargled. "Oh, grow up. Will's fine whether or not I've warmed his slippers in the morning. Ask him for advice if it's this much of a problem." Even though Nicholas was usually the one to lose his temper first, something about the unfamiliar sight of Matías losing his cool helped him remain composed. "I'm the one who has to deal with you being here, so if I have to get over myself, so do you. I know it's a shock, someone having no interest in being anywhere near you, but this isn't college anymore," he said, extending both arms around him, unsure what he was trying to show him.

"I'm not asking you to hang out every day, but I thought you could make an effort and be a decent human being for a few months. We used to be friends."

"We were never friends, Matías. Friends don't treat each other the way you did."

Nicholas felt a wave of disgust when he saw Matías's eyes soften.

"That's what it's about? After all this time?" The silence threatened to topple Nicholas over. "You've been insufferable for weeks because I blew the whistle on that psycho all those years ago?" He paused. "I don't know what to tell you, Nicholas," Matías continued, his voice quieter. An apology didn't seem to be trying to fight its way out, and suddenly Nicholas didn't want to talk anymore.

He'd spent the past five years ignoring what had happened, had rebuilt friendships without ever facing the events that had led to him losing Matías's. He wasn't ready to have that conversation now, perhaps he never would be. After all this time, the burning shame that Matías may have been right still hadn't left him. "This isn't about him."

"What is it about, then?"

Nicholas looked at him in the eyes, but the words remained stuck in his throat.

It's about how you went about it, he wanted to say. *It's about how I trusted you, how much I wanted you to see me. It's about me being young and stupid, wanting to prove that someone could love me and how you used that against me.*

Nicholas had been eighteen, a lonely freshman adrift in a sea of change. He had no Sloane, no Ajay, barely a phone call from his mother every other week. Even when Matías spent time with him, Nicholas couldn't shake the feeling that he was merely doing Will a favor—that his friendship belonged to William first, and he barely noticed if Nicholas was there.

But his professor had noticed.

At first, it was just office hours and shared cups of coffee, but soon it added up—time that no one had ever given Nicholas before. He started believing it meant something. Soon he was lying for it, hiding it. They'd gone out of town one weekend, and away from the eyes of university staff and fellow students, Nicholas had thought this was his first real relationship.

It had taken him years, but he knew now that nothing about it had been genuine, that he was vulnerable and lonely and an easy target for a man who relished in whatever power he could get. After the university caught wind of the affair, the man had peacefully moved to another cushy professor job on the other side of the country, doubtlessly finding another Nicholas there. He never wrote, barely said goodbye.

Nicholas got over that. The resentment that still clung to his skin wasn't so much about being tossed out with the bulky waste on the man's way out.

No, what still haunted Nicholas was how he'd confided in Matías; how Matías had listened like he was going to keep his secret, continuing to spend game days with him and taking him to parties as if nothing had changed; how he'd pretended not to see Nicholas's heart breaking when the professor ended things, acting like he hadn't been the one to sign the report that had made it happen.

"Nothing," was all he said.

Matías sighed heavily, running a hand through the curls that were starting to dry. In silence, he dropped the dirty ball next to the door and slowly headed toward the couch. Nicholas had to bite his tongue when Matías sat heavily, reminding himself that he wasn't the one who had to sleep on it regardless of mud stains. Looking down at his hands, Nicholas wondered if leaving the tray half-done in the sink and running away now would just be further evidence of his weak, childish nature.

"I'm sorry I pretended I didn't know what was happening. After." Matías broke the silence that Nicholas had thought final. He was looking down at his shoes, his voice low and embarrassed, like that of a man who'd never had to do much apologizing in his life.

Nicholas sighed in frustration. "That's not—"

"I know we should have talked about it. I knew it then, I just… didn't know how. I didn't know how to be there for you. I thought you'd be mad at me, and I was so mad at you too, and then you started looking at me with so much resentment and anger in your eyes. I was young too. I didn't know how to talk about it. Having to keep Will together, having to—" Nicholas scoffed at that, but Matías spoke over it. "No, don't. You don't know. You have no idea how much Will—"

Matías groaned, his loyalty to his best friend clearly coming to a head with his desire to explain himself.

"You say that like you had any interest in being there for me." Matías looked up, having the audacity to look confused by his words. "I was angry at you for ruining everything, sure. I was eighteen. Of course I thought it was love; of course it wasn't." He sighed. "But I got over that. When I found out it was you who reported it after I trusted you with it, it was like losing everything else. And then you couldn't even look at me."

After a breath, Nicholas continued, his voice raw. "You made me think it was my fault for falling for it. That I deserved it to end like that. Maybe if you had talked to me, it would have helped me understand that it wasn't just a cruel prank."

"You didn't want my help," Matías murmured. "You would have never accepted it."

Nicholas wanted to laugh, but he was so tired.

This seemed like the cruel prank, after all these years, Matías pretending that Nicholas wouldn't have gladly taken anything he was ready to give him.

From: Brianna Ann Nelson
To: Nicholas Fisher
Subject: HELP!!!
September 17, 10:13 AM

Nicholas,

I'm so glad to hear from you.

To answer your questions, I am mostly done with research for the parts on translation and cultural transmission, but I've been rethinking my outline and spent the last few days playing around with different structures.

I don't know if Jasmine told you, but I'll be working on my own on the project in the end—and I keep going back and forth between restructuring or going along with it as planned.

I think I could really use your help, if I'm honest. I was going to wait until we were closer to midterms to ask if we could meet, but if you're sure that you don't mind meeting soon, I would love to catch up as soon as possible.

Please let me know what time works for you, even if it's just for a few minutes.

Thank you again!!!

Bri

CHAPTER 10

"TRANSLATION IS, AT its core, an act of radical empathy. It requires us to imagine the world as someone else thinks it. As Goethe wrote, 'Those who know nothing of foreign languages know nothing of their own.' But more than that, they know little of the lives and minds that exist beyond their own narrow borders. Translation forces us to ask: What is lost in the act of conversion? But more importantly, can something be gained?"

Nicholas had been waiting for this section of the syllabus for a month; yet there he was at the back of the drafty classroom, his eyelids heavy from the lack of sleep. The persistent headache he'd been boasting for the past two days was making paying attention an impossible task.

"I will not bore you with platitudes about the beauty of multi-lingualism," the professor continued, her words cutting crisply through the stillness of the room. "Instead, I will ask this: when we translate, whose voice shines through? The poet's? The translator's? Or something else entirely—something that we share? Translation, you see, is not merely the act of finding equivalent words; it is the process of recreating context, bridging gaps, and stepping into someone else's mind without fully leaving your own."

Their professor was exactly what Nicholas would have expected of someone who'd spent her life studying seventeenth-century literature. Although she appeared austere at first, her strict pencil skirts and tiny reading glasses seemingly plucked straight out of the pages of a Victorian governess manual, her severity had tended to shed as the texts they studied grew older and more obscure.

"And yet, translation can be an act of violence as much as it is one of empathy. The translator wields great power: the power to erase, to reinterpret, to leave behind." Her tone had sharpened, almost a warning. When the professor leaned forward, as though daring someone to respond, Nicholas squinted, willing his groggy mind to engage.

"So why bother? Why translate at all, knowing that we will always fail to fully capture the original? Knowing that what we recreate will always be, in some sense, an approximation—an echo rather than the true voice?"

Nicholas half-expected someone to raise their hand and throw out a shallow answer about cultural exchange or universal understanding. Then, he remembered that his Wednesday morning seminar was mostly attended by people who had thought it an easy class or needed a nonfiction credit to be able to pursue their research of choice. No one ever answered or said anything halfway interesting, and in his weakest moments, it made Nicholas sad for her.

"This was a question, by the way. I know at least some of you are interested in interpretive translation, perhaps even actively researching it as we speak. Why?"

After a weary exhale, Nicholas spoke up, hoping she was ready to be disappointed.

❧

He was sitting in the library the next day when Kieran finally answered his text.

Sure. How about tonight?

It had taken him two days to respond, so Nicholas had long convinced himself he'd blown it. The rush of relief he felt was almost heady enough to agree, Will and Thursday evenings be damned. Almost.

I can't do Thursdays. But I'm free all weekend.

Let's do Saturday evening.

The sudden tap on his shoulder made him jump in surprise. He was so embarrassed by the half-yelp that escaped him that he almost didn't recognize the girl next to him, too busy scrambling to drop his phone and take off his headphones. The plastic headband almost snapped as he rushed to pull them down one side of his head.

"Sorry, can I sit with you?" she asked. She was Matías's friend, the one he'd met on the quad a week ago. Was her name Leila? She was waving her arm at the empty chair next to him, where he'd dropped his backpack.

"Sure," he said, trying to ignore the amused curl of her lip. She wore a dark green hijab today, but the rest of her outfit wasn't any more colorful than the first time he'd met her.

The long wooden table that stood in the center of the old library was so tightly packed, their elbows brushed a few times as she emptied her backpack and settled in next to him. Other than to murmur a thank you, she didn't glance at him after that. For the next two hours, she switched from watching a lecture to annotating a paper to seemingly creating a graph out of nowhere. She got so much work done that he started squirming, feeling inadequate as he distractedly stared at articles that all looked, and indeed read, pretty much the same.

Feeling his concentration slip away as the library got noisier, Nicholas grabbed a snack from the many currently buried at the bottom of his bag. That first bite of hazelnut and chocolate made him melt in his seat, and he wondered if he'd accidentally moaned out loud when he reopened his eyes to find Leila looking at him with the same amused smile from earlier. Feeling guilty for not really acknowledging her, he pulled out a bag of candy and turned it around to inspect its ingredient list. Satisfied, he handed it to her with a question in his eyes. She took it with a smile.

Another hour passed, and he sighed in relief as he typed up the last of his notes ahead of his next meeting with Brianna. This would have been a great time to head home, except he'd been trying to spend as little time as possible there since his fight with Matías. Motivated by the need for a distraction and some fresh air more than the watery cup of warm mud that awaited him, he got up to grab a coffee from the entrance hall of the library.

Leila looked up at him hesitantly. "Taking a break?"

He nodded.

"Can I come with you? I'm boiling in here."

"Of course."

They remained silent as they exited the impressive reading room, which had impossibly grown even busier since they'd sat down. At the coffee machine, he hovered over the selection panel with a questioning glance.

She smiled softly. "Nothing, thank you."

"Right. Heart health and all that," he joked to himself, remembering the six months Matías had sworn coffee off because he'd read that one article about caffeine's propensity to cause atrial fibrillation. It had lasted until Nicholas had reminded him that getting blackout drunk twice a week probably carried more risks to his athleticism than a morning cup of coffee.

Still not saying anything, the two students headed outside, standing at the bottom of the steps in front of the library, Nicholas burning his fingers through the paper-thin cup. It didn't take him long to regret not bringing an extra layer of clothing. It seemed like Chicago didn't care much that September was supposed to be a summer month.

Leila didn't seem uncomfortable or eager to fill the silence, and neither was he, but he started to realize that perhaps it was a bit odd, the two of them spending the last three hours together in complete silence. It was certainly uncharacteristic of the people Matías tended to pick as friends.

"Have you always played soccer?" was all he could find to ask, but at least she smiled again. It was a really nice smile, especially as it reached her almost-black eyes. Her features may have been made for seriousness, with her straight nose and dark brows, but when she smiled, she became an entirely different person.

"I've got three brothers. I'm sure you can guess."

Nicholas managed to smile despite the familiar pang of hurt reverberating through his chest. He often wondered if Emma would've played too, having two brothers who did.

"That's… nice?"

She laughed. "It's all right. At least they're an uneven number, so they needed me more than they hated having a girl play with them."

Nicholas hummed, unsure of what there was to say.

"Any of them still play, then?"

"No," she said with a smug smile. "Pretty much stopped when they realized I was a lot better than them." The pride in her voice would have been arrogance coming from Matías, but from Leila's mouth, it came out warmer and—in his opinion—more justified.

"Your parents must be proud."

She looked at him with a snort. "About which part—that I'm twenty-six and still in school, or that the only way I could afford undergrad was by playing a sport that puts me in the spotlight for racist abuse every day?"

Nicholas swallowed. "Does wearing the hijab make it worse for you?"

She tilted her head, not taking long to consider the question before answering it. "Yes. It's not soccer itself—it's the scrutiny that comes with it. Every time you step foot onto the pitch, you're put under a magnifying glass. People project whatever they want onto you, and it doesn't matter how well you play. If you're wearing a hijab, you're the problem before you've even touched the ball." Her voice was calm and matter-of-fact, though her gaze remained fixed somewhere past his shoulder.

No words felt adequate in the face of what she'd had to endure, and still did.

When he didn't say anything, she sighed. "Soccer's always been a space where people lose their inhibitions and say things they'd never dare in real life. You probably saw what Matías had to deal with back in the day. It's not all that different for me, just add a hijab and some extra vitriol. Obviously, it's getting better, and it's better here than where we both grew up. At least I get to play in a way that feels true to myself. Did you know that in France, soccer players just aren't allowed to wear hijabs? Even in the national team."

He hadn't. "That's… an awful lot to take on just for a sport," he said clumsily.

"Doesn't feel like that to us."

"It doesn't feel like a lot?" he asked dubiously.

"It doesn't feel like just a sport," she said simply.

As she spoke, Nicholas felt the weight of her words settle over him. He felt selfish for not realizing he wasn't the only one for whom soccer was a battlefield.

When he looked back at her, Leila was looking at him with a weary smile, nodding toward the heavy library doors.

"Back to East African languages?" she asked. She'd probably caught a glimpse of what he'd been reading up on for his meeting with Brianna. In that moment, her mannerisms and the teasing light in her eyes looked so much like Matías's that it made him wonder exactly how close they were.

"Worse. Back to Pre-Colombian epics, actually."

Her face twisted with such horror that it made him laugh out loud.

"Now, why would you do that to yourself?"

He shrugged, grinning as they climbed up the stairs, his fist mechanically crumpling the cup he was still holding. "Doesn't feel like work." She grimaced, which made him want to continue. "Wait until you hear that I've committed two degrees and most likely the rest of my life to studying the use of precolonial texts in late modern literature."

She was clearly struggling to find anything nice to say about that prospect. "Swahili doesn't sound so bad now," she concluded.

"That's just something on the side, for some undergrads. Or, one undergrad, I guess. She's got this research project, and I'm just giving her some pointers."

"How come? Are you a TA as well?"

"No, it's just some mentorship thing I'm doing in the hopes that I *don't* have to TA next year. I'm not sure I could hack it, to be honest." After a brief pause, he answered her other question. "My advisor asked me to help her. She's a good kid, just trying to find her way. Although she's a lot further along than I was at that age. Everyone but her knows she'll be fine. I think she just wants some reassurance that she can do it."

"So you're showing her that she's on the right track, and she's showing you that you can hack being a TA? That's nice."

Nicholas looked at her in surprise, thinking her answer over as he passed through the metallic turnstile leading to the main reading room. "I… suppose so. It sounds like we're both being played, when you put it like that."

"I don't think you're being played. There's nothing like helping others to help yourself."

They sat back down, the rest of their table giving them death stares for not whispering low enough, and it took Nicholas another twenty minutes before he realized he'd already read the paper he was staring at.

❦

Leila lasted another hour, and by the time she left with a nod and a squeeze of his shoulder, Nicholas realized he was too exhausted to make any useful progress and followed a few minutes behind her. He took the long way to the bus stop, waddling through buildings and greying quads and enjoying the peace of a campus that was growing too chilly to hang out on. He was looking at the golden hue trying to pierce through the heavy blanket of clouds when his phone rang. Nicholas recognized the number instantly, even though he was pretty sure it hadn't called him in years.

"Nicholas?"

"Obviously," he answered, hoping his heavy eye roll would be palpable through the phone. He hadn't said a word to Matías since their fight on Monday, but considering that conversation had been five years in the making, he had hoped it would take another decade before they needed to say anything else to each other. William was back, anyway, so Nicholas doubted Matías had even noticed his silence.

"Can we talk?"

Apprehension filled Nicholas's body.

"I won't be home for a while," he lied.

"Look, I just…" There was a heavy sigh, and Nicholas had to fight the urge to hang up instantly. "I just wanted to apologize, actually, but with our schedules, I'm not sure when I'll get to see you."

"Apologize for what?"

"For blowing up at you the other day. That wasn't me." *Maybe not anymore*, Nicholas wanted to say. But Matías had seemed like exactly the man he remembered. "And—well, I guess you were right—for leaving you behind back then too. I was young, but it's not fair to hide behind that. I didn't know how to deal with it, so I just… didn't. Left you alone with the mess. I guess I'm sorry about that too."

"Okay."

There was a silence then, and Nicholas stopped walking. The bus stop was deserted, which meant he'd have to wait a while. "If you're waiting for me to apologize too, I hope you have a good phone plan because you'll be here a while."

Matías laughed. "Of course not. I just wanted to say it. It's been weighing on me. Also," he continued before Nicholas could say something rude, "I wanted to tell you that I've got some more viewings this week. I know I've been a bit complacent with the housing situation. I haven't had much time, but I'm back on it."

Nicholas nodded but only belatedly realized Matías couldn't see him. "Okay."

"Okay. See you when I see you, then."

❧

"I heard you had someone over while I was away."

Nicholas's head whipped up from the prawn pasta he was working on. Will sat on the sofa, a glass of wine in one hand and his phone in the other, looking like he'd spent the last ten minutes working on sounding casual. Nicholas grimaced in pity. He supposed four Thursdays in a row without trying to overstep the boundaries of his personal life would have been too much to ask of his older brother.

"Where'd you hear that?" Nicholas asked over his shoulder, hoping the sound of the extractor fan would hide the strain in his voice.

Despite William's semi-regular attempts at getting to know anything about his little brother's life, the Fisher brothers were not in the habit of discussing overnight guests. "I don't mind. You can have guests when I'm here too, you know. You don't have to wait until I'm away. You're an adult, there're no rules or anything."

Nicholas started whisking the sauce with heightened efficiency, feeling the embarrassment climb up his neck, all the way to his cheeks. "Please don't tell me you're about to give me the talk."

"No, no, of course not." Will raised his hands in surrender, finally dropping his phone. If he wasn't so uncomfortable himself, Nicholas would have laughed at his brother's matching reddening face. "I just wanted to say that you don't have to hide or sneak around in your own house."

Nicholas sighed heavily as he turned off the stove and the fan.

"It was just Ajay."

"The engineer Ajay?"

"Yeah," Nicholas said, although he didn't think he'd ever told William anything about his friends' degrees. "My best friend Ajay. Sloane—our other friend—was out of town, so we just hung out and baked cookies. They cut my hair. We watched *Family Guy.* Your buddy was in the way the entire time, anyway. Not exactly the kind of shenanigans you're worrying about, I should think," Nicholas said caustically as he finished assembling both plates.

"Oh. Right." Somehow, Will looked confused, so distracted by his own thoughts that he didn't realize the food was ready until Nicholas dropped his plate in front of him. "Well, if you wanted to have them over more regularly—the rest of your friends too—you should. I could clear the apartment, if you wanted, or just... not embarrass you."

"As if that's possible," Nicholas said, trying to sound like he was joking. "But thanks, I guess."

Will still didn't press play or pick up his fork.

"Any other burning questions on your mind?" Nicholas asked with a raised brow, eager to end the talking part of the evening as quickly as possible.

"Well—" It took a while for the words to come, but Nicholas couldn't think of a joke to lighten the mood, so he kept his head down and started eating while his brother figured out what he was trying to say. "I know we never talk about that stuff, but we could, you know. I mean, if there was anyone that you wanted to have over or something, they'd be welcome..."

The tense anxiety in Will's voice made Nicholas look up. "Is this a preamble to you telling me you want to start bringing girls over?"

Will snorted. "God, no. No time for that."

"Right. Too much long-term investing and ladder-climbing to do first."

"Exactly," Will said with a smile instead of the offended grimace Nicholas had been expecting. "And don't forget about being numbingly boring and lacking in depth," he finished, a clear reference to Nicholas's current list of often-voiced grievances against his brother. They both smiled, their features looking even more similar than usual.

The silence had lost some of its awkward edge, but he could still feel his brother's eyes on him.

"Well, there's—"

Will seemed to tense in anticipation, poorly disguising his eagerness as he leaned forward to hear whatever confession was coming.

Nicholas rolled his eyes but decided to keep going. "There is a guy."

Will nodded, visibly trying to keep his mouth firmly shut lest he scare Nicholas off with any of the dozens of questions he was probably lining up. Funnily enough, it reminded Nicholas of coming out, the summer before Will left for college. His brother had been the first person he'd told, half-hoping he'd react badly so it would ease the sting of him leaving. It had quickly become clear that Will had been waiting for the conversation and preparing for it. He'd nodded, all serious, and vowed that he'd make sure "no one messed with him about that" before he left.

"It's not serious yet. We've only hung out a couple of times. But we'll see."

Knowing that he would be allowed approximatively one follow-up question before Nicholas closed himself off for another year or two, Will seemed to pick his next words carefully. "What's he like?"

Nicholas felt a surge of gratefulness when William, for all his faults, didn't awkwardly stumble around the words.

"Scottish," was all Nicholas said.

"Is he a postgrad as well?"

Nicholas nodded. "Classics. Even fewer prospects than me, you'd hate it."

But Will seemed delighted. He was smiling, which wasn't something Nicholas was used to seeing aimed at him. He used to think the only reason his brother had such a defined jawline was because of the hours he spent clenching it in disappointment at Nicholas.

"That's good," he said with a nod to himself before leaning back against the sofa. "Good, that's really good."

Nicholas eyed him dubiously, wanting to make a joke about the clear relief on his brother's face. Instead, he downed half his glass of wine and pressed play.

❦

On Saturday, with no grocery shopping to do and no one at home to roll his eyes at, Nicholas had plenty of time to think about all the ways he could ruin his chances with Kieran. He had tried to move the date to the late afternoon, since he got out of work at four, but Kieran insisted they keep it in the evening, which left him with too many hours with only his thoughts for company.

Nicholas got dressed and undressed three times before he gave up and called his friends. Only Sloane was available, but she came over, like he knew she would, and sat on his bed in silence while he ran lines with her.

"Stop wringing your fingers like that, you're going to give yourself rheumatism."

Nicholas sighed. "I don't think I want to go anymore."

"Yes, you want to go. In fact, you have to go. It's time you got yourself a boyfriend, Nicholas, and you can't meet someone by staying home all the time. Now try on the blue shirt again."

❦

Nicholas arrived at the gallery with his shoulders hunched slightly against the cold, a nervous energy buzzing beneath his coat. The gallery Kieran had suggested was nothing but a square white building, but the light spilling out into the evening was warm and inviting. Kieran was already there, leaning casually against the wall just outside the entrance. One hand tucked in his coat pocket, he looked like something out of a movie, and Nicholas had to avert his gaze, scanning the surroundings until he found something familiar to remind himself this wasn't a dream.

When he looked back, Kieran had noticed him. The half-smile thrown his way made it clear he was perfectly aware of the effect he had on others.

"You came," Kieran said, stepping forward, a note of amusement in his voice as if he could read every jittery thought that had passed through Nicholas's head today.

"Of course."

Nicholas caught up to him, unsure what to do. Thankfully, Kieran took the lead, draping an arm around his shoulder.

"Ready to look at some pretentious art?" he asked with a smirk.

Nicholas exhaled, relieved to find humor where his nerves had expected judgment. He had been glad that Kieran had offered to do something that didn't involve alcohol, but was still worried that a second date was too soon to reveal he knew nothing about modern art.

Inside, the gallery was a mix of dimly lit corners and loud splashes of color on large, unframed canvases—a stark, modern aesthetic that Nicholas suspected was meant to feel edgy. Some pieces were so provocatively abstract, he wondered if their only purpose was to make anyone who walked in feel like they were too stupid to be there. Nicholas glanced sideways at Kieran, wondering how to interpret the smirking satisfaction on his face.

"So, this is… certainly something," Nicholas said with a raised eyebrow, breaking the silence.

Kieran chuckled. "I thought it might make a nice change. I wasn't sure if this was your type of place."

Most definitely not, Nicholas thought. "I like it. It's different from what I'm used to, that's all."

They moved through the gallery in semi-silence, their fingers brushing with every other step, sending jolts of excitement all the way up Nicholas's arm every time they did. Kieran paused in front of a blank canvas splashed with random strokes of neon. Nicholas tilted his head, trying to find something to say about it, when the other man leaned in close, his voice dropping to a conspiratorial whisper.

"You know, I'm fairly certain I saw something exactly like this hanging in my dentist's waiting room. They must have missed the fact it was priceless." He gave Nicholas a wink.

Nicholas chuckled, feeling his own tension start to dissolve. "Or maybe they got a group of five-year-olds to pitch in for theirs instead."

Kieran grinned, watching Nicholas's reaction as much as the painting. "See, now you're getting into the spirit of it."

The ease in Kieran's tone softened something in Nicholas, the confidence unspooling between them. Once he realized they weren't there as a test, he found himself sharing his impressions freely, even attempting a few jokes. It didn't take long before they stopped pretending to look at the art and focused on each other instead, the conversation meandering from aesthetics to academic life. Soon, Nicholas found himself confiding in the other man about his doubts that pursuing a PhD at all had been a good idea.

When Nicholas asked Kieran if he saw himself teaching at all, he exhaled, a hint of irony lacing his smile. "Sometimes. There are days I can convince myself it matters, but other days…" He shook his head. "The truth is, I'd rather be publishing, talking to people I have something to learn *from*." He gave a wry shrug. "I don't know. I think we're expected to care more than I actually do. The students, they're fine, I suppose, but half the time, they're just going through the motions."

Nicholas was quiet, letting the words settle in the space between them. He couldn't help but notice that despite his ambivalence, Kieran didn't seem to be worrying about anything half as much as Nicholas did.

The crowd around them had grown, and soon enough the careless chatter grew loud enough to pierce their bubble, people trying to push past them to catch sight of the painting they were standing in front of.

Kieran started walking again, gesturing to a particularly bizarre sculpture—a mass of tangled wires and broken glass dangling from the ceiling. "Any thoughts?" he asked, amused.

Nicholas narrowed his eyes, pretending to scrutinize it. "Someone was definitely having a rough week."

Kieran laughed, the sound rich and deep, and for a moment, Nicholas forgot his nerves entirely.

After they'd both admitted they didn't really care for the art, it didn't take long to near the end of the exhibit. There were fewer people there, and they found themselves in a quieter alcove where the sounds of the main room faded to a low hum. Kieran turned to Nicholas, his gaze suddenly more intent.

"You know, I think you might have been the most interesting part of this evening," Kieran said, his voice low.

Nicholas felt his pulse quicken under Kieran's stare and had to look away. "And here I thought you were a big modern art fan."

Kieran didn't reply, smiling slightly. His hand brushed against Nicholas's shoulder, lingering a moment longer than it needed to. Nicholas felt his throat go dry. Every word he could think to say seemed like the wrong one. He wanted to lean in, to close the space between them, but something held him back—a self-consciousness he couldn't quite shake.

Kieran seemed to sense his hesitation, his hand dropping back to his side as his gaze softened. "No worries, I remember. Slow and steady wins the race."

Nicholas felt his cheeks warm, and for a moment, he simply nodded, feeling a mixture of relief and regret he couldn't quite make sense of.

"I had a great time tonight," Nicholas said softly, finding that, for once, the words came easily.

From: Brianna Ann Nelson
To: Nicholas Fisher
Subject: Fanmail
September 24, 11:56 AM

Hey teach,

Can't believe you didn't tell me you were a star!

Just got out of a meeting with Jasmine and she mentioned your article that just came out—congrats!! I Google scholar'ed you and found the others too.

How come I had no idea? Now I feel even guiltier about demanding so much of your time. I can't believe I know an expert on Latin early modern travel literature and all the other stuff I didn't get around to read (yet!). Wrong continent for my area of interest, but I actually want to see if I can use your paper on translation/transmission for my project. How cool would it be if I got to cite you??!

Bri

PS: Will send you my first full draft by the end of the week.

CHAPTER 11

NICHOLAS'S TENDENCY NOT to utter a single word until he'd been awake for at least a few hours caused another overhearing incident a few days later. Unlike last time, he hadn't made himself discreet on purpose. Rather, his half-awake self had turned off all his alarms and slept through most of the morning, a relief after the insomnia of the last few days.

Nicholas was halfway through finding the motivation to get up before the day was fully wasted when he realized that Matías was not only still in the apartment but also seemed to think he was alone. It sounded like he was half dancing around the living room, what with all the noise he was making, and whistling a tune that had been all over the radio lately.

When Matías's phone rang and he picked it up, speaking in fast but intelligible Spanish, it took less than five minutes for Nicholas to realize the last conversation he'd overheard had been nothing but a lackluster rehearsal. In a few minutes, the atmosphere in the living room took a sharp turn. Matías's words were angry, the lightness of his whistling long forgotten.

"*Do not drag Mom into this*," he almost screamed, and Nicholas wondered if the vibration of the walls came from the volume of Matías's voice or if he was actually kicking it from the other side. His worry was quickly replaced by annoyance that he cared at all about Matías's temper tantrums.

"*I'm not listening to this*," Matías spat out.

There were some more angry words, but with every one of them, the annoyance that had been pooling at the bottom of Nicholas's stomach morphed to bitter resentment. Matías had never been anything less than effusively happy, yet on the other end of the phone was someone who could undo all that with just a few words.

"*We're done, then*," Matías finished. It seemed like he was trying to sound cold, but to Nicholas, it sounded irreparably sad. "*You can keep your money. Good luck with the election. I'm done. If you can't accept—I've done it all, I've tried to be perfect, but I don't think it'll ever be enough. So we're done.*"

His tone was final.

Nicholas heard what was unmistakably Matías's phone crack against the wall, followed a few minutes later by the sound of him leaving the apartment. He didn't come back for hours.

Nicholas went to class and back. When he got back home, late in the afternoon, the first thing he did was scan every room looking for a sign of life. There was none.

The place had grown cold and dark by the time he decided to reheat the plate of chili left in the fridge and eat half of Matías's cereal bars. No one came home to claim them. It was the first Thursday Will missed since Matías had moved in.

The quiet shouldn't have bothered him. Matías was a grown man; of course, he was allowed to do what he wanted to distract himself from the things he didn't want to think about. He was probably out partying with Will, surrounded by girls and trying to forget what had clearly been his father telling him he didn't want anything to do with him anymore. It was for the better, Nicholas reminded himself. He certainly didn't want to have to deal with an angry, despondent Matías this evening. There was no reason to feel betrayed or stupid for spending the afternoon thinking of ways to distract the other man tonight.

When he got to work the next evening, Marge was running wildly around the library, waving around hastily printed rosters while trying to dodge the Friday evening crowd that was stocking up on books for the weekend. Apparently, one of the librarians he'd never bothered speaking to had needed to fly to Maine unexpectedly to visit his mother, and they now found themselves even more grossly under-staffed than usual, with no way to remedy it until the man came back at the end of the following week.

Luckily for Marge, spending every waking minute at work for the foreseeable future sounded like exactly what Nicholas needed. Matías and his brother had dragged themselves home in the middle of the night and made it impossible to go back to sleep, and Sloane and Ajay were growing too busy to listen to him whine about any of it. Being paid to read and organize books all day long seemed like the perfect solution to avoid having to deal with a self-destructing Matías invading his living room and taking Will down with him.

"I could kiss you right now," he told his boss when she asked him if there was any chance he could pick up longer shifts for a few days.

"Do not get my hopes up, boy," she answered with a relieved laugh, ruffling his hair.

Oliver's absence—Marge had reminded him of his name with an unimpressed sigh—meant that Nicholas had to take over his tasks, which all seemed to revolve around shelving and inventory. It wasn't as bad as he'd thought, even though he missed the reading circle and its preschoolers who liked to gather around him like hungry bees. He liked the small humans; they were uncomplicated and a lot sharper than anyone ever gave them credit for. They were curious without judgment—born from a desire to understand rather than to categorize. They made it easy for him to be soft, even though he didn't think he deserved the adoration in their eyes when they looked up at him.

When he got home, he was surprised by the low rumble of voices and background music he could hear from the landing outside their front door. Usually, William and Matías met up downtown directly—or so Nicholas assumed—when they were going to spend the night out at bars or parties or games or whatever else extroverted best friends did on the weekends. Sometimes, they stopped by the house to get ready and have a few drinks, the remnants of which Nicholas came home to after he'd closed the library, but they were usually gone by then.

He was tired after the extra hours but knew he had no choice but to face the crowd if he wanted to make it to his bed. When he opened the door, he was welcomed with a chorus of hellos, uttered with varying degrees of enthusiasm. He smiled in relief when he saw Leila's serious expression among the faces looking up at him. There weren't as many people as he'd feared; Will and Matías were sitting on the couch, Leila and Gabi were on the floor, and some guy he'd never seen before was on the other side of the coffee table. There were snacks everywhere, surprisingly no liquor around the table, and… a pile of board games.

"Game night? And I thought I was the only senior resident around here," he half-joked, looking at his brother. His tone had come out kinder than they were both used to, his subconscious probably aware of the audience around them.

"Sorry," Matías said around a mouthful of… something, distracting Nicholas into looking at his lips. "It was decided last minute, or we would've texted you," he said. "Wanna join?"

Nicholas quickly counted heads. "I doubt you'll find a game for six people."

"It's fine, we'll do teams," Leila cut in before anyone could satisfy themselves with that answer. "You should play with your brother. I'll play with Gabi, and law school can be a team, since they're so smart," she finished with a fond grimace.

It was almost funny, the way Matías and both brothers snorted in unison when Leila proposed they pair up. But Nicholas had barely talked to anyone all day, and he was in the mood to win.

He spoke up first, looking down at his older brother with a clear challenge in his eyes. "Sure, no problem."

"I'm scared," Matías said flatly, looking back and forth between the two.

William and Nicholas, while usually unable to talk to each other for long without ripping each other's heads off, were a lethal team when paired together. It didn't take long for that fact to become obvious to everyone who didn't already know it—so, everyone but Matías. Only Leila's calm reminders that the point was to have fun kept them from ruining everyone's evening.

Bored of pretending the Fisher brothers could be beat, Nicholas quickly stopped paying attention to what was going on at the table. It seemed like he wasn't the only one who had things on his mind; he caught Gabi glancing at Matías with concerned eyes so many times, he almost started doing it too. She even coughed in warning when his play forced Matías to skip his turn twice, as if that hadn't been on purpose, as if letting him win this childish game was the least Nicholas could do for his roommate.

So, whatever had happened between Matías and his father, everyone knew about it, and this was their attempt at distracting him. It seemed to work too; the Texan was laughing along to most jokes—and there were a disturbing amount—and trying his best to care about whatever faux debate his friends were engaging him in.

Still, there was a faraway look in his eyes that came back whenever he thought no one was looking.

Even Will, perhaps the only person on the planet who liked winning more than Nicholas did, was obviously making sure they weren't doing too well. Nicholas gave him a sharp look. If they knew one thing, it was that no knock-knock joke or board game win could take away the pain of losing your family.

They didn't let Matías win.

♋

Whatever had kept Matías out of the house so intently when he'd first moved in, whether it was classes or house-hunting or social engagements, it was obvious that attending any of it was no longer a priority. Nicholas was up before him on Monday morning, and he came home wondering if the man had bothered going to school or even showering.

"No viewings today?" Nicholas asked by Wednesday afternoon. Matías looked up at him from under his forearm, which was made slightly difficult by the way he was lazily sprawled across the dark gray sofa.

"No," he answered, a rasp in his voice that made Nicholas wonder if these were the first words Matías had uttered today. Where was Will?

Nicholas nodded, leaning against the counter pensively as he bit into… an apple, before looking at it with a frown. Since when did they keep fruit in the house?

"Well, I'm going to play ball for a bit. Do you want to come?"

That finally got a reaction other than a flippant grunt from the older boy. Matías sat up, staring at Nicholas in confusion.

"Are you coming, then?" Nicholas asked again impatiently.

It was a testament to how much Nicholas did not want to study that he was ready to do this. There was also the small matter of Matías monopolizing Will all the time—if he stopped going to soccer practice altogether, Nicholas could say goodbye to ever watching the rest of *Golden Girls*. He was trying to be understanding of the guy's need to process what was obviously a family-related mental breakdown, having had a few of them himself. But if Matías didn't rejoin the world of the living soon, he would be the one having a breakdown, and his tended to be a lot more explosive.

All he needed to do was get Matías outside, remind him of his undying love for physical exercise and the outdoors, and he'd be out of his hair again. That was the plan.

Matías was still motionless, but his face was undergoing a tumultuous journey. "You're… what? Playing what ball? I'm confused."

Nicholas rolled his eyes in exasperation, but he felt mostly relief. "Soccer. It's a great day for it, before it gets too cold and soggy. Are you coming?"

Matías was looking at him with such intensity that Nicholas was forced to look away, which was when he noticed the book lying on the floor, next to the sofa. It was another one of his.

"Okay," Matías answered carefully, clearly stunned into agreement.

"Okay. Be ready in five minutes," Nicholas said dismissively despite not being anywhere near ready to… play soccer… outside. In early October. He winced as he remembered how cold it was getting. At least the sky was the kind of gray that could potentially hold until evening before it broke open and started pouring down.

Five minutes later, Nicholas ran out of his room in clothes that could pass for workout-appropriate with a little bit of imagination, heading to Will's to steal his cleats. From the corner of his eye, he noticed Matías already in full gear, holding the ball and waiting patiently on the couch.

"Give me a minute," he threw out. He couldn't find his old goalkeeper gloves, even though he knew they had to be somewhere since he remembered seeing them in the move. Growing marginally more irritated with every passing minute he spent looking for them, he tried to remember the only reason he was doing this was to get Matías out of the house and over whatever was going on with him.

By the time he found both of them, hidden in a box under his bed where he had also found a compass and some artwork he'd ordered online but never hung, ten more minutes had passed. Matías still didn't say anything, and Nicholas had to work to keep his face straight when he registered the shock on Matías's face at the sight of the gloves. He walked out of the apartment without looking back, pushing out the thought that he found it weird that, in all the years they'd been teammates, Will had never told Matías that Nicholas used to play too. Maybe Matías had just thought Will was being polite when he asked his little brother to join their scrimmage games, not knowing he'd spent a decade asking Nicholas the same question.

They came out into the biting mid-afternoon air, and Nicholas shook his head to dispel the questions. None of it mattered as long as Matías stopped moodily monopolizing his couch. He turned around expectantly, signaling for Matías to lead the way. Obviously, he hadn't played soccer since moving in with Will, so he had no idea where to go.

He thought he caught the shadow of a smile on Matías's lips, but it was quick to vanish, and the two set off on an awkwardly quiet fifteen-minute walk through a series of residential streets that all looked identical. At least Nicholas didn't have to worry about his companion being overly conversational for once.

As it turned out, Matías wasn't bothering to go anywhere that could at least pass for a soccer field, instead taking Nicholas to one of the muddy local parks. He supposed they didn't need much more than an empty square of patchy grass to kick a ball around for an hour, especially since this one was almost deserted.

"Let's go over there," Nicholas said with a nod, grabbing the ball from Matías's hands. It was clear Matías wasn't expecting them to play any actual soccer, and Nicholas had to try hard not to get offended when Matías started kicking the ball slowly, like he was stuck entertaining a six-year-old until his parents returned. It took him several minutes to realize that Nicholas was, in fact, fully capable of catching every pass, and another five for Nicholas to stop sending the ball back with murderous force every time, hoping Matías would get the hint. Finally, laboriously, they found a good rhythm.

"I can't believe you can actually play," Matías said through a laugh when he wasn't able to stop one of Nicholas's feints. It was hard not to smile back.

"Picked up a few things over the years," he said casually, kicking at the grass. Nicholas wasn't ready to admit that once upon a time, Will hadn't been the only one who took the sport seriously. Mostly because he didn't want to explain why he'd stopped.

"Clearly," Matías said, sounding almost proud.

He didn't know how long it took, but finally, the tension in Nicholas's body started to ease as Matías's passes became stronger. Soon enough, they were moving faster, dribbling around each other and letting hands grab at shirts in an embarrassingly childish attempt to show off their skills. Granted, Nicholas had barely played in fifteen years and was facing a college athlete who lived and breathed the sport, but Matías did not make it obvious.

They couldn't do much, just the two of them, but they tried their best, running after each other until they were both sweaty and had to throw their jackets to the side.

"This is definitely a free kick, man, what the hell?" Nicholas screamed after Matías tried to trip him.

"Absolutely not. Do you even know the rules?" he asked, to which Nicholas raised his head in outrage, choking on the expletives fighting their way out. But when he looked up, Matías was grinning. It was wide and childlike, and it was the first time Nicholas had seen it in a while.

"Oh, I know the rules all right," he answered, getting in position.

"Do your worst," Matías almost sing-songed as they set up for the free kick.

Then, they were playing for real.

Matías seemed to remember he could speak, which Nicholas soon grew to regret when he started to explain drill after drill. Unfortunately, Nicholas's fitness level meant he had no energy for anything other than trying to keep up, so he went along with them.

But Matías was flushed now, and he was smiling. It was like the biting wind and fifty degree weather were blowing away the grey veil that had settled over his features in the past week. The tip of his nose was growing just as red as his cheeks, and he kept shedding layers, which made Nicholas want to jump in the nearby pond.

Instead, he kept running.

"Do you need to practice your shooting?" he asked with a grin after Matías missed. "I'll be goalie." He was starting to grow sore and tired.

Matías quirked an uncertain brow, but then Nicholas grabbed the gloves he'd thrown on the ground earlier.

"Okay, then."

While he was getting in position, Nicholas let himself look at Matías. He didn't remember soccer shorts being this short, or maybe it was just Matías's muscular thighs that made them look so indecent.

He wondered what they would look like wrapped around him.

With a choking sound at the realization of where his thoughts were headed, Nicholas forced his brain to go blank until all he could see was the ball that would soon be rushing toward him. This was his secret weapon. Even at eight years old, it had been clear to everyone in the team: Nicholas was a goalkeeper. The razor-sharp focus and the distance from the action had spoken to him from the beginning, and even if it had been months since he'd put them on, the battered gloves lining his hands still felt familiar. When Nicholas caught Matías's first feint, diving to the left and catching the ball they'd both thought was a sure goal, he looked up to see Matías's mouth forming a wide "O" of surprise. He caught himself laughing.

It was a pity that he'd been too scared to embarrass himself in front of Matías to ever accept Will's invites, because the endorphins rushing through his body almost made Nicholas think he would have liked to do this again.

The thought had nothing to do with Matías's entire attention being on him, his words and his focus and his eyes for Nicholas only, with no phone or teammates or pretty girls to distract him.

The daylight started to dim and Nicholas's sweat started to cool from his relative stillness between the makeshift goalposts. As soon as Matías caught sight of him shivering, he grabbed their things and told him they should head home.

They walked back lazily, Matías's face slack with satisfaction.

"I didn't know you could play like that."

"Well, don't tell anyone. They wouldn't believe you anyway."

Matías snorted and flashed him a grin, which Nicholas mirrored before he could stop himself.

He felt stupid, so he looked away.

☙

They were almost home when Matías spoke again. "Thanks for that, by the way."

"Whatever," Nicholas shrugged.

"It was nice. I really needed it."

Nicholas chuckled, although he'd hoped it would come out more derisive than it did. "Oh, I know." He saw something in Matías's eyes then—hesitation. Nicholas panicked. If Matías tried to tell him what had been happening to him these past few days, Nicholas would have to admit that he already knew, that he had a tendency to eavesdrop and that he understood Spanish perfectly for unknown reasons, and it would all be incredibly embarrassing. "You were stinking up the whole apartment, I had to do something. Now you have no choice but to shower."

From: Elizabeth R. Green

To: Nicholas Fisher

Subject: Checking in

October 4, 2:25 PM

Dear Nicholas,

I hope this email finds you well. I know your second year can be just as busy as the first, if not more, but I do hope that in your case, no news means good news!

Jasmine Miller-Reed tells me that although you haven't checked in with her formally either, you have been meeting and exceeding her expectations as a mentor. I'm very pleased by this—as I mentioned, the department will be much more willing to discuss teaching credits if you can prove a real commitment to getting a well-rounded education.

It would be my pleasure to have a meeting next month, so we can discuss any progress on your dissertation, thoughts about next year, etc. If you would like to have this meeting with Dr. Miller-Reed instead, that would also be agreeable; she might better know the balance between your mentorship responsibilities and your own work.

Best,

Dr. Green

CHAPTER 12

HE WAS OUT grabbing coffee with Sloane that weekend when his phone chimed. Only when he saw the name on the screen did Nicholas realize what he'd forgotten while he was busy worrying about Matías. *Kieran.* It had been two weeks since their date at the art gallery. Outside of a few text conversations, Nicholas hadn't been able to make time for Kieran, busy as he'd been with his extra shifts at the library.

It's Saturday. Do I get to see you tonight or do I have to wait until next week?

"Who's that?" Sloane asked, making him realize he'd stopped in the middle of the sidewalk. When he looked up from his phone, he found her with her face tilted up toward the weak sun, the golden light reflecting on her closed eyelids. She always did that, closing her eyes and taking in the sun's rays like a highly opinionated plant.

"Kieran," he answered, pocketing his phone and catching up to Sloane before he could reply to the other man.

"Oh!" she lit up, turning toward him. "How's that?"

"Good," he answered with a smile, walking up next to her. They kept going in silence, one hand buried inside their coats and the other wrapped around a cup of coffee.

"Any more details you'd like to share?" she asked after a few seconds.

She'd come to pick him up after his shift so they could catch a movie before whatever Saturday night plans she had came around, a habit that had started at the beginning of their friendship. But Sloane's tightly packed schedule this year and her trying to prove that she could handle a joint degree meant they hadn't found the time to go to the movies together since classes had started.

Today, however, the independent place they loved was showing a rerun of *Sin City*, tickets were half-price, and Sloane had cleared her schedule.

Even though it wasn't yet cold enough to justify it, she was wearing a coat so big that it would have swallowed Nicholas whole. On her, it managed to remain an accessory, something she'd thrown over her large shoulders; her pale skin and red lipstick gave her a regal air.

"Not particularly. Last weekend was fun."

He tilted his head to look at her, almost laughing at her raised brow.

"Are you going to see him again?" she asked, her tone still light but edged with impatience.

"Yes, of course."

"Come on, Nick!" she burst when he didn't say more. "Give me *something*! This is the first guy you've seen more than once in *months*, and you've barely told me anything. I need to know. You usually tell us all your date stories," she almost whined.

She was right. Between everyone's busy schedules, the extra hours he'd picked up at work, and the dozens of research-related emails currently awaiting his attention, he hadn't been a very present friend lately.

There was also the small problem that he didn't know how to talk about how things were going with Kieran without disappointing them.

"Sorry. It's going well, I just have a lot on my mind. But I'm going to try to see him again soon."

He saw her frown, but she kept walking. He half-heartedly hoped the interrogation was over, but the thoughtful look and slow sips of coffee told him otherwise.

"So… what do you two talk about?" Sloane asked, her voice casual but curious.

Nicholas shrugged. "Mostly academia, I suppose. He knows a lot about how it works—just, the politics of it all. It's really interesting to have someone who went through it, especially with all the choices I have to make soon."

Sloane nodded slowly, her eyes fixed on the street ahead. "That's great. It's nice when someone has their thing." She took another sip of coffee. "What else do you like about him?"

Nicholas blinked, caught off guard. "I mean, obviously he's really handsome. And smart, and he's just… interesting to listen to. Feels like he knows everything about everything."

Sloane gave him a sideways smile. "But does he make you laugh?" Her voice was gentle, almost tentative.

Nicholas frowned. "I don't know, I guess. Dates don't always have to be fun, do they? I like that he's… solid. Grounded." Nicholas was growing suspicious of this conversation. "I thought you liked Kieran," he added, a question in his voice.

Sloane looked at him, her brow raised. "I don't know him. But I know *you*. I'm just… trying to figure out if you're having a good time or if you're pushing yourself to make this work. You know, to check some kind of box."

"I'm just trying to do the right thing," he mumbled, feeling a twinge of defensiveness.

Sloane stopped in her tracks. "What does that mean? The right thing for who, Nick?"

"I don't understand what you're expecting from me," he started, frustrated. "You've been pushing me into his arms for weeks and now you're telling me to think twice?"

"I've been pushing you to give it a shot, because I want you to be happy. So that's all I'm asking. Are you happy?"

"That's a very loaded question."

"Okay, try this one: are you truly excited by the prospect of getting to know him better, or are you just going through the motions? Because to me, it seems like you put more effort into choosing a place for coffee with me than seeing this guy. And treating him like a chore, another item on the to-do list—that's not fair."

Sometimes, he forgot how hard it could be to be loved by Sloane. She held the people around her to a moral standard proportional to how much she cared for them, expecting them to meet it at all times. It always made Nicholas feel like a failure when he couldn't.

Nicholas felt a pang of frustration rising. "I don't have to be gushing over him every second to like him, Sloane. This is real life, not some movie."

"I know that," she said, her voice soft but unrelenting. "But even real life should make you happy."

"So what, you're saying I shouldn't be with him?" Despite himself, he felt irritation rising. "You guys have been going on and on for months about how I need a boyfriend. And now that I'm giving it a shot, I need to stop trying so hard and let it come naturally? I'm not sure how to please you here."

He could see the surprise in her eyes, the way they darted around while she realized what he'd just said. She grabbed his arm. "Oh, Nick. I'm sorry if we ever made you feel like you *had* to find someone." Her voice was softer now. "We love you just as you are. You don't have to make yourself date anyone. That was an awful thing for us to ask."

"I'm not *making* myself," he answered in a rush, staring ahead at the blinking lights of the movie theater visible in the distance. "But even if I'm trying, I'm still me. I don't think I'll ever go weak-kneed and gushy over some guy, even if I like him—"

"Do you?" she cut him off.

"Do I what?"

"Like him?"

He frowned in confusion. "I mean, we really do have good conversations. The rest comes with time, doesn't it?"

She shrugged. "It doesn't matter anyway. You're allowed to not like him. You don't even need a reason. But you do owe it to yourself to be honest. Let yourself call it quits if he doesn't do it for you, or if it's just not the right time."

They kept walking in silence after that. There was something heavy at the back of his throat, and the back of his mind too. He knew the reassuring squeeze on his arm was Sloane trying to tell him that she loved him, that she didn't think he was a terrible person. But it was hard to believe she'd remain of that opinion if she knew about every other time he'd taken the coward's way out to avoid facing difficult things.

☙

Nicholas's favorite way to ignore what he didn't want to think about had always been to drown himself in work. Except it didn't work at all in this instance. It was his week to take care of the literature review for his Thursday seminar, on which he would get feedback from... Kieran. As he spent Sunday afternoon working on it, the anxious weight of mixing a personal relationship and a piece of homework left a bitter taste in his mouth he was all too familiar with.

He replied to Kieran by Sunday evening.

Sorry I've been so busy. The weather's supposed to be really good tomorrow, should we grab lunch? After the lecture maybe?

He wasn't sure Kieran would want to be seen eating lunch with him on campus, but then he remembered: he wasn't an undergraduate anymore, and this wasn't a professor.

Sorry, not much for campus lunches.

We can go downtown? Nick wrote back.

ᛒ

Nicholas lasted three days waiting for a response. When he realized Kieran wasn't planning on giving him one, he wondered if maybe this was it, if the other man had finally gotten bored of him. Monday's lecture came and went without Kieran glancing his way once, but Nicholas's last unanswered text was a small thorn lodged in his mind, prodding at him.

He knew he hadn't been giving Kieran the effort he deserved; even Sloane had noticed, he remembered with a wince.

By Tuesday, it dawned on him that maybe Kieran cared enough about him to have been hurt by his silence. It was a long shot, but the thought made him feel sick with the bitterness of knowing he might have made someone feel like second choice, a position he knew all too well.

By Wednesday afternoon, Nicholas's feet took him to the humanities building. The door was slightly ajar when he arrived at the office a few of the department assistants shared, and he knocked gently, feeling an anxious pang as he waited.

"Come in," came Kieran's low voice from inside, and Nicholas pushed the door open slowly. Kieran was at his desk, eyes on a stack of papers, the sunlight filtering through the window and glancing off his hair. He didn't look up right away, not even when Nicholas stepped into the otherwise empty office.

"Kieran," Nicholas began, his voice coming out strained. Kieran glanced up then, and something unreadable flickered across his face.

"Oh. Hi," he said, a smile pulling at his lips, though it didn't reach his eyes. "I didn't expect you to drop by here."

"Yeah, I…" Nicholas trailed off, feeling an awkwardness settle between them. "I just thought maybe we could… talk," he said, his voice more uncertain than he'd like.

Kieran leaned back slightly, tilting his head, his eyebrows raised as if to say, *Go on*.

Nicholas shifted his weight, feeling an unexpected surge of frustration. "I just wanted to apologize for not being so available lately. I am getting really busy, and…"

"Oh, right. Well, I'm busy too, as you know," Kieran said, gesturing to the messy desk in front of him. There was an edge to his voice that Nicholas couldn't quite place. Maybe it was impatience. "Doesn't mean I can't take the time to send out a text."

Nicholas felt his stomach sink. "Right. I get that. That's why I wanted to make up for it with lunch."

Kieran snorted, and all of a sudden Nicholas felt smaller than he had in a long time. "Yeah, well, not that I don't enjoy a casual lunch every once in a while," he replied, a faint smirk tugging at the corner of his mouth. "But after over a week of radio silence, I suppose I was expecting a bit—well, more."

Nicholas blinked. He felt like he was losing his grip on the conversation, and didn't know how to get it back. "I know it's no art gallery, but I told you, between work and studying, I'm really struggling to find time for, well, anything else, really. Thought it'd be better than to wait until next weekend."

Kieran gestured vaguely, a flicker of impatience in his eyes. "Hey, if you're too busy, I get it. Maybe it's just not the right time for you to make any promises."

"Right," Nicholas said slowly, his voice laced with disappointment. He'd come here to clear the air, but now he felt a cold sense of clarity settle over him. "Maybe you're right." Kieran raised an eyebrow, daring him to continue. "I want to get to know you, but I can't make any promises right now."

"You can't promise an evening a week?"

He wasn't sure if it was Kieran's words or simply his tone, but something resonated inside Nicholas's body. Maybe he just didn't *want* to promise one evening a week, not as much as he wanted to hold up his other promises—that his friends got him on Sundays, that Thursdays were for Will, that Marge could call him if she needed an extra shift covered.

"Not really," he breathed out.

A flicker of something passed over Kieran's face, but it was gone as quickly as it came. He leaned back, the usual quiet confidence back on his face. "All right, then. If that's how you feel."

Nicholas nodded, suddenly feeling more sure of himself. "Yeah. That's how I feel."

Kieran shrugged, glancing down at his papers. "Well, I guess that settles it. No hard feelings."

It stung more than he wanted to admit, the casual dismissal, but Nicholas pushed it down.

"Okay," he said, the finality sinking in. He lingered a moment longer, and then, before he could stop himself, asked, "I'll see you soon?"

Kieran didn't even glance up. "Sure," he said flatly.

Nicholas felt a strange hollowness settle in his chest. The detachment in Kieran's voice confirmed what he'd feared—that this was done, and not in a way he could salvage. He'd hurt Kieran somehow, that much was clear, and he could understand the pull to be cutting and indifferent when wounded.

Hearing it now, directed at him, made him wonder how Will had managed to deal with it from Nicholas their whole lives.

Discussion Board: CLAS 46903

Posted by: Kieran Donne

Subject: Week 7 Literature Review Feedback

October 10, 1:57 PM

This week's literature review demonstrates an approach I would recommend avoiding. The class should get familiar with Mr. Fisher's work in order to familiarize yourselves with what to avoid in your own research. Overall, this work is limited by two key issues:

- **Overly self-referential analysis:** The review frequently drifts into personal interpretation at the expense of critical distance and clarity. It's vital to let the primary sources speak without imposing a subjective lens that detracts from the objective analysis we strive for in this course.

- **Gaps in foundational sources:** For any of you aiming for depth, please note that Mr. Fisher's selection of literature here leaves critical voices absent, resulting in a superficial treatment of key debates. Stronger reviews will engage with broader research rather than focusing too narrowly on interpretations that align with personal views.

To those working toward a strong final project: while there is value in drawing connections, centering too much on one's own perspective limits both insight and rigor.

Note for all: Study widely and avoid these tendencies in your own research.

CHAPTER 13

BY THE TIME NICHOLAS managed to drag himself away from his laptop and pack up his things from the classroom he'd stayed back in, the late afternoon traffic was at its worst.

Nicholas spent the whole ride home trying to keep his temper in check, but he couldn't keep his hand from shaking as he repeatedly tried to insert his key into the rusty lock of their front door. His vision was starting to blur, and he had to take a few deep breaths before entering the living room, knowing that Will would probably be back from work already.

He'd been the last one to read Kieran's feedback. He'd forgotten he was even expecting it, thought he was walking into another discussion session with his classmates that he could afford to barely pay attention to, like every other week. Instead, he had been met with pitying looks and more nods than he'd gotten in the two months the seminar had run.

Nicholas kept his head down as he opened and closed the door, heading directly to his room. Even a few hours after he'd discovered what Kieran thought of his work and what the whole class now knew, the sting still hadn't lessened.

He made the mistake of looking up on his way to his room, accidentally catching his brother's eyes. Whatever he saw on his younger brother's face made William lock his phone instantly and sit up straighter. Unfortunately, even a fight with his brother wouldn't have been able to make Nicholas feel better in that moment, so he just rushed to his bedroom without a word.

He had to hold his breath to make sure he wouldn't be heard laboriously trying to calm down in the ensuing silence that enveloped the apartment. He wasn't a crier, and he wasn't planning on changing that any time soon. He'd done enough sobbing in his early years, his face going all red and splotchy while he screamed obscenities at his dry-faced family.

He also found that there was rarely anything worth crying about once you'd known real pain.

But today, his chest was burning with an intoxicating mix of anger and embarrassment that threatened to drown him. It was an ugly and familiar feeling, and even bitterly trying to rub the flush off his cheeks wasn't enough to make him feel in control of the situation. The worst part was the crippling doubt. No matter how many times he reread his submission, Nicholas still couldn't figure out if Kieran had lashed out because of the way things had ended between them, or if Nicholas genuinely had no place in a research program.

He had another hour until he had to leave for work, but none of the things he usually did to pass the time managed to hold his attention. He paced around his room, picking things up and wondering how he'd ever found any collection of words distracting enough to quiet his own panicked thoughts. In the end, he gave up and sat on the edge of his bed until his stomach growled, shaking him out of the haze he'd lost himself in.

He took a deep breath and headed to the kitchen, thankful that at least Matías wasn't home to see him in this state. It was only his brother, who probably wouldn't bat an eye, since their tumultuous teenage years had made dramatics a regular occurrence in the Fisher household.

There was a fresh box of donuts on the kitchen island he was sure hadn't been there before, but he ignored it. He pursed his lips, wondering if he would have to make do with fruit again.

"There's nothing in the fridge," Will said neutrally from the couch. "I just went and got us some donuts. It might have to be breakfast for dinner tonight."

If there was one thing in this world that William Fisher did not do, it was have carbohydrates for dinner. Nicholas turned around, trying to come up with something appropriately rude to say, but then William opened the box. They really did look good. Without a word, he grabbed the two that looked the sweetest and let out an embarrassing moan of appreciation as he bit into the strawberry glaze.

He loved breakfast for dinner; it reminded him of all the years Will had been the only one making sure they ate before going to bed, sneaking whatever sweet treats he could find into their room. Feeling his whole body relax as the sugar entered his bloodstream, Nicholas threw himself on the other side of the couch with the firm intention of ignoring his brother until he had to leave.

He ate in silence, wondering if the sugar rush would make him feel better or worse.

"Do you want to talk about it?" Will asked after a while. It was a brave question, considering he must have known the odds of Nicholas telling him he could stick his concern where the sun didn't shine.

"No." There was no bite to his answer, just weariness and the exhale of a long-held breath.

Nicholas almost laughed at the surprise in Will's eyes. He wondered why his brother had even asked if he expected to get his head bitten off. They stayed silent for a bit longer, Will leaning back against the back of the sofa.

Nicholas leaned forward, grabbed a third donut, and proceeded to inhale it as obnoxiously as possible, speaking with his mouth still full. "Remember that guy I told you about? The classics one?"

"Of course." There was a careful edge to his big brother's voice.

"Yeah, that's over."

"I'm sorry. Are you… okay?"

"Yeah, yeah. I ended it," Nicholas said, waving a hand dismissively at the air between them. He paused. "I don't think he is, though."

Will hummed like this was a situation he had personal familiarity with. Nicholas wouldn't know, since they never talked about such things. Smartly, William didn't ask any more questions, just waiting for the drip of information to turn into a flood all on its own.

"He's a teaching assistant," Nicholas continued, not sounding as casual as he'd hoped to.

"*A* teaching assistant or *your* teaching assistant?" The edge in William's voice had changed to something that sounded almost dangerous, which confirmed how much of a bad idea confiding in him was. Still, now that he'd started, Nicholas wasn't sure he could stop.

"Mine, I suppose."

"Did he blackmail you or something?"

Nicholas grimaced at the dramatics. "No. Just a bit of academic retaliation, is all."

Will stood up suddenly, his concern turning into indignation in the blink of an eye. "What did he do? Did he fail you? I swear to—"

"Not yet, the final paper isn't due for a few weeks. But if his attempt at public humiliation in the class discussion board is anything to go by… I think he will, and there's not much I can do about it."

"*Nicholas.*" It was strange to hear his full name in his brother's mouth. Almost everyone called him Nick. In the mouths of his family, "Nicholas" had become a prelude to unpleasant conversations.

"I'll get over it, it's just a few credits," he lied. As a second-year graduate student, he had all of two classes per semester, and not enough research responsibilities yet to be able to do without the credits. Between that and his teaching aversion, Nicholas definitely could not afford to fail any classes.

Will was now pacing around the living room. It almost made Nicholas want to reassure him.

"Can we report him? Could he affect your other classes? Surely there's a rule that says TAs can't date their students. If not, they're going to hear from—"

Nicholas sat up in alarm, cutting off his brother's rambling words. He hadn't meant to start a riot about university policies. Again.

"*You*'re not going to do anything. Stay out of it." Will looked like he was about to argue with him, so he continued. "Seriously. This is only the consequences of my own actions. I've been dragging him around, half—"

"This is *not* your fault, Nicholas," Will said with a vehemence he usually reserved for soccer and investment plans.

Nicholas frowned. "Obviously, I didn't make him be an ass and call my work subpar in public, but I did hurt the guy."

"*You* hurt *him*? Nick, he used you."

The words echoed off the walls, or perhaps it was just inside Nicholas's head. He looked at his brother then, really looked. Despite Will's lighter hair and stronger jaw, his face was undeniably Nicholas's own—the kind of resemblance that had always announced them as siblings, even when they hadn't wanted it to.

There was a long beat of silence.

"What is your problem? He didn't *use* me. I thought I could commit to more than I had time for and then I hurt his feelings and he retaliated the only way he could. When you think about it, this is just proof that I dodged a bullet." Somehow, Will getting so worked up about it was the first thing to finally help him calm down. The world would not be able to withstand both Fisher brothers being angry at the same time. "I'll just ask for a meeting with my advisor and see how we can damage control—"

"We can *damage control* by making sure he gets fired and expelled."

"Would you calm down?"

"*Calm down*? This your education we're talking about, Nicholas."

While a small, childish part of Nicholas felt vindicated by his brother's anger, he also knew it was wildly disproportional to the situation. Sure, Nicholas's feelings had been hurt by Kieran's decision to humiliate him and denigrate his work to the whole class after their conversation in his office. But everything wasn't lost yet; he could always go to Michaelson directly, appeal a potential failing grade, or just talk to the guy and try to convince him not to fail him when final papers came around.

"Since when do you even believe in my education, Will?"

His brother was standing against the opposite wall, flexing his knuckles like he was genuinely about to find Kieran and get into a fist fight with him. Which he had never done before; actually, Nicholas had never seen his brother this angry, even for the things that mattered, even when he would have liked him to. He had no idea why news of an unknown TA throwing a wrench in the gears of Nicholas's PhD was the one thing to break the veneer of quiet composure he'd so unbearably held onto all these years.

"Listen, I take it back, all right? I don't know what I was thinking, telling you about it, but you need to stay out of my life, especially when it comes to school. I have worked too hard for this to have you ruin everything. I'll handle it."

"I'm *trying* to stay out of it, but it's hard when you keep putting yourself into these situations, Nick! What is wrong with you?"

"What situations?"

The silence was deafening.

"You know what I'm talking about." Will's voice was low, barely a whisper, but it managed to be dismissive nonetheless. Something tingled in Nicholas's spine. It was urgent and dangerous, and it was breathing in his ear that this would be the perfect time to run away.

"I'm sure I don't."

There was no possible way that Will knew that this wasn't the first time his personal life and his education had come crashing together. Will had never asked what happened between him and Matías, why Nicholas had stopped hanging out with the two of them halfway through freshman year.

Will sighed, deflating instantly. "Look, I'm sorry I implied it was your fault. But I can't just stand here and do nothing while your ex makes you fail one of your two classes this quarter."

Nicholas shook his head, trying to muster the anger he wanted to feel instead of the fear and confusion currently threatening to over-whelm him. "Yes, you will. You're going to keep going about your life and do absolutely nothing," he continued through gritted teeth.

"Because that worked so well last time, did it?"

"What are you talking about?"

Will looked away. As his brother's words sunk in, Nicholas felt his ribcage trying to push its way up his throat. Will was hiding, looking everywhere but at his brother, like he hoped that Nicholas wouldn't be able to ask again unless their eyes caught.

"What do you mean?" he asked anyway.

"You know what I mean."

"I sure hope I don't."

Will sighed irritably but didn't respond.

The Fisher brothers hadn't always hated each other. Every now and again, they still forgot they were supposed to, when a passing kindness would remind them of the early childhood of laughter and complicity that had been shattered by their sister's death. But they never forgot for too long. They had been eight and twelve when it had all ended. In the blink of an eye, Nicholas was broken and their mother was a ghost and their father was the reason for it all, but still, he was invited at the dinner table. William stopped laughing but he never stopped living, a nonchalance the middle-turned-youngest Fisher could never forgive him for. He'd never been able to forgive any of them, actually.

Nicholas swallowed around the dryness that was burning his throat.

"Did you know?" When no response came, he tried again, screaming the words this time. "What happened freshman year. Did you know?"

It had been years since he'd screamed in William's face, the way he used to all the time trying to snap his family out of their daze.

"I did," his brother breathed out, but it was Nicholas who got the wind knocked out of him.

Somehow, despite his already low opinion of William, he had never entertained the possibility that his brother knew about the professor who had lured Nicholas when he was eighteen and told him *he* could be his family. It wasn't something he could bear thinking about, that his brother had just shrugged off the knowledge like it didn't bother him.

Thankfully, ignoring the truths that made them feel anything more than indifference was a skill the Fishers had perfected a long time ago.

"So why the concern now?" he asked like he was curious, like his brother dismissing the affair as inconsequential wasn't threatening to bury him in quicksand. "Why are you being so extreme about this when you didn't care when I was eighteen?"

The cold fury slowly invading William's face reminded him of their father's quiet anger so much he had to look away.

"Don't you *ever* say that I didn't care again."

Nicholas scoffed, getting up too, long used to his brother's spineless posing. If he hadn't cared enough about his dead kid sister to miss soccer practice once, why would a fifty-year-old using the pedestal Nicholas had put him on for his own twisted amusement have affected him in the slightest?

But William wasn't done.

"I was going to *kill* that man," he said coldly. "I'm not joking, Nicholas—the only reason that degenerate is still alive right now is because of Matías. I know you think I'm heartless and a waste of space, but the one thing I won't tolerate is hearing that I ever stopped caring." The glint in William's eyes was not one he'd ever seen before, so he kept quiet. "You have no idea what it did to me, to hear that my kid brother was being used like that by someone he trusted and looked up to."

Will's mouth made an ugly grimace of disgust before speaking again. Nicholas didn't interrupt him. He wouldn't have known what to say anyway.

"Maybe I was selfish about it. I let you hate Matías for reporting him, so you wouldn't hate me; I pretended I didn't know so you'd have someone in your life who didn't remind you of it. Matías told the university because if he hadn't, I would have killed the guy, and he said you'd carry the weight of that for the rest of your life. He begged me to let them handle it, to let that be enough. He took the blame because you'd need someone you still trusted, and you couldn't lose both of us.

"So I left it alone, I never mentioned it again; I looked out for you, if you needed help, if you needed support, and I know I haven't always done a great job, but you seemed fine. You got over it. Except now it's been five years, and you're telling me you're still sleeping with guys who have the power and authority to destroy everything you've worked for. So, I ask you again, Nick, what is wrong with you?"

Will was out of breath now, his chest rising and falling at an alarming pace.

Nicholas decided that ten minutes before he needed to go to work was not the time to have an existential crisis that put into question everything he'd ever thought to be true about his brother.

"Well, I'd appreciate it if you didn't kill this one either," he said with all the arrogance and dismissal he could muster. Feeling emptied of what little energy he'd brought to the fight, Nicholas turned around and headed to his room to grab his bag. "Just keep your savior complex out of my life from now on."

"I would love to, when you stop making all the wrong choices!"

Nicholas slammed the door, but not quickly enough to miss the disappointment in his brother's voice.

From: Jasmine Miller-Reed

To: Nicholas Fisher

Subject: Meeting

October 15, 5:12 PM

Dear Nicholas,

I'm very glad to hear from you and would be happy to organize a meeting—how does next Monday sound?

Let's discuss everything you've mentioned in your email then, but I'd be glad to join your advisory committee. I'm sure Dr. Green will be happy to do the switch. Lots of exciting things coming up for you, and I've heard great feedback from Brianna. Don't worry too much about credits!

Best,
Jasmine

CHAPTER 14

NICHOLAS WENT BACK to Kieran's office after his elective the following Wednesday. It had been a—long, sleepless—week since they'd ended things, and he thought the sting might have dulled enough that they could have a productive conversation about what had gone wrong with his work. Either way, Nicholas needed to know exactly where his chances of passing the class stood before his meeting with Miller-Reed.

The door was wide open, and Kieran was standing next to his desk, gathering his things.

"Hey," Nicholas started, clearing his throat. "I was wondering if you had a minute to talk about my literature review?"

Kieran barely looked up from where he was packing his bag. "Sure. It'll have to be quick, though. I have somewhere to be." His voice was neutral, with none of the coldness Nicholas remembered from last week.

"I just wanted to make sure, you know... It just came across pretty harsh." Usually, Nicholas would have spent days agonizing over having to ask. But in the wake of what had happened with William, this felt like child's play. "I just wanted to make sure it wasn't... personal."

This made Kieran look up, his eyes rapidly scanning the room around them. "Look, I'm sorry to break it to you, but I was just being honest. I wouldn't tank your feedback over a couple of dates. I'm not that petty. So just... do better next time."

Nicholas forced a steady breath. "Right. Just thought I'd ask."

Kieran adjusted the strap on his shoulder. "Well, now you know. See you in class, Fisher," he finished before walking out.

Although he wanted to find a hole and hide in it for the rest of the year, at least Nicholas had his answer. If—when—he didn't pass the class, it would be because he simply wasn't good enough, not because he'd hurt someone's feelings.

☙

Hot air billowed from somewhere above Nicholas when he walked into the dining hall. It wasn't so busy today, or perhaps it was because it was already mid-afternoon, which he told himself was a good enough reason to grab as much cake as his two hands could carry.

He ignored the questioning looks his friends threw at his tray and sat down heavily in front of them.

Ajay looked up, their dark brows partaking in a complicated dance while they finished chewing. "Is this your lunch?" they asked, looking dubiously at the three plates of dessert in front of Nicholas.

"Yes."

"Any interest in eating a vegetable one of these days?" Sloane asked.

"Not particularly."

Ajay made a humming noise. "Figures."

Nicholas hadn't told his friends about Kieran's feedback or the fight with his brother, but something about the half-heartedness of their dig at his eating habits told him they knew something was wrong anyway. They weren't the only ones. After almost a week of living in an icy cold apartment where neither of the Fisher brothers was able to even look at the other, Nicholas worried Matías was about to explode from secondhand discomfort. Between Matías's own moroseness ever since the phone call with his father and the volatile tangle of emotions that were blurring past and present, the walls of their home felt brittle.

Matías's way of dealing with it, apparently, was with alcohol and cheap costumes.

"He did what?" Nicholas choked on his pie.

"He called me about your guys' Halloween party," repeated Ajay. "Told me to come and bring Sloane, and any of your other friends."

"But we're not having a Halloween party."

"You are. He said, 'we're having a party,' and I said, 'who's we?' and then he said, 'Nicholas, Will and I.' Do you need a full transcript?"

Nicholas was left speechless. Even by Matías Romero's standards, this was an abysmally bad idea. So much so that he didn't know where to start, so he picked the first thing that came to his mind. "Why are you guys even talking? Does he have your number?"

As far as he knew, Matías had been horrible to Ajay after they'd slept over, and that was the last time the two had been in contact. Nicholas felt a pang of guilt for forgetting about it.

Ajay looked at him with a frown. "I gave it to him when I was over. Then he called me to apologize about that morning at your place. We're not 'talking.'"

"Apologize? When?"

"The next day," Ajay said like it was old news. "Said he'd been in a mood and hoped it wouldn't hinder our potential friendship. It was all very diplomatic, I'm sure he'll make a great lawyer."

"I had no idea." After a short silence, which his friends didn't try to fill, Nicholas said softly, "Why is it that just when you think you know someone, they turn out to be a stranger?"

"Maybe because you like to put people in a box after you've met them once, whether or not they fit in there?" countered Ajay.

"Aj, be nice," Sloane cut them off.

"Fine," they said with a faux pout. "Well then, rather than hurting your pretty brain thinking about your archnemesis not being scared of apologizing when he needs to, you should use it to come up with matching costume ideas for the party you are evidently throwing. I vote we go as the *Totally Spies.* You can even go as Jerry, if you want."

"We're not going to the party."

"Oh, Nicholas. Wrong again."

☙

Unfortunately, classes didn't stop, even when Nicholas stopped believing he had any chance of passing them. But even if a few people had dropped out of Michaelson's class throughout the course of the semester, he certainly wasn't about to become one of them. He made sure to read his classmate's literature review and the feedback that followed, trying to understand how he could have performed so badly. When the next discussion session came, he sat in the front row.

"Are you sick or something?" asked the chatty third-year who always participated in class when he settled next to him.

Nicholas shook his head once. "Just trying to pay attention."

"Man, relax. Your thing was fine." Nicholas frowned, unsure how to respond to this poor attempt at comforting him. "What'd you do to piss him off, anyway?"

"Hm?" Nicholas could feel heat invade his cheeks.

"Must have been pretty bad for him to destroy you like that. I know nothing's ever good enough for Mr. Perfect, but that was tough, even for him. What did you do?"

Nicholas shrugged; the words Kieran had used in his feedback were still resonating inside his head. "Overly self-referential analysis and gaps in foundational sources, I think it was."

The boy snorted. "You're funny."

"Too bad we're not in clown school."

"Come on, man. Relax. Read the other reviews if you want. Your work was just as good. Maybe the guy was just having a bad day. Honestly, I don't know if you were paying attention last week, but it freaked all of us out. If what you did wasn't good enough, then there's no way anyone is passing this damn class."

Nicholas was about to disagree, but someone coughed at them from the front corner of the room. He didn't listen to a single thing anyone said after that.

༄

No matter how many times he turned the situation over in his head, Nicholas still didn't know who to believe. Maybe the guy from his class—he still didn't know his name—was just trying to be nice. Cheer him up when it was clear he wouldn't pass. But even if he'd been right—and Nicholas wasn't sure he could afford to believe that—it didn't actually help. Kieran was the one grading their final papers. If he had it out for him, Nicholas would still fail, even if he wasn't as mediocre as he'd convinced himself he was over the past week. Either way, Will would have a field day.

Nicholas knew he had no choice but to tell his advisors. Failing his letter grade course put everything that was supposed to come next in jeopardy. Also, after he'd finally told them what had happened, his friends had made him promise to talk to someone about it, lest they stage a protest outside the humanities building.

They had first suggested he go directly to Michaelson, but there seemed to be something insurmountably childish about arguing against a fate he'd brought upon himself to someone he held in such high regard.

Instead, he was waiting in the carpeted corridor outside Miller-Reed's office, wondering if the walls really were caving in on him from all sides or if it was just his body betraying him again. At least there wasn't anyone around to witness him twisting his fingers around the wrinkled hem of his t-shirt. Everything around him was quiet, the office tucked away on the ground floor and surrounded by rooms whose purposes remained unclear.

Miller-Reed was late, which didn't help his budding apprehension, but then a young girl with red-rimmed eyes exited the office sniffling, and he thought perhaps he wasn't the only student who'd been sent her way in the middle of an existential crisis.

"Nicholas, come in."

Her smile was warm, unlike the room, although the familiar smell of chamomile made the cold almost bearable.

"Tea?"

"Yes, please." He could feel a draft coming in from one of the windows.

"Sorry about the temperature. I arrived on Monday to find the radiators weren't working, and I'm sure you can guess how tortuous it is to get anything fixed around here," she said dismissively. She tried to readjust the blanket on her legs discreetly, before looking up at him. "How have you been?"

Nicholas took a deep breath, which he had to release when no words came to him.

"I see. Should we go in order? I remember you mentioning a few things in your email."

He took a big gulp of the tea she handed him, but only managed to burn both his tongue and throat in the process. He knew for a fact that Brianna had already kept her professor appraised of their progress in detail, and he didn't have much to tell her regarding his dissertation, especially because her area of expertise couldn't be further from what he was interested in.

"It seems that I have a... credits problem."

She was looking at him kindly, but her continued silence made it clear he would have to force the words out himself. Mustering some of the bravery he always witnessed in Ajay and glossing over most of the pertinent details of the situation, Nicholas finally managed to explain that he would probably fail his current class and needed four credit hours to somehow fall into his lap by the end of next year.

Instead of asking why exactly he was so certain of the outcome when he had yet to receive any grades for the semester, she hummed, leaning back against her chair and thinking his words over.

"Well," she finally spoke. "The best I can do, as far as solutions go, is to let you apply for a TA spot with me next semester, which will be credited. Now," her tone grew more severe, "since you haven't taken my class, you'll have a lot of catching up to do on the topic. And you'll need to show evidence that you have some aptitude for working with undergraduates. I also still want you to go through the department application process, which I believe closes quite soon." She paused, looking at him sternly.

The tea had finally gone from scalding to just uncomfortably hot, so he busied himself with drinking while he gathered his thoughts.

Nicholas hadn't even known one could be hired as a TA during their second year and found himself staring back at her blankly. He'd expected her to ask a thousand questions and to enjoin him to work hard enough to get the credits he'd signed up for. Instead, despite her inflexible tone, she was effectively handing him a solution on a silver platter. He wondered, briefly, if she would still think he deserved it once she got to know him.

"Of course," she continued, "I could always give you some pointers to help you pass this class of yours instead. I could help you with the final paper, since I see that you haven't gotten any grades yet, and I'm sure Professor Michaelson would be understanding if there was anything he needed to know."

Nicholas wasn't able to keep the bitterness completely out of his voice. "There's nothing that can be done, unfortunately."

"Well, the spot is there, if you'd like to apply for it." She infused that last part of her sentence with something akin to a challenge he didn't really understand.

The last of his tea was barely enough to wash away the bitter taste of being handed an opportunity he clearly didn't deserve. At least he still had to apply for it. Pretending he might get it based on merit was the only way he would even consider this.

"Does that sound satisfactory to you?" she asked when he remained silent.

"Yes," he exhaled, feeling something drop inside of him. "Yes, that's… yes. Thank you."

"Good."

"Thank you."

"Of course."

He wasn't sure what he was supposed to do next, other than thanking her again. "Where should I start?"

She nodded, grabbing a piece of paper and scribbling down a few titles. "Send your application to the department as soon as possible. Then, read those, and I'll email you the syllabus later today."

His fingers were shaking as he grabbed the note, and he felt a surge of gratefulness when she didn't ask why.

☙

Nicholas was sweating under his coat by the time he managed to win his duel against the rattling front door. He was trying to close it behind him without dropping any of the five books that hadn't fit in his backpack, precariously leaning the pile against his chest, when Matías materialized in front of him.

"Need help with that?" he asked, one hand already reaching for the books while the other was swatting Nicholas's own away.

Nicholas rolled his eyes, but he let Matías take them and put them on the counter. He dropped the backpack that had been digging into his shoulder on the floor unceremoniously and when he looked up, Matías was riffling through the titles with a frown. Taking off his wet shoes, scarf, and coat with a huff, Nicholas decided to leave him to it, certain he would have something to say about his incomprehensible academic choices soon enough.

"Any reason for your newfound interest in translating poetry?" Matías asked skeptically, holding up a thick volume in each hand.

"Translat*ed* poetry," Nicholas corrected.

"I thought you didn't like poetry."

Nicholas tried to hide his surprise. "I never said I didn't like it. I just don't know much about it." He sounded defensive to his own ears, but Matías just grinned.

"No, seriously, what's this new hobby about?" he asked, still trying to decipher what he was reading. "What happened to the ancient books with tiny fonts you usually like?"

There was no reprimand in his voice, just curiosity.

"It's not a new hobby, it's research."

"I thought your research was on prose, and movement and… things."

Nicholas ignored the panic rising in him at the thought of Matías knowing him so intuitively. He had no recollection of ever mentioning anything about his research to him. "What about you? You've got to be the only law school student hanging around at home on a Monday afternoon. Don't you have midterms to study for?"

Matías waved off his comment as if it was inconsequential. "Yeah, yeah." He paused. "Is this about those undergrads you're helping?"

Finally, he turned to face Matías fully. Ajay's words came back to him suddenly, and he didn't like the feeling it gave him, to be known so well while there were so many parts of this Matías that Nicholas wasn't privy to. It made him feel even more inadequate than usual.

"How do you know about that?"

Matías shrugged. "You must have told me."

"It's not, it's for another thing," Nicholas said, trying to convey that he would appreciate it if the conversation ended there. Of course, Matías pretended he couldn't hear the dismissal in his tone.

"What other thing?"

"What is this about?" Nicholas asked with a heavy sigh, tired of pretending like it was normal for them to chat away about his research over the kitchen counter. Granted, they had been slowly doing better since Matías's apology, but Nicholas was still wary enough of the other man not to have broken his habit of avoiding his existence yet.

The curiosity in Matías's voice made him feel a dangerous desire to tell him everything he wanted to know. This was why having a reason to antagonize the guy had been so important in the first place. Except now, all of Nicholas's avoiding and antagonizing was busy being directed toward William, while the Texan was clearly going through enough with his own family without adding Nicholas's drama to the mix, if the circles under his eyes were anything to go by.

The choice in front of him caused something to stir in Nicholas's chest. He could either be rude, like he always was—another reason for the recent but near-constant frown on Matías's face—or he could be the one person who supposedly didn't know about his father, the one who Matías went to when he wanted to think about something other than his family giving up on him.

"I was just wondering," Matías shrugged, his talkative bravado dissipating in front of Nicholas's eyes. Nicholas gathered the books he'd borrowed at Miller-Reed's recommendation, brushing against Matías's rock-hard chest as he did so and trying to ignore the heat that seemed to emanate from him.

When he looked up, Matías had a small smile, his dimple barely visible. "Oh, I started reading Chekov, by the way."

"Which one?"

"*The Seagull.* I think you said that was a good place to start, right?"

He had, years ago. "Are you liking it?"

"Er," Matías said, his cheeks coloring faintly. Nicholas would have missed it if he hadn't been looking at his face so intently, so he stopped doing that immediately. "I'm sure it'll pick up soon," he continued, clearly trying to convince himself more than anyone else.

"It will. And if it doesn't, no one's forcing you to finish it."

The look Matías gave him was somewhere between blame and disbelief. It was true that mocking athletes for not being able to get through modern classics was very much a habit of Nicholas's—or at least, the Nicholas he'd been at eighteen, when reading big books was, he felt, the only thing worth a damn about himself.

"Do you want to play some soccer?" Matías asked Nicholas before he could make it to his bedroom.

"Why would I want that?"

Matías shrugged. "Just thought you might, is all."

"Well, I don't." Then, because he'd heard the harshness in his own voice, "I've got too much to do." It wasn't a lie—he waved at the pile of books in front of him. "Especially if I'll be busy throwing a Halloween party this weekend," he said pointedly.

Matías just grinned, the light finally reaching his eyes; yet he completely ignored Nicholas's attempt at finding out more about his scheming. "Did you know that physical activity improves your concentration? I read a study," he said instead, apropos of nothing.

"You—what?"

"I read a study about it. Something about blood flowing to the brain, I can send it to you if you want. So, really, I would count a quick game as work, when you think about it. Or at least investing in the quality of your focus for the rest of the afternoon."

℘

By the time they headed outside, the drizzle that had enveloped the city all day had turned everything wet. It was almost impossible to run at the park, and Nicholas quickly slipped on the mud as he tried to dribble around Matías's feet, pulling the other man on his way down and calling it an accident. Once they were both soggy with mud, there was no point in holding back anymore and their game became a dirty one, fingers wrapping around arms and feet knocking against chins.

It occurred to Nicholas that this was the first time he'd touched Matías so shamelessly, hidden under the cover of a sport where contact was inevitable, if not encouraged. He was stuck thinking about the feeling of Matías's hard stomach against his palm when he missed a pass headed straight for his abdomen, doubling over in embarrassment more than pain when it hit him at full speed.

The look of pure panic in Matías's eyes when he ran up to him was so entertaining, however, that he waved off his apology with a smile and contented himself with making Matías pay for coffee on their way back.

∽

Sloane was waiting for him outside of his classroom on Wednesday, which she had never done before. He had no time to ponder why, since she immediately grabbed his arm and proceeded to recount every single minute of her meeting with the English department faculty. It had apparently involved a lengthy discussion on the origins of bookbinding and absolutely no mention of her dissertation. She was still talking when Nicholas walked ahead to hold the heavy emergency exit door open and a wave of freezing wind hit them both.

"I still have no idea whether this was a good or bad meeting," he admitted when she stopped talking long enough to grab her woolen hat out of her bag.

"Oh, sorry I should have started with that—it was great," she smiled, her eyes lighting up as she continued. "They couldn't give me an official answer there and then, but I believe you're looking at the newest student of the English department."

"What? That's fantastic!" he said with a grin, hugging her tight as she let out a startled laugh. "Ajay's going to hate it." The lack of a single scientific bone in either of their bodies was a well-known source of despair for their engineer best friend. "Now, tell me about your thesis."

"Oh," she said dismissively, "it's way too early to think about that." They both snorted. "I want to look into bookbinding a bit more first."

He draped his arm around her shoulders, although the layers of coat and scarves made it hard. The temperatures had dropped almost overnight, turning the grounds slick as they trudged their way to the warm café just outside campus where they served tea and pastries sweet enough to sustain him for hours.

It was fuller than they were used to, books and computers finding their way out of the classrooms and libraries they belonged in, as they tended to do during exam season; but then Nicholas saw the mini strawberry bavarois-type cakes on display and any complaint about the place died in his throat.

"You're chipper today," Sloane said when they sat down.

"How could I not be?" he asked with a grin, gesturing to the two desserts in front of him and rubbing his hands in anticipation. She'd opted for a much more hour-appropriate falafel sandwich, which probably explained her guarded expression.

"Should I make a list?"

"I told you, my meeting with Miller-Reed really eased my mind about the credit thing. Even if I don't get the TA position, I think she'll help me out."

"Sure, but getting the position should definitely be your goal. And if you do, you'll still have to digest an entire syllabus and TA a class you've got no interest in. And you're unfairly failing a class you were really passionate about. Not to rub it in," she rushed to add, "but you're allowed to be narked about it. I know I am."

Nicholas took his time to eat a generous spoonful of the pink cream, closing his eyes to enjoy the flavors. It was sweet enough to convince him that absolutely no actual strawberry was responsible for the color, but he hummed in satisfaction all the same.

"I'm not sure what you want me to say. There's nothing I can do about it. It's been two weeks, you should be happy I'm done being all moody and unbearable."

She pursed her lips. "You know I don't mind when you are. Although you did do a really good job at not being too unbearable this time around."

For some reason, her words made him feel warm. "Practice makes perfect and all that."

"Practice… at being moody?"

What seemed like an entire cohort of undergraduates noisily entered the café at that moment, running in from a sudden downpour, and they both shuddered as a gust of wind made its way to their table.

"I meant practice at distracting myself from my own feelings by dating men that will leave my academic career and mental well-being in shambles, actually. And practice at dealing with the consequences when that goes to shit too, I suppose."

Distractedly, he stuffed a few pieces of fruit in his mouth. He was wondering where exactly these strawberries had been grown to taste the way they did when he met Sloane's shocked gaze. She kept opening and closing her mouth, something crossing over her face every time she seemed to have made a decision on what she was going to say. He thought she would have been impressed with his self-awareness, but then he remembered she didn't actually know what he was talking about.

He was tired of his friends feeling like they had to walk on eggshells around him.

"It was a long time ago," he added, taking pity on her.

"What was?"

"There was this professor when I was a freshman." The way she immediately dropped her sandwich and straightened up made him doubt he wanted to hear what she had to say to that, so he continued, trying to sound nonchalant. "You can imagine the rest. I don't mean to be cavalier about the Kieran thing, but it just pales in comparison to being eighteen and finding out you weren't the first or only freshman your favorite professor was… mentoring." He laughed, but there was only weariness in his voice. "And don't go saying it's the same thing happening again, because it's not," he finished, more sternly than he intended.

"I wouldn't."

"I know. Sorry. Will just implied that it was the same thing happening again, which was definitely not—"

"Will knows about the professor?" Her voice was careful.

"Apparently, he's known all along. That's what I found out when we had our big fight. Which I didn't tell you about either. He spun some heroic tale about how he wanted to kill the guy, but Matías kept him from doing it and reported him instead, which got him fired because I wasn't the first one. But then the university made it go away as long as he moved—anyway, it was all very dramatic, but it was a long time ago, and I don't think it can be compared to some guy our age acting out because I dumped him."

She looked like she wanted to say a million things. But all that came out was, "No wonder you didn't want to be Elvis for Halloween."

From: Brianna Ann Nelson
To: Nicholas Fisher
Subject: Trick (you edit my essay) or treat (you edit my essay)!
October 25, 4:23 PM

Teach,

Thanks again for yesterday. Sorry I was spiraling about everything. It's good to know even the greatest minds of our generation (you) went through the freshman scaries too.

Here's my ENGL 12307 midterm essay. Thank you so much for agreeing to look it over and not tell Jasmine. She scares me so much... Or maybe it's the weight of my own expectations... Who knows?

Let's meet again before Thanksgiving break so I can show you the presentation.

Happy Halloween!

Bri

CHAPTER 15

THE JOIE DE vivre Matías Romero had always carried around every-where with him was almost entirely back at the prospect of throwing a party. Nicholas had been assured that he didn't need to do anything apart from actually showing up, which suited the younger Fisher just fine, considering he was still not talking to his brother.

Anyone else would have parted with their resentment long ago, would have made concessions for the sake of cohabitation. But not them. They had been raised in the same haunted house, after all. Nicholas might wear his armor for all to see, spitting insults and constantly displaying his discontent, but under the cloak of easy smiles and small conversation, the teeth of Will's temper were just as sharp. Knowing that had once brought him a cold sort of comfort; his big brother might look normal and easygoing, but he would fight for him when push came to shove. He no longer had such illusions.

"You better start looking like you're enjoying yourself, or I won't be the only one with a hole through my stomach," Sloane snapped, handing him a drink from where they were standing in the corner of the living room.

Nicholas huffed. Somehow, both of his friends had vetoed all of his costume ideas and had revoked his right to suggest any more when he had proposed they go as rock, paper, and scissors. Now there he stood, in a three-piece suit complete with bow tie and glasses straight from the nineties. Although he appreciated that his costume provided him with an excuse to dress nicely for once, he needed to be standing directly between his two friends for the cult classic reference to make any kind of sense. Neither Ajay, who was dressed as Lisle Von Rhuman, nor Sloane, sporting Helen Sharp's red dress and holed-stomach, had this problem. Although she looked so beautiful, her generous curves highlighted by the tight dress and her skin glowing against the bright red fabric, that Nicholas had no problem staying right behind her.

Soon enough the living room was full of mostly familiar faces. Nicholas had feared this would be another iteration of Will and Matías's frat parties, but it seemed like the guest list had been carefully picked out to include actual friends of each of the three boys. Yet, despite the warm atmosphere of entangled conversations and well-thought-out costumes, Nicholas couldn't help but feel Matías's absence.

He was probably still getting ready after spending the afternoon setting everything up. The living room was decorated with spider webs and a worrying number of candles, bowls of suspiciously dark drinks littering every available surface. Nicholas tried to distract himself by trying out every mixture he stumbled upon, catching up with Gabi and Leila and that one woman from Will's work he'd met before and actually liked.

He knew when Matías finally entered the room, not because he saw him but because of the way everyone's composure changed when he appeared, their eyes lighting up and smiles widening.

"There he is," Leila said almost breathily, the relief clear in her voice even if it contrasted with her Maleficent costume. Nicholas decided this was a good time to find a corner to stand in and wait out the wave of excitement that had taken over the living room. It seemed like everyone else had been feeling their host's absence too.

Matías was dressed as Woody. Or—partially so. He had the cowboy hat and the boots, the jeans, even the belt. He just appeared to be missing the shirt under the cow-print vest, a rather important part of any outfit in Nicholas's opinion. His caramel, ridiculously sculpted chest was out for the whole world to see, and Nicholas had to drink an entire glass of… something before he could regain some control over his own thoughts.

He found a wall to stand against while everyone drowned Matías in warm love and loud accolades. Looking at it from the outside, it was clear that they were all subtly fighting for his attention, strategically using the few seconds they got it to say something that would make him stay. A rather ugly feeling pooled at the bottom of Nicholas's stomach, but he tried to convince himself it wasn't the growing desire to sever whatever string was tethering Matías to each of the guests and tie it around himself instead. He didn't resent the undemanding intimacy he didn't know how to take for himself. No, his irritation came from the way everyone touched Matías like he was theirs to take.

But instead of ruining his own night any further, Nicholas took off his jacket and found Sloane; he danced and he drank and he ate every single strangely-colored bite he found. People joined in and out of their little circle, but Sloane remained right by his side until he was out of breath and his hair was sticking to his forehead.

When she excused herself to go to the bathroom, Nicholas closed his eyes to find the world spinning. He needed to sit down, but all the available surfaces were already claimed, so he went to his bedroom.

Perhaps spending the evening rotating between every single type of alcohol in their house hadn't been his brightest idea.

After what could have been seconds or hours, someone knocked lightly and Matías's mess of curls appeared through the doorframe. He was looking hot too, his forehead glistening and his hat long forgotten somewhere.

"You all right in there?"

Nicholas nodded, which was followed by a groan when he felt his own brain move around inside his skull. Matías just laughed, disappearing again. Before Nicholas had time to process anything, he was back with a tall glass of water. He walked toward the younger man, softly closing the door behind him before sitting next to Nicholas on his bed.

"Drink this."

Nicholas frowned—the goal tonight was to get so drunk his vision was too blurry to see Matías's chest and his eyes and his smile. Drinking water didn't seem like it would help with that.

But then there were fingers on his face—no, on his glasses. Matías grabbed the plastic glasses on the tip of his nose, discarding them somewhere behind Nicholas. They had been so dirty, his vision was almost back to normal now that they were off.

But Matías was still touching him, the whole left side of his body too close for Nicholas to be able to think about anything.

There had been more and more touches since the soccer games, around the house mostly, casual and fleeting, and Nicholas could remember every single one of them.

"There. Drink the water, Nicholas."

Still not trusting his voice, Nicholas did, but not without a heavy eye roll sent Matías's way.

There was silence, for a while. Matías's eyes caught on Nicholas's hand as it wrapped around the glass and brought it to his lips.

He coughed suddenly. "I like your costume."

Nicholas snorted. "It's just a suit."

"It's from *Death Becomes Her*, isn't it? I saw you standing with your friend earlier, then I got it."

Nicholas nodded.

He felt at peace, despite the pounding headache and the blurry edges of his vision. He knew the seconds he was afforded this, the weight of Matías's thigh against his own in this quiet, dark room were measured, and he knew no words would make the moment last longer. He'd spent all night watching people try.

"Would you take it, if you could?" Matías asked.

"Huh?"

"The potion. From the movie. The one that makes you young forever. Would you take it?"

Nicholas gave him a soft smile. He looked at Matías, remembering him at eighteen and twenty-one and, now, twenty-five. How time had already given him three different versions of Matías Romero. "Probably not."

Someone opened his bedroom door looking for Matías, and his time was up.

℘

By the time people started trickling out of the apartment, Nicholas had gone all the way to drunk and back a few times too many. He was sprawled on the couch, half-listening to the conversation going on behind him. William was wiping something outside of his field of vision, no amount of alcohol in his blood able to keep him from "getting ahead of the cleaning."

As people had grown tired and the party had moved from raucous dancing to lazy conversations all around them, Matías had made it clear that he knew, and could not care less, about the fact that William and Nicholas were fighting. He walked around the apartment address-ing them both and ignoring the avoidant gazes, refusing to let their antipathy affect his night. Every open question he asked them seemed to say: everything is out in the open now, and aren't we all relieved?

Nicholas was trying to find the motivation to get up and walk the few short steps to his room, aware that they were already a few hours into Saturday, which was a workday for him, when one of Matías's law school friends—Josh or John or Jack—tried to catch his attention.

"What about you, Nicholas? Any plans for Thanksgiving?"

Of course he had plans, including but not limited to: reading an entire syllabus, writing two essays on translated poetry and hoping it was not all for nothing, and perhaps, starting to look for a new place so he wouldn't have to rush through dingy viewings when Will finally kicked him out.

"Work. Study," was all he said.

"Aren't you going home?" Matías asked, cutting off whatever his friend had been about to say.

Nicholas just hummed—he'd been hoping not to, counting on his brother to come up with an excuse as to why he had to stay in Chicago. Instead of telling him that, he decided to return the question.

"Are you?"

The look that crossed Matías's face couldn't really be called anything other than painful. "Um, I'm not sure, actually. Maybe, maybe not."

Even when he had first met him as Will's best friend, Matías Romero hadn't talked about his parents often. But when he had, the respect he held for them had always been clear, and he had certainly never missed a holiday at home in all the years Nicholas had known him.

He saw his brother still from the other side of the kitchen counter, and something instinctual inside Nicholas knew what was about to happen before his brain did. "Actually, Mom and Dad said he should come to ours, since we're so close."

The Fishers had tried to get Matías to come home with Will for the holidays since they'd met him as a loud and messy eighteen-year-old and instantly proceeded to fall in love with him. Nicholas had even joined in on the nagging once or twice, back when he was still in high school and the stolen bites of college breaks were the only times he'd get to experience a house that felt alive. There was no reason this year would have been any different, when it seemed like Matías finally knew what it was like not to want to go home.

Still, something deep and dark opened up inside Nicholas's chest when he tried to recall the last time his parents had asked him to come home and came up empty.

"I see," Nicholas replied sharply. "Well, the Fishers do love a charity case. Although," he said without looking at Matías as he got up, "you should make sure they don't hear about whatever made your actual parents not want anything to do with you. Wouldn't want it to happen twice, would we?"

Will was in his face in an instant, and for a moment, the look in his eyes made Nicholas wonder if he was finally, after years of screaming at each other, going to hit him for the first time. His brother seemed to be wondering the same thing, but before he'd found the answer, Nicholas threw him a venomous smile and closed the door to his bedroom behind him.

⁕

Surprisingly, lashing out at Matías did not make him feel any better, but it did bring the number of people who hated him to a neat three.

Instead of dwelling on how much worse Matías avoiding his gaze felt than Will's and Kieran's glares, Nicholas went back to leaving the house early, haunting the campus library and the 129, not coming back until late in the evening.

His friends tried to be there for him, but they didn't know what he'd told Matías at the end of the night. Every time they looked at him with concern, Nicholas felt like nothing more than a fraud, because they didn't know he deserved none of it. So he stopped replying, letting them grow as frustrated and disappointed in him as he was feeling toward himself. At least it was November now, and everyone's schedules were so packed he could hope they didn't notice he was avoiding them.

Being aware that the loneliness creeping over him was his fault did not help with his mood, but keeping busy did. For the following week, Nicholas picked up more shifts at work, staying long after closing time to help Marge. He was trying so hard to fill his schedule with things that didn't involve sitting with his own thoughts that when she tried again to suggest he pick up some slots for the free tutoring program the library offered, he almost agreed. Instead, they made a display about non-Christian holidays and traditions and a schedule of activities for the week leading up to the holiday closure.

She didn't mention his eagerness to help, only said thank you for the extra hours, but the half-dozen cups of hot chocolate she would bring him on an average shift made him wonder just how bad he looked.

At least he didn't have to fake being busy for too long—he had concepts to research and article proposals to submit, on top of his decision to put so much effort into his final for Michaelson that it would be good enough to appeal Kieran's decision when the TA inevitably failed him. Then there was Miller-Reed's syllabus to study and the TA application to send off, which were both making him feel so inadequate he caught himself wondering more than once why he didn't just quit academia and ask Marge for a full-time job.

His ever-chirping inbox was almost enough to distract him from the gnawing feeling that things didn't have to be so hard. He was used to the consequences of his own temper by now, all too familiar with the cycle of hurt, spitefulness, and alienation he'd spent years engaging in with clocklike precision. What was entirely new was the distressing pull to apologize for it. He had a sinking suspicion that the guilt from hurting Matías so deliberately was the reason for how he felt. Of course, he denied it to anyone who asked, blaming his horrendous mood on Kieran's pettiness and general exhaustion.

Yet the feeling he got every time he saw the Scot was closer to indifference than the paralyzing apprehension he felt at the idea of going home, knowing that Matías wouldn't look up from what he was doing or ask about his day anymore.

After over a week of avoiding everything, Nicholas was starting to think about asking Sloane for advice on how to apologize for being a royal prick. But these thoughts were interrupted when Brianna came up to him one day at the main library, a grimace of disgust on her face.

"Did someone kill your puppy or something?"

Nicholas bit down the colorful retort he would have given anyone else. Even though Brianna did everything in her power be treated with the same carelessness as an adult, he couldn't help but see her as the scared teenager she was—although he wasn't stupid enough to call her that to her face.

When he had first met her, she'd reminded him of Emma, all curious glances and polite expectation, but now that he knew her a bit better, he could see she was all him.

Over the past few weeks of working with the freshman, he'd learned a little bit about what stood behind her loud jokes and attitude. Nicholas couldn't help it; he saw himself in the rough edges and the lonely hours she spent hunched over textbooks, convinced she'd never be good enough for the future she wanted.

"I didn't know the school offered a comedy major."

Brianna snorted. "You've been looking miserable all afternoon. I can feel your bad energy from over there, and I'm trying to study."

"What are you studying for?"

"Computer science," she groaned. The eclecticism of her courses always startled him.

"It seems like it's going well," he said, his voice dripping with sarcasm.

"It's just so annoying," the teenager huffed. "And I hate the class. I'm practically the only girl, and the teacher is always talking like he's some big prize, with the graphs that don't make sense and all. Whenever I ask a question, he just looks at me like I'm stupid."

"Mind the furniture," Nicholas said sharply when she started kicking his chair in frustration. It was a habit from working the children's desk at the library, where they had the budget to order new furniture approximatively never. "Right, then, bring it over here."

Brianna looked at him with clear confusion etched on her face.

"Bring your homework over here. Maybe I can help."

Her face showcased a range of expressions, all of which sat somewhere between derision and disbelief. "I thought you hadn't looked at a number in years. I bet you can't even tell the time."

She wasn't wrong about the first part. "Well, then there's no risk of me looking at you like you're stupid, at least. Bring it over."

It was true that he would be no help with the actual work, but he knew the look on her face too well, the one that usually came with thoughts of "I'm not good enough for this place," and he'd be damned if he let her go back to her booth to spiral on her own.

Brianna brought her laptop—and her attitude—next to him on the long wooden table he was sitting at. He took one look at the lines of code on her screen and winced, but she just rolled her eyes and got to work in silence.

By the time he had to go to work, Brianna's frown had disappeared, and an air of satisfaction radiated from her. It was the first time that week he felt anything other than miserable.

❧

It took almost two weeks for Nicholas to stop spending his evenings working from a diner until he was sure everyone was asleep. It was Thursday, so Matías would be at practice anyway, and avoiding the house so much was starting to dig a hole in his finances. After a quiet bus ride home, he ran up the stairs and almost threw himself inside the apartment, eager to escape the storm brewing outside. He got the book he'd been holding out from under his jacket, where he'd had to put it to protect it from the snowy rain that had threatened to blur its pages during the few short steps between the bus stop and their front door.

He went right back to reading it, walking through the living room blindly even though he could feel his brother's presence. The lights were on, and the faintest smell of tomato sauce lingered in the radiator-warm air. He assumed today wasn't going to be the day they broke their four weeks of silence since Will's revelations—until he realized his brother was standing in front of his bedroom door and let out an embarrassing yelp as elbows hit shoulders. He looked up ready to lash out, happy to swap a few well-paced insults. But the look on William's face was guarded.

He wasn't moving out of his way, and the first thought in Nicholas's brain was that the day he got kicked out of the apartment had finally arrived. He didn't let himself be hurt that his brother couldn't even wait until break.

"Right," he started flippantly. "I'll be out by the end of the week."

Nicholas avoided his brother's eyes and tried to walk around him. "Don't start, Cosette."

The surprisingly pertinent reference, more than the veiled insult, startled Nicholas into pausing.

"I need to talk to you," Will said as he headed toward the kitchen.

Nicholas only followed him because having a conversation about anything was such a sharp deviation from their usual modus operandi that he was almost curious to see what would happen next. He dropped his bag and coat but decided to remain standing. Despite their negligible height difference, he always felt small when talking to his brother.

He wasn't sure what a nonchalant person would do with their arms, so he just stood there, his fingers itching for something to hold. Will was leaning against the counter on the other side of the room. He didn't seem to have a problem figuring out where his hands were supposed to go.

"I won't apologize, and I know you won't either." Somehow, Nicholas wasn't sure this was how reconciliations usually started, so he braced himself for the rest. "This isn't about wanting you out of the house, so don't start playing martyr either."

"What's it about, then?"

"It's about whatever is wrong with you needing to be sorted out and fast." His whole body tensed, but William was only just getting started. "You know I don't care about your constant rude comments and that insufferable temper of yours, or the fact that no one can talk to you without getting their face chewed off in response. I have spent half my life being mad at you and the other half relieved that you have enough anger in you for the rest of us. I'm used to it."

Nicholas regretted not sitting down—but his brother kept going. "We both have our flaws, and we've learned how to live with them, because we're family and there's no other choice. I know you never forgave me and Mom for how we acted after the accident, which is fine." He seemed to be expecting Nicholas to object, but nothing came. "There's plenty of things I never forgave you for either, but it's my responsibility to keep them to myself.

"The *point*," Will continued, frustratedly raking a hand through his dirty blonde hair, "is that Matías isn't like us. He's… he's normal, Nicholas. In a way that we can't ever hope to be. He's honest and he tries to be kind and he would never do or say anything with the sole purpose of hurting another person. I know you disagree," he continued, even though Nicholas still hadn't said anything or really emoted in any way, "but I think that's because you knew him at his worst. Senior year was hard for him; his father was always asking him for the impossible and he had to make choices he hated just to make him proud and…" William sighed heavily. "I know you've been on bad terms since then, and that's mostly my fault. I didn't speak up when I should have, and then it was too easy to pretend we could all just forget about it. But it's been years, Nick. I thought you'd understand that he only did it to protect you."

"It wasn't just that," Nicholas tried to say, but all that came out was a broken whisper.

"What?"

"It wasn't just that he went to the administration behind my back. There were other things, things he said and never apologized for."

Will sighed heavily, and for a moment Nicholas thought he looked much older than twenty-six. "So what? He hurt your feelings? What could he have said that was so shitty you're still holding him to it five years later?"

Nicholas sat down on the couch, leaning back in exhaustion. It hurt that in all the fights they'd ever had, it was the one that impacted Matías that made William actually talk to him to find a solution.

They let the silence float around them for a beat, but it wasn't long until William tried again. "You went too far at the party. He didn't deserve that."

Nicholas rolled his eyes. "Oh, come on, Will. You make it sound like I pushed a five-year-old down the stairs. I know he's had the perfect life, but surely a few harsh words can't have affected him that much."

"They can, coming from you."

Nicholas let out a chuckle at the words, but he was left speechless by the enormity of the lie. Matías Romero had only ever tolerated Nicholas because of William; he'd hung out with him in college because he was William's little brother, he'd reported the professor to protect William, and he was nice to him now because he was sleeping on William's couch. None of his polite regard had ever been more than responsibility toward his best friend.

The silence stretched, and his brother sighed again, which was getting rather irritating. The conversation didn't feel over, but Nicholas certainly wasn't going to be the one to ask for more.

William spoke up again, seeming to remember something. "You know that I never heard you say a single bad thing about him, in all the years you've known him? Until this year, that is. Ever since you met him when you were in high school, you always wanted him around. You'd call me brainless and irresponsible and all kinds of nasty things whenever I came home, but you never included him in that." Nicholas felt his face flush. "I only realized you were mad at him back in college because you stopped hanging out with him, not because you ever told me he'd done something wrong. You never said anything," William insisted, his voice rising.

Nicholas was playing with the fraying hem of the cushion resting on his knees. His hands were cold, despite the warmth of the apartment.

"You've never—he's never seen this version of you aimed at him, Nick. He doesn't know how cruel you can be, and I don't think he can handle it."

"You're really overestimating our relationship, Will. I've never had the power to hurt him."

"You're wrong."

"I'm done with this conversation," the younger Fisher replied sharply, getting up to leave.

"Please," William said from behind him. "He's hurting, and he's not like me. He can't just shake it off and ignore you for a few weeks until he's forgotten why he should."

Nicholas didn't think he'd ever felt so tired. He didn't even have enough energy to attempt to detangle the truths from the lies in William's words.

"Look," he finally spoke, turning around. "Maybe you didn't realize or understand why I was so mad at him in college, but he knew. He knows. I confronted him when I found out he reported the professor, and he made it clear that he didn't respect me enough to ever be affected by what I had to say. He's not the untouched angel you think he is, Will, and however cruel you think I've been, it wasn't any more vicious than the things he told me when I was nothing more than a stupid kid."

Will looked at him for a long time.

"Nick. I'm sorry that I don't know what I don't know. But what I do know is that, for some reason, he really cares about your opinion. And somehow, he doesn't think you're the kind of person who hurts others just for fun, so he's probably convinced himself that he deserved it."

Nicholas flinched. That sounded exactly like what he'd felt at eighteen, when Matías had blown up in anger and told him exactly what he thought of him and his disgusting affair, and Nicholas had believed he deserved it.

"But that's stupid. I hurt you all the time," he said, his voice deflating. "Surely he doesn't think you deserve it."

Will dismissed his words with a wave of his hand. "That's different."

"It is?"

"Yeah. You hurt me, and I hurt you, and that way we can be sure the other doesn't forget we exist."

He'd never thought of his older brother as being particularly perceptive, but his words created an uncomfortably familiar echo in Nicholas's head. He stayed silent, taking it in and leaning against the wall next to his bedroom door.

"His family's bad, then?" he finally asked in the heavy silence.

"Yeah. It was never great despite what he said, but he didn't want to see it. There's been some… developments in the past few years. He definitely sees it now."

"What if he doesn't forgive me?" Nicholas had hoped the words wouldn't come out, but they did.

He snorted. "He will."

Will spoke like this was the most obvious thing in the world.

Nicholas made it to his room in a daze and flopped on top of his bed. His face still buried in his pillow, he blindly padded for his phone, typing the familiar keys once he found it on his nightstand.

He had some apologizing to do.

From: Nicholas Fisher

To: Student Employment

Cc: Jasmine Miller-Reed; Elizabeth R. Green; English Department Inquiries

Subject: Teaching assistant application

November 8, 11:35 AM

To whom it may concern,

Please find attached my application to join the English Department's teaching assistant program, with the kind sponsorship of Dr. Jasmine Miller-Reed. All supporting documents are also attached to this email.

I am looking forward to hearing back and remain available for an interview or any further information you may need.

Best regards,

Nicholas Fisher

CHAPTER 16

WHEN NICHOLAS ASKED his friends to have lunch with him the next day, they agreed without hesitation, which he knew he didn't deserve after ignoring them for almost two weeks. He'd spent the morning at the library researching sources for Michaelson's essay, and was almost not late by the time he joined his friends at the Chinese place they liked behind campus.

"Look who the cat dragged in. Are we friends again, then?" asked Ajay when he sat down.

"We were always friends," Nicholas answered easily. "I was just being a shitty one."

Ajay made a humming noise. "True. What was that about?"

Nicholas made a face. "Oh, you know. Just that pesky habit of mine to push people away when things get hard. I'm sorry I didn't return any of your texts."

"That'll do it," Ajay agreed. "I suppose you're forgiven, but only if you quit the quivering voice. It almost makes me want to give you a hug."

All three smiled. Finally. Soon enough they were discussing how Sloane was planning to catch up on two years' worth of English credits, and Nicholas got lost in the conversation, even allowing himself to take some space in it. He was listing which professors she should avoid and which ones gave easy credits, attempting to distract himself from the almost painful elation he felt that his friends weren't angry he'd disappeared on them. Being so easily forgiven, so clearly wanted at the table instead of simply accepted was exhilarating.

After he'd ordered, Nicholas turned around in his seat to look for a clock.

"Somewhere to be?" Sloane asked with a mocking glint in her eye.

"Not really. I need to get home, though."

"No library today?"

"No, I've got to catch Matías." Her grin told him this was the right answer, even though she couldn't possibly know why.

"Are you boys friends too, now?" Ajay asked around a mouthful of ramen.

"Not really. I… said some things." He ignored the unsurprised snort from his friend. "And I'd like to apologize."

That made them both look up, rather dramatically, he thought.

"Apologizing, do you hear that? Our baby's all grown up," Ajay told Sloane, mock emotion in their voice as they tapped the corner of their eye with a folded napkin.

Nicholas threw his napkin at them. "Not *that* grown, thank you very much."

❧

He managed to catch the bus early enough that he should have been able to get home around the time Matías's class finished, which would leave him plenty of time to prepare what he wanted to say, and maybe even breathe once or twice.

Nicholas Fisher was rather good at ignoring people and knowing how to hurt them; he was not, however, good at apologies. A small voice at the back of his head told him it might be time to change that, considering how often he tended to hurt those he cared about.

Not that Matías was part of that group.

Of course, he should have known that making a plan was the most surefire way to have it fail. He opened the door to find Matías shirtless at the stove, one hand on a pan and the other holding a spatula. His headphones were on his head, his hair definitely hadn't seen either end of a brush yet, and the caught-in-headlights look on his face when he looked up to see Nicholas in the entryway could have rivaled Bambi's.

Nicholas's eyes kept alternating between the clock on the oven, which did indicate it was well past four in the afternoon, and Matías's chest, which was still annoyingly broad and tan.

"Did you just get up?" was the first thing Nicholas thought to ask, his voice accidentally wrapped in judgment. He clearly looked like he had, and Nicholas caught himself wondering whether Matías had gotten another phone call from his father or if the ghost-like air around him was Nicholas's own fault.

The embarrassment was painfully obvious on Matías's face. Great. Should Nicholas apologize for his comment now or add it to the list for later?

It seemed like later would have to be now; Matías dragged the headphones off his head and left them to hang around his neck. Even if they weren't currently on speaking terms, he wouldn't stoop so low as to keep listening to music while someone was talking to him. It made Nicholas smile, albeit sadly, to know that both he and Will would have turned the volume up if they'd been in his position.

Perhaps his brother had been right—Matías wasn't like them.

"Give me a minute, and I'll clean up the living room," Matías said finally.

Nicholas turned around to see that wrinkled sheets were still spread all over the couch. He suspected that if he were to slip into them, he would find a lingering warmth there.

"I'll take care of it."

He had been right; when he bent over and started gathering the blankets, they smelled of fresh sleep and Matías, and breathing felt dangerous until they were piled in a corner and the couch looked like one again.

Nicholas kept his eyes tightly screwed on what he was doing, even when Matías protested in confusion. He hadn't once touched the makeshift bed, but he'd seen Will take it apart or put it back together countless times. Even though he knew he was just trying to delay whatever had to come next, Nicholas told himself that no good apology could happen on an unmade bed. Or at least, not the kind Matías would accept.

When the living room was back to looking like it didn't house a six-foot-one man and all of his possessions, Nicholas started hitting the cushions in the middle the way Will liked to do. When he looked up, Matías was staring at him. His face was dancing between confusion and amusement, although he appeared to think he was hiding it.

Matías's omelet was done, but he seemed unsure about where it would be safest to eat it considering Nicholas's inexplicable behavior taking over the living room.

"Thanks," he finally said, walking toward the sofa with his plate. Matías sat down in silence, his movements still guarded, almost like he was eating with a wild animal next to him that was too volatile to risk moving too suddenly. Nicholas knew he was acting strange, hovering without saying a word, but he wasn't sure how to get back to normal. He'd also never known Matías to do well with silence. He always had the need to fill it. Why wasn't he filling it now?

"I'm sorry," he blurted out after walking to the kitchen and back once more, not only louder than he'd intended but also somehow more aggressively, like the silence had been accusing him of something.

Matías looked up, his fork halfway to his open mouth. Nicholas could see the hesitation in his soft brown eyes, so he waved his hand in a gesture that he hoped conveyed something along the lines of "please keep eating, this is going to take a while" and took a deep breath. "I'm sorry for what I said the other day, and for being a bit of a dick since Halloween. Or before, I guess. Actually, always," he said closing his eyes. "You… It was mean. I apologize."

He was prepared for a range of reactions to his apology. A small part of him hoped it would be smooth and painless; Matías would say thank you, he appreciated it, and they would go back to their semi-regular awkwardness. Or perhaps the anger would fade as swiftly as it had arrived, and they could go for a game outside—although he hadn't really dared to hope for that. Most likely it was going to be one of the scarier options. Matías wouldn't forgive him, would tell him he'd gone too far this time, listing all the horrible things Nicholas had ever said or done to justify why he didn't want anything to do with him anymore.

He was prepared, he thought, for every eventuality.

But not this one.

Matías's whole body seemed to deflate, his eyes staring down at his feet while his head hung limp from his shoulders. Surely the seconds kept ticking forward, but to Nicholas, there was nothing but this moment. The more cowardly parts of him wished time could freeze, etched forever in the fragile stasis of not knowing whether he was finally going to get his wish and have Matías leave his life for good.

What if he did?

"I'm sorry too."

"You're… sorry too," Nicholas repeated rather listlessly.

"I'm sorry about the things I said to you. A long time ago. I know that's why you're still mad, and probably why you've been a dick this whole time. What I said back then, it was… mean." Repeating Nicholas's own words seemed to be Matías's attempt at alleviating some of the tension with humor; unfortunately, this was highly unsuccessful as far as the younger man was concerned.

He'd waited so long for these words, but now they burned. He hadn't foreseen that it would feel so much worse to know that Matías remembered what he'd told Nicholas, after all this time. That they hadn't been throwaway insults but were perhaps harsh truths whose only fault was a clumsy delivery.

"And not true," Matías added as an afterthought.

Nicholas knew it was time to forgive Matías for the things he'd said five years ago, but the memory of these words had played such a big part in his life that he couldn't help but feel the cruel injustice of an apology wiping away years of damage. Yet he knew he couldn't stay angry forever; it was exhausting, spending his days refusing to see Matías's efforts and trying to convince everyone and himself that he was a bad person.

They stayed silent for a long time before Nicholas was able to get back to what he'd wanted to say.

"And I'm sorry for whatever you're going through at home. It must be pretty bad if you'd rather spend Thanksgiving with the Fishers."

"And *I'm* sorry I didn't apologize earlier. I didn't know how. I hoped maybe you would… forget about it." Matías winced at his own words, which reassured Nicholas that he didn't have to point out the obvious flaw in that assumption.

A small part of him wanted to laugh at this deluge of apologies; like the dam they'd spent years building between them and the things they'd done to each other had finally broken and regrets were all crashing in.

"Did you really think I was damaged goods?" Nicholas couldn't help but ask in the ensuing silence, his voice barely more than a whisper.

"Fuck, Nicholas." Matías rubbed his face in his hands with more strength than was necessary. It messed up his eyebrows, and Nicholas tried not to smile. "I don't remember saying that."

Nicholas shrugged—perhaps he'd extrapolated, but he would forever remember the venom in Matías's words—the kind of disgust they called forth was clear, regardless of semantics. "What about dirty and twisted, then? You said those."

"I'm so sorry." Matías seemed to be in physical pain, and it shouldn't have given Nicholas the jolt of satisfaction that it did. "Maybe I was just talking about myself."

He had no idea what that meant. Their roles had always been clear to him. Matías was perfect and well-adjusted and desirable, and Nicholas was small and fucked up and that was at least half of why the Texan would never look at him twice. Too many realizations had already happened in the past two days. He couldn't add the fact that maybe Matías didn't see himself the way everyone else did to the list.

"So you're coming for Thanksgiving, then?"

Matías smiled, a shy smile that was familiar but rare, so soft that Nicholas had wondered if he'd made it up in his head. "If you'll have me."

Nicholas nodded. "You should tell our mom now, she'll want to have time to practice her *papusas* recipe before you arrive."

The expression in Matías's eyes was so soft, it would have been easy for Nicholas to convince himself he could look at them safely. Still, he didn't risk it; now that they were both done with their apologies, it was time to run away again, and Nicholas tried to shake himself into leaving Matías and his omelet alone. But when the man spoke up again before he'd reached the door of his bedroom, all he felt was relief.

"I found a place, by the way."

"A place?"

"It's twenty minutes away, but it looks decent. I'll move before we head to Milwaukee. Sorry for staying for so long."

All Nicholas could do was nod, tapping his doorframe nervously and wondering why he'd thought eating so much at lunch had been a good idea as a faint feeling of nausea rose up in him.

❧

"… Any questions?" Brianna concluded.

Nicholas slow-clapped and even tried to whistle in an attempt to hide his pride. She had just given him a near-perfect twenty-five-minute presentation of everything she'd been working on for the past two months, and he did rather think it was far better than anything he could have produced at eighteen.

She looked at him with her arms crossed over her chest, and he easily recognized the familiar tendency to act aloof and untouchable when all you felt was small and scared.

"How did that feel?" he asked her.

"Scary," she exhaled, throwing herself on one of the chairs around him in relief. "Do you think it's ready?"

Her voice sounded so vulnerable.

"I think it's more than ready. They're going to be really impressed. They might ask you to TA a class next semester, at this rate."

She rolled her eyes, but he could see that she was pleased at the comment.

"I need to get into grad school, first. Can I hit you up for a reference when I apply?" she asked as they both got up and started putting their things away.

"I'm not sure some grad student's opinion is going to weigh much on their decision, unfortunately."

"I suppose, but three years from now, you'll be a professor, so it would definitely help." Nicholas frowned. "Oh, don't look at me like that. We both know you're meant for it."

"I'm not planning on becoming a professor."

She didn't look convinced, but she also didn't seem to care much either way. He'd quickly realized that the Brianna who understood he wasn't going to let her fail had a lot more attitude and opinions than the Brianna he had first received uncertain emails from.

They wrapped themselves in their winter layers, heading outside through the heavy back door of the study room they'd miraculously managed to book for an hour. The cold hit them like a wave; the frozen wind that had settled with Nicholas's mood over Chicago had finally turned into the first snow of the season. It was ridiculously early and announced the kind of winter that would hold until April.

"So, what now?" he asked after a few seconds of walking silently side by side. He realized with a pang of sadness that this was probably their last time meeting. It reminded him of moving out of his old, moldy apartment; the bittersweet taste at the back of his throat that moving forward was good, even when it was tinted with sadness.

"I think I'll rehearse it a bit more and get an early night. Then, I need to forget all about what I've spent months working on to focus on finals," she sighed. "What about you?"

"I was speaking more generally."

Brianna snorted. "I'm a freshman a month away from my first finals season. Short-range vision is the only thing I've got right now."

Nicholas knew this was far from true, but he let it go.

"Touché. Well, let me know if you need any more help before Wednesday. Your presentation is in the afternoon, right?"

"Don't you have a thesis to write?" she asked instead of answering.

He shrugged. "Not yet. I just have articles and final papers. But I'll be all right. I…" He was about to say more, to explain that there was too much going through his mind to muster the apprehension he'd felt during every other time his academic plate had reached the fullness it now experienced. But he had to remind himself that Brianna was closer to being his student than his friend, and he owed it to her to act like it. His friends, who wanted nothing more than to hear about the twisted mechanics of his moods, were waiting for him at Sloane's. "Well, this week is mostly for doing the rounds anyway."

"The rounds?"

"The rounds of everyone I need to check in with before I stop answering emails until January," he joked.

She looked at him like she knew he was keeping her at arm's length, but he liked to think she would appreciate it one day. "All right, teach. Well, don't help too many needy freshmen. You already look enough like a vampire with these dark circles. Heroin chic hasn't been fashionable since the nineties, you know."

Nicholas just scoffed. He knew very well that whenever he was tired, his already-pale skin and bony features only became more obvious. He wasn't sure why Brianna drawing attention to it didn't hurt him as much as it usually did, though.

"Thanks for everything. I'll keep that email address handy for when I need it, if that's cool." She burst out laughing when she saw him staring uncertainly at her raised hand. "You're embarrassing me, now," she noted. Offended, he gave her his best impression of a high five. "There you go. Bye," she sing-songed, walking backwards away from him.

"Break a leg," he called out when she'd already turned around.

"What, like, now?" she asked with a grin over her shoulder, pretending to stumble on the pavement that would soon turn icy.

He shook his head and turned around, knowing there was one last thing he had to do before he could leave campus. Thankfully, Leila was a creature of habit, and he knew where she would be at this time on a Monday—heading to lunch in the dining hall closest to the library so she could go and study as soon as she was done. He ran to catch up with her outside of the science building when he saw her.

"Calm down, Tonya Harding," she said when she caught sight of him. "Maybe skipping up and down a frozen pavement isn't the best idea two weeks before break?"

"I'm not skipping."

The look Leila cut him would have, he was convinced, driven a weaker man to his knees. Her eyes were so dark, he wondered how he could feel the difference in the way they were looking at him, but he did. It had been this way since he'd bumped into her in the library last week, something in her voice colder than he was used to. He'd pretended he couldn't hear it. "Just thought I'd let you know I made up with Matías."

His suspicions that she was annoyed with him about hurting her friend were confirmed when the veil of annoyance that had been draped over her features dissipated. He hadn't been sure how close Leila and Matías actually were outside of soccer, but he had his answer now—apparently, they were close enough that Matías had told her about his abysmal behavior at the party.

He wondered if Sloane was the same brand of quietly disapproving when she stumbled upon people who had hurt or annoyed Nicholas.

"Did you, now?" she tried for a casual tone, but he could feel she was holding back.

"Yep. Apologized and everything, then he apologized; it was all very sentimental. You would have hated it," he assured her.

Even though they'd spent the last month studying together every time they had the chance, Nicholas still barely knew anything about Leila. She'd never seemed interested in catering to what he might want her to be or make any effort to convince him into a friendship, which he respected more than she knew. All they did was sit side by side for silent hours, refusing to yearn for connection but forced to realize that company wasn't always a bad thing.

"Then what happened?" she asked neutrally, her eyes screwed to the ground ahead of them.

"Well, that's about it, really. It's taken us years to say some of that stuff, so I think it was plenty of progress for one conversation. He's coming to ours for Thanksgiving, though," he added matter-of-factly, as if the thought hadn't been blinking at the forefront of his mind like a neon sign for days.

They reached the slope leading to the dining hall, which had gotten the better of many a coccyx last winter, and he held out his arm for her to grab if she wanted to. She did not, but when he looked at her face, he saw her pleased expression. "That'll be good for him."

There was a knowing look in her eyes. It was on the tip of his tongue to ask her why the man who'd always spoken so highly of his parents had chosen to spend the most family-centric holiday of the year with the dysfunctional Fishers, or why he'd been sleeping on his friend's couch for two and a half months. But he didn't want the answer to come from anyone but Matías, so he stayed silent.

"So you're back to being friends now?" she continued.

Nicholas shrugged. "I don't know," he admitted, doing a decent job at pretending he hadn't spent the weekend alternating between asking himself exactly that and burying the thought as deep as it would go. "I guess we'll see. It's been so many years since the last time we were friends, it's more like we're starting over."

"Starting over is nice, sometimes."

Before he could answer, they'd reached the door to the dining hall. "Are you coming tonight?" she asked before they parted.

"Coming where?"

"We have an open practice. Everyone's welcome."

He frowned. "Why would I do that?"

"Thought you might want to."

"It's below thirty degrees out."

"It's indoors."

He couldn't find anything to say to that, but he didn't know whether he was relieved or disappointed when she didn't ask him once more.

"See you around, then." She bumped his fist before heading inside.

On the bus to Sloane's, he told himself he was glad Matías hadn't asked him to come see him at practice. He had too much work to do to waste an hour sitting around on uncomfortable benches in a drafty arena, anyway. But it was getting harder to lie to himself, to pretend that he wouldn't have happily pushed working on his thesis until next year just to see Matías smile when he came to watch him during practice, like friends did. He knew it wouldn't do him any good, but for the first time in years, Nicholas closed his eyes and allowed himself to picture it.

From: Jasmine Miller-Reed
To: Nicholas Fisher
Subject: ENGL 12307 Presentation
November 15, 4:56 PM

Dear Nicholas,

I want to start by acknowledging receipt of your teaching assistant application. I will keep you appraised of my decision as soon as possible.

As I'm sure you are aware, Brianna gave the class her research presentation on Wednesday. It was a great success, and she has exceeded my expectations. She also made sure to insist that you were instrumental in steering her in the right direction for this.

While I know the upcoming week will be one of the busiest for you this season, and the one after that will be break, I propose we meet to discuss credits and further plans at your earliest convenience in December.

I'm sure I will also have more information on the TA placement by then, and you might have a better idea of your credit situation for the semester as well.

Enjoy your holidays,
Jasmine Miller-Reed

CHAPTER 17

TRUE TO HIS WORD, Matías moved out the following Saturday. Nicholas's many deadlines, Miller-Reed's updated syllabus, and all the holiday activities he'd signed up for at the library when he thought he was going to be lonely and miserable all month kept him too busy to really feel his absence—or at least, they did for the first two days.

Nicholas tried to tell himself that the pull in his chest each time he came home to a cold and dark apartment was neither loneliness nor yearning. He made himself appreciate the pristine living room, the lack of sheets and pillows all over the house, and his brother's renewed absence now that he didn't share a home with his best friend. Nicholas watched TV and read on the couch, stood by the windows and looked at the city lights, enjoying the space he'd spent so long wanting all to himself. He even found time to wonder why it was that the living room walls were suddenly painted a bleak cream color, when he'd been convinced they were a light yellow for months.

Supposedly, Will had heard about his apology to Matías because he was back to acknowledging his brother's existence. He off- handedly informed Nicholas that their old roommate was spending most of his time studying or taking exams, for which he seemed to resent law school heavily. His best friend's unavailability made Will crabby and annoying, and with no buffer between them or reason to be kind, the brothers went back to snapping at each other about the state of the apartment and calling it conversation.

With the amount of stress he was under, Nicholas was too exhausted to find comfort in the intimate anger he'd always been able to muster up toward his brother. Instead, he tried to be tolerable the few times he was able to make it out of the hole of unintelligible articles he was buried in, which resulted in William cooking them dinner for three days in a row and taking over all the chores that had been Matías's. The constant correlation between keeping his temper in check and people being nice to him in return was becoming impossible to ignore. Thankfully, he was too busy to dwell on it further.

"How's Matías's new place?" Nicholas asked Will one evening. He was trying to put together an edible meal from all the food Matías hadn't bothered to take with him in the move. Nicholas couldn't remember what they had ever put in the empty shelves he'd left behind.

Will grimaced. "You can imagine. His roommates are weird and the insulation is terrible. He sleeps with a hat on."

"Jesus," Nicholas breathed out. He knew too well what that was like, and he was stingingly aware that the only reason he wasn't in Matías's position was because his brother had given him the one free bedroom in his freshly renovated apartment. The pang of guilt was quick to follow. "He can still come over, you know. There's heating here."

"I think he's trying to give us some space."

Nicholas rolled his eyes. "Space to do what? It's hell week for me, anyway. I'll be barricaded in my room, writing. There's no reason to be wearing a hat indoors," he added with a face of distaste.

Will looked at him for a beat and simply nodded, pressing play on the show they hadn't watched in over a month. "I'll let him know."

✄

The next day, someone rang the doorbell in the middle of the afternoon. Will was at work and Nicholas was planning on ignoring it, but whoever it was seemed intent on mistreating the thing. He had no choice but to get up from his desk, grumbling complaints all the way to the door. He was about to give the stranger outside of his apartment a colorful piece of his mind, but the words died in his throat. On the grubby and run-down landing stood a red-faced Matías in soccer gear, smiling from ear to ear and holding a ball under his arm.

"Hi," he said rather enthusiastically.

"Hi," Nicholas answered stupidly. "Will's not here."

"I know." This he should have expected, considering it was the middle of the workday. "I came for you."

Something in Nicholas's expression made Matías burst out laughing.

"Heard you were holding siege in here with your big boring books, so I came to drag you out for a game."

"What about your big boring books? Aren't you supposed to be learning the Constitution and such?"

Matías shrugged, unaffected. "That's what crunch time is for."

Nicholas remembered the older boy's senior year, when he'd ended up getting even better grades than Will even though Nicholas had rarely seen him do any actual work. Matías was both annoyingly smart and the kind of prancing procrastinator that spent his afternoons lying around, too lazy to work until the threat of a deadline physically loomed in front of him.

Matías's eyes might have been shining with eagerness from where he was standing, but the dark circles that surrounded them were unmistakable. Nicholas felt a pang of compassion, wondering if there was anyone helping him navigate his first law school finals season.

"I don't really have time for a game right now," Nicholas said obligingly.

"Have you been outside today yet?" Nicholas winced, which was answer enough. "Well, you have to, at least once. So what you actually don't have time for is arguing about it until it gets dark."

Dazed by the commanding tone, Nicholas nodded and moved aside to let the man in. It was an odd feeling, to let Matías make the decisions and accept them with barely a fight. It reminded him of how they used to be, how Matías had taken him under his wing when he'd shown up to college, teaching him the ways of adulthood, dragging him to fraternity houses and bacchanalian soccer team parties, not giving a speck of attention to the fact that Nicholas had no interest in being one of the cool kids. He'd say stupid things like "meet everyone once, and then you can decide who your friends are" or "say yes to everything in your first year," and all Nicholas could do was nod along hoping to see pride or approval in Matías's eyes.

"Tea?" Nicholas asked then, at least trying to pretend he wasn't eighteen anymore and could make some decisions.

"Do you have any oat milk?"

"I do."

"All right, I'll make it. Go change."

All Nicholas could do to that was obey. He didn't even feel anything when he closed his laptop and left his books behind; not the choking weight of responsibility, no panic at all the things that still needed writing and reading. All he felt was relief and a childish sort of excitement he didn't want to look into.

He had expected that they would walk to the park in their usual silence. But it soon became clear that the peaceful strolls of the last times they'd done this had, in fact, been incredible feats of restraint from Matías. It only took a few seconds before the man launched into a long-winded description of how much he hated constitutional law and how angry it made him that you couldn't really understand "anything about anything" without suffering through it first. Then, he discussed how expensive groceries were getting and the mold invading most of the comfortable armchairs in the libraries across campus without once stopping for breath.

As the two boys walked through the city, Nicholas let himself listen with only one ear while he looked at the streets around them. The layer of almost-snow seemed like it would never thicken, but at least it had grown less slippery during the week he'd spent in his room studying. Even though college students were all buried in mountains of confusing feedback and repetitive articles, the rest of the world seemed happy and distracted, holding its breath until the holidays.

This time of the year, everyone was still excited about the newly cold weather, especially with the warm lights everywhere and the constant, if faint, scent of pumpkin spice in the background. Nicholas thought that the buildup was always better than the holidays themselves, and the city seemed to agree. It was still shrouded in cheerful promises, far from the unmet expectations that the next few weeks would bring.

When they got to the park, a group of teenagers was occupying the square clearing they usually claimed. Nicholas went on to see if he could find an empty spot somewhere else and a makeshift goal post. But he'd barely walked three steps before Matías had struck a conversation with the half-dozen boys and started laughing loudly with them.

"Nicholas," he called over his shoulder, "let's play with them for a while, they have to leave soon anyway."

Nicholas shook his head in annoyance he didn't feel, heading toward the side of the pitch Matías wasn't on.

It was good to move after the week he'd had; soon enough his constantly aching upper back and the tired skin under his eyes faded into the background of his beating heart and burning thighs. He had fun, admittedly, especially once they let him play goalie. It was a welcome change to be so unquestionably good at something, stopping balls that rushed in his direction instead of spending months writing articles he was never sure were visionary or terrible. Although his position in the goal did mean he caught himself looking for Matías rather than paying attention to the ball more than once.

Nicholas's team was in the lead by the time the teenagers had to leave; apparently, even thirteen-year-old boys had busier evenings than he did. Over the course of the short game, they all seemed to have become great fans of Matías's, and Nicholas couldn't resent them for it. He was impressive in his element, skilled and fast and comfortable enough that he always managed to remain humble.

What surprised Nicholas was that almost every boy who had been on his team came up to him to shake his hand or clap him on the back, saying things like "thanks, man" and "come back whenever" on their way out. He tried to hide his smile as he walked back to Matías.

"So that's what they call a D1 athlete these days?" he teased.

"You do realize that you had one more player than us, right?" Matías did not seem fazed by his loss in the slightest.

"You're saying all it takes is one thirteen-year-old, and you're over-whelmed?"

"He was at least fourteen."

Nicholas laughed, and for a heartbeat he caught Matías's crinkling eyes as he did the same. There was something there, something almost hungry. He stopped smiling.

"Think you got one more shootout in you, or are you done?"

"Sure."

Matías proceeded to take off the last few layers of clothes he had on, leaving only his t-shirt to cling to his sweaty chest. He grabbed the ball from under Nicholas's arm, getting so dangerously close to him in the process that the younger man could feel the heat emanating from him.

"Actually, how about you take them? I'll teach you," he said with a challenge in his eyes, still moving back.

Nicholas laughed, too distracted by the rise and fall of Matías's chest to be as affronted as he should be. "Teach me?"

Matías hummed.

"I'm only in the goalpost because we both know we wouldn't get any playing done otherwise," Nicholas noted, "since I'm pretty sure you can't catch for shit."

Matías opened his mouth in outrage. But before he could say anything in response, Nicholas dropped the ball and started proving his point, dribbling past the other man and rushing for the goal. He was clearly showing off, accidentally letting yelps of joy escape him when Matías started running after him.

In a move that would have had every referee in the world throw-ing cards redder than Nicholas's cheeks, Matías grabbed him from behind before he reached his objective. Matías's laugh wrapped itself around Nicholas's gasp of surprise when he felt strong hands on his waist, more than enough to make him lose the ball, and any sense of control of what was going on. He turned around to face Matías, out of breath.

Matías wasn't blinking.

"I didn't know they allowed holding these days," Nicholas's voice came out hoarse.

Matías's hand was still on his shirt. His chest was rising and falling rapidly, but everything else about him was so still, he could have been a painting.

All the world was this: standing so close to Matías Romero that he could feel the heat radiating off his body, or maybe it was just the nerve endings from the fingers on his ribs echoing everywhere inside him. Nicholas knew this was as close as he was ever going to be allowed, and he didn't even mind.

Of course, that was when it started raining properly, big cold drops falling on Matías's curls and rolling down his skin. It would have taken a tornado strong enough to carry Nicholas away for him to leave this moment; but he didn't know what to do with the fact that Matías wasn't moving either. The rain seemed to make the already grey afternoon even darker, and all Nicholas could see were corners and shadows. A streetlight from the other side of the park fence lit up one side of Matías's face, which felt more manageable than being hit with all of it at once, so Nicholas allowed himself to look.

Matías was also looking, his breath held. Nicholas had to move, or he was going to do something he'd regret. Maybe it was the darkness cloaking everything making him delusional, because he thought Matías was looking at him like he would let him.

"We should probably go," the Texan's voice was soft. The fingers that had still been on his waist moved to graze Nicholas's arm, lightly, like this touch would be enough to snap Nicholas into movement.

It did, and Nicholas started pulling away, but then Matías raised his hand. It was hovering next to his face, Matías's eyes locked on the strand of hair that fell just in the corner of Nicholas's eye. Before he could say anything, Matías's fingers pushed the strand of hair off his forehead, and he whispered, "I miss your long hair."

"Well, I like it better like this," Nicholas said belligerently, breaking the rising tension.

Matías burst out laughing, pushing his head back to look up at the sky with joy etched onto his face, which Nicholas found confusing but irrelevant. "Fair enough," he said when he looked back at Nicholas. "You should keep it like this then. Beautiful either way."

Well, Nicholas couldn't be held accountable for breaking then, could he?

He drove forward. For a man who had been called avoidant and fearful and never brave, he didn't feel the electric rush of nerves he would have expected. He smashed their mouths together with speed and no precision, rushing before his brain could process what he'd done. But Matías did not move away. He let him go through with what he'd decided to do, tiptoeing around their closed-mouth kiss for a few seconds before he grabbed the back of Nicholas's neck. He tensed, but then Matías pulled him forward and every part of him was touching a part of Matías and the pool of panic inside him turned to silence.

Matías was kissing him back, and he wasn't stupid enough to think he'd ever get to live this moment again, so Nicholas stopped thinking altogether and closed his eyes.

He grabbed Matías's t-shirt with a fist; soon enough there was a hand on his waist while another was trying to hold onto his too-short hair. He could feel the tense restraint in Matías even as Nicholas caught his lower lip between his teeth and Matías groaned in appreciation. This gave Nicholas some courage, and he started to take a little bit more. He put a hand against Matías's cheek, against the perfect face he'd spent so long trying his hardest to hate.

He kept expecting Matías to snap back to reality and walk away from him, to realize what he was doing, but instead the other man offered up more of his mouth—his arms, his lips—with a hum, hand still lost in Nicholas's hair. So Nicholas squeezed the back of Matías's neck. It was like both of them were challenging the other to walk away, to call it too much, the most confusing game of chicken Nicholas had ever played.

When they finally parted, soaked and cold, Matías grinned. "Sorry," he said, the picture of a man who had never felt regret in his life. Nicholas opened his mouth, trying to form coherent thoughts that weren't about how red and puffy Matías's lips looked, even in the dim light. Matías didn't seem to care either way. "Been wanting to do that for a while."

Nicholas bit down the confused whimper that threatened to come out of him; swallowed once, twice, and tried to remember if breathing was better through your nose or mouth, but that just made him think of Matías's mouth again. Shaking his head, Nicholas managed with effort to snap out of the daze he was in. Surely this was a dream, or some sort of prank, and the sooner he could go back to reality, the healthier it would be for everyone. Matías was still staring at him.

"Should we go?" his voice came out small.

Matías nodded. "Let's get you home."

He tried to squash the feeling of disappointment he knew had no place here as Matías wrapped layers of clothes back around himself; he was shivering after all, and the rain was unrelenting. But Nicholas Fisher had never been a fair man when it came to his brother's best friend.

They ran home—because running was easier than talking, pushing each other into puddles and against walls like all the questions Nicholas wasn't asking could be forgotten if they laughed loud enough.

When they reached his apartment, they were out of breath and Matías's cheeks were flushed and his gaze had lost some of its dangerous edge. Nicholas stood there, tempted to ask exactly what had happened in the park. That's when he realized that whatever it had been, a kindness or a joke or a mistake, hearing Matías spell it out for him would probably hurt more than just safekeeping the memory and accepting the fact that it would probably never happen again. There were a million reasons why Matías could never actually be interested in him, and Nicholas didn't need him to awkwardly but not unkindly list them out.

It was like a mirror descended on the street, and he could see himself at eighteen again; begging for the attention that was only granted to him as a second thought by his older brother's kind but uninterested best friend.

Nicholas wasn't eighteen anymore.

"Do you want to borrow an umbrella?" he asked Matías, making it clear that he expected him to go straight home—wherever that was now.

"That's all right, I'll take the bus," Matías said, his expression undecipherable. He looked more pensive than either mad or glad; but Nicholas didn't waste any time trying to understand what it meant. He already knew there was a long weekend of insomnia and overthinking ahead of him after today's events—maybe he'd add the faraway look in Matías's eyes to the list of things to ponder.

"All right," he said with a smile he hoped was friendly, before bumping his shoulder against Matías's in goodbye and heading up the stairs without looking back.

That was what friends who sometimes kissed did, right?

From: William

To: AJ, Leila Khayat, Matías Romero, Princess Sloane, +3 more

Dear friends/family of the Fishers,

You are officially invited to Will & Nick's Friendsgiving bash on Saturday, November 23. Please reply to this chain with your attendance and whether you are bringing anything (unnecessary). There will be vegetarian/ non-alcoholic options, and Nicholas will be cooking so please come with an empty stomach and a forgiving mindset.

See you then,

Nick & Will

CHAPTER 18

WITH THANKSGIVING BREAK approaching, it was like the collective breath the student body had been holding for weeks was finally released. By Friday, most undergraduates were too busy packing or celebrating the few days of freedom they were about to be granted to bother showing up to campus at all. The number of crying students in the commons decreased drastically, and library seats finally freed up long enough to reveal what color they were.

Despite their university's generous policy of giving students the entire week off, most postgraduates still had deadlines and responsibilities, but they took them in stride. They had long learned that the word "break" would remain relative until they held their diploma in their hands.

This didn't seem to be a problem for Matías, who seemed to have dragged everyone out with him after practice last night, if William's hungover grunts at breakfast were anything to go by.

"Earth to Nicholas?" Ajay caught his attention with a paper napkin ball to the face. He'd agreed to have lunch with his friends, whose compromise for working through Thanksgiving Break was to take the time to have three meals a day, but he was exhausted. As was to be expected, he'd barely slept since the kiss. Even spending his days working on Michaelson's essay and his evenings proofreading Brianna's summer internship application had not been enough to quell the onslaught of questions plaguing his mind.

Nicholas had replayed the scene at the park until the vinyl was scratched, and he still had no idea why Matías had kissed him back, although his current theory was that Chicago had been hit with a kind of toxic rain that had made Matías so delirious he'd thought he was kissing a woman.

But he was fine not knowing, Nicholas told himself. So what if he felt haunted by the memory to the point of being consistently nauseous and so tired he had trouble reading the simplest sentences? There would be plenty of time to get over himself and disappear into Morpheus's arms when he got to his parents' house next week.

Except that Matías would be there too.

"Did you end up seeing the antique shop guy again?" Nicholas asked Sloane, hoping to distract her from his lack of participation in the conversation so far.

"Heavens, no." Sloane answered indifferently. "The charm wore off once I saw his friends, and his house, and... well, maybe the secrecy of it all was more appealing than he was."

"I want a secret love affair," lamented Ajay.

"You could never have a secret anything. How would you remind everyone you're better than them if they can't know the reason why?" Nicholas pointed out.

"That's true. You'd be much better suited to it, with all the staring broodily into the distance and reading sad, old books."

Nicholas snorted. "After my last attempt, I think I'm going to steer clear of those for a while."

He looked at Sloane, who unfortunately did not seem to find his words as funny as he did.

"Steer clear of what?" asked a familiar voice behind him. He would have recognized it anywhere, the warm and almost fond notes foreshadowing a wide smile and kind eyes. When he turned around, Nicholas was surprised to see Matías holding a tray full of food.

Despite the freezing weather outside, he was wearing a ridiculous sweater that hugged his shoulders in a way that left very little to the imagination, and Nicholas had to physically shake his head to stop himself from mentioning how stupid he looked.

Apparently, last night's shenanigans had ended up with Will accidentally going home with Matías's wallet. When he'd explained the problem to Nicholas over breakfast, it was with such a weight of expectation in his eyes that Nicholas'd had no choice but to offer to return it to Matías when he went to campus.

But before Nicholas could get his wits about him and remember where he'd put the wallet, the older boy had set his tray down next to his and taken the seat across from Sloane.

"Secret love affairs," Ajay answered matter-of-factly, waving hello at Matías distractedly like they didn't mind his unannounced interruption.

"Ah, of course. I'm not very good at those, personally," he said, laughing to himself as he started eating.

Nicholas's heart was beating abnormally fast as his body tried to compute what was happening. He'd hoped things wouldn't be awkward and had convinced himself that he and Matías would go back to tiptoeing around a friendship neither really wanted. But as he saw the brunette's famously charming grin working overtime in Sloane's direction, he wondered if even that had been a mistake.

"Sloane, right?"

Nicholas realized that outside of their Halloween party, the two had never properly met. And even then, Nicholas had spent the whole night stuck to Sloane, which had at least had the benefit of keeping Matías at a distance.

He remembered why that was important when he saw the pleased look on his best friend's face. Anyone who met Matías for the first time tended to wear that same dazed expression.

"That's me. Nice to properly meet you."

Matías's face lit up when she talked. "British!" was all he said, which made her laugh at a pitch so high Nicholas didn't think he'd heard it before. "The love affair thing makes more sense now."

"Does it?"

"It does," Matías assured but did not explain. Everyone around the table smiled, except Nicholas who tried to take subtle deep breaths as he plucked out Matías's wallet from his bag and handed it to him.

"Here you go."

"Oh, thanks so much, man. Sorry for making you come all the way over for this."

"All the way… to lunch?"

Matías had the audacity to look embarrassed. "I hope it wasn't too much trouble."

"Now that you mention it, the dessert selection is terrible here."

"No chocolate?"

"None."

Matías gasped. "*Sacrílego*. I'll see if I can steal something from the law building. We've got this big buffet thing to celebrate… something. Are you going to be around later?"

"I'll probably be at the library with Leila."

"Cool, I'll find you."

Matías dug back into his food, unaffected by the growing silence around him.

"How was work yesterday?" Matías asked after a few seconds, unaware that there was anything odd about Sloane and Ajay's silence.

"Good. Some of the local teens ended up helping me set everything up." Matías frowned, and Nicholas cut him off before he started reciting child labor laws. "I know, it's not ideal, but they insisted. And if they don't have anywhere else to go in the evening, then I'd rather have them put together some bookshelves than be out looking for trouble…"

"Maybe they just want to help you out like you've been helping them."

Nicholas rolled his eyes. "Sure, between the preschool story time and the middle school math homework I understand even less than they do, they get a lot out of me."

Matías dismissed his words. "Tell that to that freshman you've been helping like she's the one paying your tuition."

Nicholas forgave him for a lot when he said that.

The silence came back, everyone focusing on the food in front of them.

"Sorry," Matías finally broke it, looking up from his plate after he'd engulfed two thirds of it and finally catching eyes with Sloane and Ajay. "I feel like I interrupted. Please go back to the secret love affairs. I'll be quiet."

They did go back to discussing the unavoidable demise of Sloane's latest paramour, and Matías didn't seize the conversation again, letting Ajay and Sloane's stories wash over him. Every now and then, he would turn to Nicholas to remind him of someone they both knew or a situation they'd both witnessed, oblivious to the looks of everyone around him. It was like they shared a hundred tiny secrets, and Matías wanted to make sure he remembered that.

He left as quickly as he'd arrived; one second, he was putting his fork down, and the next he was apologizing and saying he was expected somewhere else, unaware of the whirlwind of emotions he left behind.

"It was nice to see y'all," he added before heading out, tapping Ajay on the shoulder amicably on his way.

The three friends were left to sit in silence, and Nicholas wondered if the others were also experiencing that stunned feeling Matías always left him with whenever he dipped in and out of Nicholas's day. When Sloane finally spoke up, her words were so careful it was like she was walking on cracked glass.

"That was nice." Nicholas only shrugged. "You guys seem to be getting along, now."

"I kissed him."

He'd expected the silence that would follow to be stunned, thought he would look up to shock and maybe anger. Instead, they were both smiling.

"Did he kiss you back?"

"I suppose."

Sloane squealed.

"Look, it's not like that. He probably just felt sorry for me or something. It won't happen again. I don't even think he's into guys."

Both of their faces fell.

"For what it's worth, a straight man kissing another man just because he feels sorry for him has to be one of the most unlikely scenarios I have ever heard, and you know I love a good plot twist," Sloane said.

Nicholas almost laughed. "Well, it's not like he actually likes me. Not like that, at least."

"Right, because footballers just hand out sympathy kisses all the time," Sloane teased. "Keep telling yourself that."

Ajay spoke up, their voice more serious than Nicholas has heard it in a long time. "Do you remember when you first told us about him? You painted him as this big narcissist, like the world was a stage and he spent all his time trying to charm the audience."

Somehow, this sentence annoyed Nicholas, but he could not begin to understand why. "So?"

"So, we just had lunch with him, and he barely talked to either of us. He was polite, sure, but he clearly only had eyes for you. We are very interesting people," Ajay insisted, "and yet he had his head turned toward you the whole time, trying to catch your attention with all of his stupid stories."

Nicholas scoffed dismissively. "Whatever you think you saw, it's not like that. Believe me. To him, I'm just a sad little boy with a ladleful of overworked trauma and a tendency to cling onto every sick, old man who looks at me twice," he continued, fiddling with the crumbs that had dropped onto the table so he wouldn't have to see the pity in his friends' gazes.

He only looked up when the silence had stretched so long it made even him feel uncomfortable. The two faces looking at him were a blend of disbelief and horror.

"What? That's what he told me."

"What *he* told you?"

"Well—maybe I'm exaggerating a bit. A lot. After he reported that professor and I told him it hurt coming from him of all people. There was other stuff mixed in there, about how it was time I liked someone my own age, but I stopped listening after a while." He felt a jolt of pride at the dryness in his voice, considering how little practice he'd had saying any of it out loud.

"That's a horrible thing to say," Sloane murmured.

Ajay was silent, which was when Nicholas realized they didn't know what he was talking about. Well, they'd have to ask Sloane, because he was done talking about it.

"Yeah, well, I did say his good guy act shouldn't be trusted," Nicholas noted, colder than he'd intended.

"You did," answered Sloane. "I'm sorry we fell for it anyway. I really… I can't imagine, you having to listen to me defending him. I had no idea he was so cruel."

Nicholas felt panic rise in him, as sharp as it was unexpected. "What? He's not *cruel*. He's a good guy, generally speaking. That was different."

"It was different because it was you?" Sloane asked softly, so clearly trying not to break him that it made him want to snap his silverware in two.

"No, it was different because he was. Everyone around this table has said things they wish they could take back. He's apologized, and you said it yourself, it was years ago."

Nicholas felt the way he imagined a race driver losing control of his car might. He'd spent so long trying to convince his friends that Matías really was a bad person, but now that he'd forgiven him, it felt critical that they did too. Unfortunately, it seemed like Sloane was trying to make up for the weeks she'd spent arguing that surely Matías couldn't have been that bad.

"Maybe we have, but it didn't take us years to apologize." Ajay was wearing the skeptical expression he'd wished they'd adorned back in September.

"Just give him a chance. You'll see."

"I'm confused," Ajay cut him off. "Are we supposed to give him a chance or believe he's the kind of person who'd kiss you just to fuck with you?"

Nicholas wanted to scream. "That's what I'm trying to figure out."

❧

Nicholas was glad that Leila was also the kind of person who did not consider a school break a break from schoolwork. He loved his friends, but the three of them were almost incapable of getting any work done when they were together. Instead, he'd planned on meeting up with Leila in the main library that afternoon, hoping its high ceilings and long wooden tables would inspire him to finally focus on something other than the kiss.

It was even emptier than they'd expected; so much so that when they grew tired of their respective papers, they were able to turn toward each other and have a hushed conversation from the comfort of their own seats without receiving a single angry glare.

"I know you're a good cook, but you should make Friendsgiving a potluck thing. Cooking for eight people just isn't as easy as our moms made it look. You'll be spending two days in the kitchen."

"Not you too. I like cooking, I'll be fine. If you're all so intent on helping, just make sure to keep Will off my back."

"Not me too?"

"Matías said something similar. About me being too busy to cook for everyone."

"What else did he say?"

Nicholas frowned in confusion. "A lot of nonsense, surely. You'll have to be more specific."

She didn't say anything more and when he looked up at her, Leila was grinning; but it was the expectant look in her eyes that did it.

She knew about the kiss, Nicholas was sure of it.

It dawned on him that, in many ways, she was Matías's best friend. Will had grown into something else long ago, something closer to family; and anyway, the guy certainly wouldn't be Matías's first choice to discuss kissing his little brother, would he?

"You know," he exhaled. He tried his best to sound stern, wanting to hide the joyful thing blooming in his chest at the realization that Matías had told someone about what had happened. He didn't know how to be anything other than a secret, but as he caught her expectant smile, he realized maybe it wasn't so bad to be known.

"Yes." Leila did not bother hiding the glee from her own voice. "He told me yesterday."

The sudden and budding happiness accumulating in his muscles made him want to jump around, maybe even go for a run, until he could form coherent thoughts again. Instead, he groaned in annoyance. "We're not talking about it."

Leila laughed, but then her face turned cold and calculating when she realized he wasn't joking. "Are you planning on running away from this?"

He gaped at her. "I'm not—there's nothing to run *from*. I—I'm not stupid, I know it didn't mean anything."

She looked quite displeased by his words. "I thought you were supposed to be smart, Nicholas. Does he need to put his intentions in writing and ask your father about courting you before you take him seriously?"

Nicholas could feel that he was saying all the wrong things, but he had no idea how to go back to the lightness with which they'd been talking just a few minutes ago.

"It was one kiss," he rushed out. "Among many for him, I'm sure. I'm just being realistic when I say I don't think anyone is going to be writing sonnets about it anytime soon."

"Among many?"

"Well, you know. He's out every weekend. Sleeping out too."

She rolled her eyes at him, the annoyance in them turning into something softer, and Nicholas bristled with how close it was to pity. "He's never told me about kissing anyone in the semester I've known him. And I know he pulls all-nighters with his law school friends before exams."

"Look, I really don't want to talk about it anymore." Nicholas's tone wasn't as kind as he would have liked, but frustration felt safer than any of the other things threatening to burst out of him. "I don't know what the kiss was about, if he was bored or curious—"

"Curious?" she cut him off angrily. "Matías Romero is the bisexual mascot of Chicago soccer, and you're going to disrespect him like that?" Leila hit his head with her pen. "I'll give you curious," she muttered.

Nicholas's brain, unfortunately, chose that moment to freeze entirely.

"He… is?"

"Of course, why do you think his dad cut him off?"

The ice inside him turned to fire. "He what?"

She was clearly growing angry, and Nicholas couldn't tell if it was because of what she was saying or his cluelessness about it all.

"Since when?" he couldn't help but ask, his voice small.

"Where have you been, Nick? I thought you guys were close. He had this boyfriend in California, and I know for a fact that your brother has met him." Nicholas was too stunned to even move, but she wasn't done. "He's coming to your house for Thanksgiving, and you don't know that it's because his dad cut him off after he came out? What do you guys even talk about?"

"Mostly just… books. And soccer." Nicholas was silent for a few seconds. "I guess we don't actually talk about him a lot."

"Well. You may be pretty, but you're not very sharp, are you?"

"All right, enough with the insults already. I didn't know."

She took a deep breath. "Sorry. I get protective."

He let out a small smile. He would never admit it, but he was glad for it. Matías had many friends, but few that saw him as anything other than unbreakable.

"Let's get back to it," she said gesturing to the work lying open in front of them, going back to her notes even when he didn't move.

It was a kind thing to do, to turn away as he processed what she'd just told him, to keep her eyes focused on her screen as he stared off into space and did not even bother turning his computer back on.

After most of the shock had worn off, he got his phone out and texted his friends.

Matías is apparently bi, out, and has had a full boyfriend in the past. Will even met him. SOS?

He huffed at Ajay's unsentimental succession of multicolored emojis and Sloane's, *Sounds like he wants a new one too.*

Why did it seem like no one else's world was currently being shifted on its axis?

The light outside soon started dwindling and Nicholas's stomach growling, which convinced him to call it a day.

Leila didn't object when he asked her if she was ready to go, and they exited campus in silence, the wind too loud and their layers too thick to make any attempt at conversation comfortable. A few seconds before they got to her bus stop, he paused, looking down at his too-thin sneakers as he tried to find the words that couldn't seem to escape the tip of his tongue.

"So, Leila…"

"Hm?"

"Do you have some advice, by any chance?" he asked in a voice so low he wondered how she managed to hear him over the noise of the traffic next to them.

"Advice about?"

"What I should do. With—you know. What it meant. To him."

She laughed, but there was none of the mocking edge he'd expected. "I've spent the past three months listening to him stress himself out about how to make you like him. At this point, I think you could wear a papier-mâché hat and call yourself the new King of England, and Matías would still worry he's not good enough."

Nicholas stood, his mind blank. Surely this was all a prank.

Leila sighed. "I am partial to grand gestures. Maybe a dance or a song of some kind, most definitely in public." She burst out laughing at his face. "But I think all you really need to do is figure yourself out."

He looked at her questioningly.

"Whatever's holding you back from going for it, you should sort it out first. He's been through a lot, and he really cares about you. He'll wait. But don't hurt him again."

Nicholas bit his lip. "I don't know how not to hurt people."

"You could tell him that."

"That I hurt people all the time?"

"That you're scared. Be honest. Be vulnerable."

Nicholas felt his pulse quicken. "I think I liked the flash mob idea more."

"You'll think of something," she said confidently before waving him goodbye.

Of course, the only thing Nicholas could think about right now was running for the hills.

From: Andrew Michaelson
To: CLAS 46903
Cc: Kieran Donne
Subject: Final Paper
November 22, 1:57 PM

Dear class,

Following the overwhelming number of confused emails I have received regarding our final paper, even though you should already be done or proofreading by now, I am once again attaching the prompt and requirements to this email. As a reminder, all your questions can be answered by reading it thoroughly; if they can't, they don't bear asking—especially during Thanksgiving Break.

The paper is still due one week from now, on December 2, at 3:00 p.m. The goal of this early deadline, as I have explained multiple times throughout the past month, is to have time to learn from the editing process together once I hand them back to you.

Please refer to Kieran if you need anything further regarding the paper or the course. And for those who made the mistake of not starting earlier, good luck—do try to find time to enjoy your break too.

I will see you all next Monday.

Dr. Michaelson

CHAPTER 19

"BUT WHAT DOES it all mean?" Nicholas asked again, loudly. Annoyingly, neither of his best friends bothered replying; perhaps they thought he could draw from any of the answers they'd offered up the last five times he'd asked. They had all been comically unhelpful, revolving along the lines of "maybe he likes you" or "he's attracted to you."

Sloane took pity on him. "How about you ask him?"

"I can't do that," he balked. "You don't get it. Whatever went through his mind, it's never going to happen again."

Both of his friends had the audacity to grimace, but it felt critical that they understood how out of his depth he was.

"Remember how I was with Kieran?" he asked, and they both looked up in annoyance. "Well, I am the opposite when it comes to Matías. I don't know how to be casual about this." He caught the look of shock on Sloane's face, but he brushed it off almost angrily. "Sixteen-year-old me would have killed for that one kiss. But that was before I knew it could ever happen. It was always a distant fantasy, a way to torture myself. And then we became friends, and that was enough. I never actually thought I stood a chance. I never thought this could happen," he repeated, low and pensive.

Sloane dropped the silk blouse she'd been inspecting and looked at him, really looked, but whatever she was about to say was cut off by Ajay's harsh voice. "Well, then you're as stupid as you are blind."

"Why do I pick friends like you?" Nicholas asked in a voice that was dangerously close to a whine.

"Because you can't stand anyone else."

Nicholas sighed heavily and let the silence settle, watching his friends try to reduce the piles of clothes on the floor into a selection that would fit into one suitcase. Sloane was leaving for New York the next day, and obviously had not started packing yet.

When he spoke again, his voice was quiet and defeated. "I don't deserve this."

"Stop that," Sloane chided him. "We're not having this, Nicholas."

"Have you seen him, all handsome and well-adjusted and perfect? And have you met me? There is no universe in which we make a believable pair."

Through the haze of self-pity, he felt thankful that they didn't mock him. Sloane's words were unflinching, but they weren't unkind. He wasn't sure he could have handled that. "He's just a guy, with probably as many flaws as the rest of us, even if you don't want to see them. He's not a god. And even if he was, that's exactly who you'd deserve."

He was about to dispute this, but then she tried to put heels that were clearly not meant to see the light of day between October and May in her suitcase. He got up from the bed and finally started to take an active role in the packing, which was in dire need of pragmatism. Even though Ajay called his suggestions "horrendous" and Sloane "plain," the East Coast-bound pile went from sporting zero to two coats, and no one walked out in anger during the hour it took them to agree on the final selection.

"Are you guys still coming for dinner tonight?" Nicholas asked after they'd finally managed to close the suitcase while Sloane sat atop it. All three of them were sitting on the floor, breathing heavily while looking at the tornado of discarded clothes around them, wearing expressions that varied from weariness to disgust.

"Are you and your brother going to behave?"

Nicholas huffed. "I'll be busy in the kitchen, and he'll be hosting. It's all going to be very civilized, you'll see."

They both said yes, as he knew they would. If they were as shocked by the Fisher brothers hosting a dinner together as he had himself been when Will had first floated the idea, they didn't show it.

It had started with Will wanting to have a few people over for Thanksgiving before everyone left town for the week. For the first time, Nicholas wanted his own friends there too. He wanted his brother to witness that he had built a life for himself that he would miss while he was away, that there were people who loved him. That he wasn't eighteen and in need of a savior anymore. When he'd asked Marge for the Saturday off, she'd agreed quickly with a proud glint in her eye that was almost suspicious.

Before anyone could say anything more about it, his phone pinged loudly from the desk he'd left it on. Even though both of his friends had been largely indifferent to his dramatics after the revelation of Matías's sexuality, he saw how they tensed, looking at the phone like it held something of Pandora's. Nicholas froze for a few seconds, before stumbling upright and unlocking it with embarrassing speed.

"It's Leila." Even he could hear the soft disappointment in his voice, but he knew it wasn't fair.

"Is Matías coming tonight?" asked Ajay.

"Yes."

"Well," they continued kindly. "At least you won't need to sit around wondering what's going on for too long."

Sloane nodded her agreement. "Just see what he does this evening and follow his lead. I'm sure you'll get your answer. And we can keep an eye on him too and tell you what we think."

Ajay snorted. "When has that ever worked? I've been saying this man was looking at Nick like he wanted to make him his breakfast, lunch, and dinner for weeks, and it's not like anyone listened."

Nicholas's "What?" was uttered with such force he surprised even himself. Ajay winced, but did not seem inclined to further expand. "You never once told me that," he continued accusingly.

"Did I not? I must have just told Sloane. It was pretty obvious."

"How was it obvious?" Nicholas asked, dazed.

"Well," Ajay smiled, looking worryingly overprepared for this question. "It was clear that my opinion mattered a lot to him once he realized how close we were. Until he saw me walk out of your room in the morning and turned into a little green-eyed monster," Ajay said matter-of-factly. "Then there was the whole tearful apology for his behavior. And all of the looking at you like you hung the moon and smiling stupidly every time you take a breath. And the fact that the meaner you get, the fonder he looks. It's either he likes you or psychotic behavior." They looked at Sloane. "I thought this was common knowledge."

She chuckled. Nicholas groaned, burying his head in her pillows. He was way out of his depth.

❧

By the time guests started ringing the bell to his apartment that evening, Nicholas was considering throwing himself out of the window or putting his own head in the oven instead of the pie that was currently sitting there. With a scoff and a kiss on both of his cheeks, Sloane told him to stop comparing himself to women whose suffering he could never truly understand, so he went back to his béchamel sauce.

For the sixth time that day, his phone lit up with Matías's name. Apparently, Will was too busy rearranging the living room and setting up little pieces of cloth around the table in case people weren't sure where to eat to take care of much else. He did, however, have enough energy to repeatedly shout at Nicholas to tell Matías to bring whatever he'd forgotten.

It had started as soon as Nicholas had come back home from Sloane's. He'd found Will fighting with a folding table of unknown origin and panicking about how much wine they'd bought. Nicholas had gaped at him when Will had asked him to tell Matías to bring some more red, but he hadn't known how to say no to that request without starting a fight.

So, even though they hadn't interacted without an audience since that day at the park, Nicholas had grabbed his phone and told himself he could act like an adult.

Good afternoon. Will asks if you might bring some red wine on your way. No worries if not. Thank you.

It was embarrassing how long it took him to craft a text that was both polite and didn't scream, "*We just kissed, and I don't know what to do about it.*" Matías didn't seem to have this concern, and quickly replied a casual, *lol yes.* As Will's requests for forgotten supplies multiplied, the laughter turned into repetitive thumbs ups, and Nicholas soon grew too busy to worry about it.

Nodding to himself, he turned the oven off and left the pots to simmer, glancing at the living room where Ajay, Sloane, and two of Will's friends were chatting around a cheese board. Everything was fine, even though his best friends were currently being charmed by his brother, who had traded his anxious yelling for gracious smiles and interested questions.

Nicholas headed to the bathroom to change out of his cooking clothes. He put on the white shirt he'd set out the night before and some cologne, ignore the rising embarrassment at how unlike himself he looked in the mirror. He told himself it was Thanksgiving; if there ever was a time to wear a white button-up shirt, it was today. The voice that reminded him that this argument had never once worked on him in all the years his mother had tried it could take a hike, along with anyone who thought his shirt's very tight fit was anything other than accidental.

After spending another ten minutes trying to make his hair look intentionally messy rather than untamable, Nicholas finally rejoined the group. He couldn't help but be startled by how easy it was to identify which friends belonged to which brother. Ajay was wearing what he assumed to be a modern take on a bright blue Sari, while Sloane's corduroy dress matched the color of her hair, an interesting choice when paired with her green shoes and earrings. Next to them, Will and his two friends looked as appropriately boring as he did in his stupid white shirt.

But the whole group was engaged in lively conversation, and his friends were laughing, no sign of tension in either of their shoulders. That was enough for him.

"Nice shirt," Sloane commented with a proud glint in her eyes when he sat down. "What's the occasion?"

He gave her a deathly glare. "Thanksgiving."

Nicholas had never been good at small talk, but if there was ever a way to get through it, it was probably sitting between the two people in this world he found most interesting, with a large glass of good wine in his hand and his brother, master of small talk and playing to the gallery, as the mediator across from him. He had to admit it wasn't as unpleasant as he had remembered big groups to be. Will's architect friends were of a different caliber than the boys he'd surrounded himself with in college, and their sharp wit and open-minded jokes soon convinced Nicholas that the day might not be so torturous after all.

Then the bell rang.

⌘

Nicholas was back in the kitchen, trying to handle the three pans simultaneously cooking on the stove without bursting into flames himself or staining his shirt with the wine sauce he was mixing on the side. He kept casting worried glances at the cheese and crackers on the living room table. They were disappearing rapidly, and he was really hoping these starters would be done before everyone was too satiated to even care.

The loud voices of the eclectic group, which had been quick to find common ground with the help of fresh wine, were so distracting when combined with the loud cooker above him that he nearly jumped out of his skin when he felt a hand drape against his side. It was the kind of absent-minded touch that wouldn't have been out of place coming from Sloane or Ajay, yet he knew right away that it wasn't either of them. The hand wasn't a size he was familiar with, unlike the tall presence he could feel behind him.

"Need any help?"

Nicholas could already feel his clumsy grip on sanity slip away, yet all he could think about was how to make sure Matías didn't stop touching him.

"Just… keep everyone out of here." Nicholas was perfectly capable of handling a three-course meal for eight people; he was, however, less confident about his ability to remain polite every time someone grabbed his attention to offer help they weren't actually capable of giving him.

Matías nodded, giving Nicholas a wide berth as he started cleaning the countertops, working around him in tandem without saying another word.

Nicholas moved to grab the pile of small plates sitting on the kitchen island, spreading them out and adding some salad on each one. "Could you turn the oven off and take both dishes out? Oven mitts are over there," he asked without looking up from what he was doing, swallowing a large gulp of wine as a congratulatory indulgence for not having stumbled on his words.

Matías took everything out of the oven, stirred what needed stirring, and did not ask about anything other than what Nicholas needed him to do in between bouts of washing up. They kept working around each other in silence, not touching again, no matter how much Nicholas yearned for it.

Once they were done, even he had to admit the starters all looked rather good. He felt a jolt of pride looking at the eight plates of roasted salmon with walnut and pomegranate salad in front of him.

Breathing in heavily, Nicholas finally let himself relax, so much so that when he turned around to reach for the paper towels behind him, he knocked his glass from where it was perched atop the microwave with the back of his arm.

Because he was always aware of exactly where Matías was standing, he knew before he saw that the entirety of the contents of his glass were now dripping down the front of the other man's shirt.

He stood there for a second, frozen and silent. Nicholas felt dread invade him; dread that Matías would be angry, or worse, disappointed. He braced himself, knowing that even an irritated snap would sting right now, but when he finally looked, he saw that Matías was grinning down at himself. He'd managed to catch the empty glass before it clattered to the floor and was now holding it up proudly.

"Well," he said, glancing back at the mess on his white shirt. His sleeve was stuck to his arm, drowning in red wine, which had spilled onto the front of his shirt and some of his pants. "I guess it's a good thing I'm so well-acquainted with that washing machine of yours."

"I'm so sorry," Nicholas blurted in a single breath, jolted into action. He grabbed a handful of paper towels and thrust the rest of the roll to Matías, who put down the empty glass and started dabbing at his lower sleeve, which had taken the brunt of the spill. This left Nicholas awkwardly patting at the front of Matías's shirt—now impossibly clinging to his chest—his pants, his thigh. Nicholas's cheeks burned. When he'd done all he could to mop up the worst of the mess, Nicholas looked up, flushed and frantic, only to realize that Matías wasn't moving. He just stood there, letting him fuss, a faint but undeniable blush warming his cheeks. Their gazes held for a moment too long before Matías seemed to snap out of it and took a step back.

"Don't worry about it. Let's finish this up, and I'll throw the shirt in the wash." Nicholas nodded, trying to find somewhere to look that didn't involve Matías's wet shirt clinging to his skin in ways that left even less to the imagination than his usual tight fits.

"I'll bring these out," he said, waving at the plates in front of them. Matías nodded and followed him to the living room under a chorus of impressed whistling, the room unaware of the storm raging inside Nicholas's mind. When everyone had found their seat, he allowed himself to look back at Matías, and found that his burning gaze was on him. It was a dangerous way to live, he thought, being looked at in this way, but any further warning was cut short by Will catching sight of the state of Matías's shirt. "Shit, man, do you need a change of clothes?"

Matías shook his head. "Nicholas is going to lend me a shirt, no worries."

Nicholas, who had been unaware that this was the plan, had to work hard to hide the surprise from showing on his face and headed to his room in silence. He sighed heavily looking at his overflowing drawers, wishing he had better clothes for perhaps the first time in his life.

He was still standing there, rummaging through washed-out tees and plaid shirts when a soft knock on his door was followed by Matías's larger-than-life body entering the room. He pushed the door delicately back against its frame, not closing it but not leaving it open either. It was suddenly so quiet in the little square room, he wondered if William had gotten acoustic drywall installed overnight. The happy chatter of the room adjacent faded away to a murmur and all Nicholas could hear was his own heartbeat.

"I don't know what kind of shirt you like," was all he could find to say with an edge of panic in his voice.

But it made Matías laugh. And wasn't that just worth it all?

"I don't have a strong opinion on shirts. Anything's fine."

Somehow, Nicholas doubted that. He'd noticed the way the past five years had taken Matías from the typical self-important rich boy who wanted to make sure you knew it to a man who had spent years searching for himself and had come back with an answer that left everyone speechless.

Nicholas had no idea how to match that. He handed him a white tee.

Somehow, the entire sequence of events that had led up to this moment had not prepared him for the fact that Matías would proceed to take his own shirt off, stand in his bedroom half-naked with an extended arm, and look into Nicholas's eyes with a hint of satisfaction that reminded him of the arrogant soccer star he'd first met.

Nicholas allowed himself to look. The lines of Matías's body were hard, there was no denying it. But something told him if he were to touch it, Matías's skin would feel like silk. He still didn't look away as Matías's incredibly tan body wriggled into a shirt that looked tighter on him than it had any right to. The younger man still couldn't tell whether this whole thing had been on purpose or not. All he knew was that his own clothes had never felt so heavy.

The warm brown eyes staring into his were irreverently amused. Matías didn't seem to be feeling any shame about standing there being practically ogled; in fact, he seemed to enjoy giving Nicholas a show. Finally, he held up the dirty piece of fabric in a ball with a question in his eyes.

"Just dump it anywhere, I have to do laundry anyway."

"Okay."

"Sorry again."

Matías shrugged, like he'd gotten over the stained shirt before it had even happened.

Nicholas looked at every corner of his room, cracking his knuckles in apprehension. He knew he only had a few seconds until they had to go back to the living room. This was probably the only time today it would be just the two of them; yet Nicholas had no idea how to find the courage to do anything about it. Somehow, finding themselves in this small, quiet bedroom felt very different than the middle of a windy park.

"You don't need to be scared of me, I'm not going to kiss you again."

"You're not?" He sounded desperate and disappointed, and when he saw the satisfied smirk on Matías's face, he realized that he'd fallen right into his trap. Nicholas scoffed. "Well. In that case, we should go back."

Matías hummed in what sounded like agreement but did not move to leave. Instead, he extended one hand toward Nicholas's face, so slowly that the younger man would have had plenty of time to step away if that didn't sound like a grave mistake. Matías's hand, warm and almost soft, wrapped itself around the side of his neck, his thumb on Nicholas's cheek, bringing him slightly closer. It was all Nicholas could do to keep his whole body from sagging in relief.

There were the familiar sparks that had electrified him during their kiss, and the stomach-churning yearning that invaded him every time their eyes met across a room; but there was something else too in the way Matías's hand held his face: comfort and peace, neither of which he deserved.

"I don't know how to do this," Nicholas whispered.

"Do you want to try?"

"What about Will?"

"You let me worry about your brother."

Nicholas sighed. Matías was good at selling dreams, at making people believe life could be easy if you let it. And he was perhaps the only person Nicholas could almost believe. Maybe if he managed to crawl inside the other man's radiance, let himself be swept away by his influence, one day Nicholas could become someone for whom happiness was an option. But as soon as he let himself hope, reality came crashing back onto him.

He wasn't the kind of person who got the happily ever after.

"Let's go eat," was all he said. Matías finally let go of him, but not without kissing him on the forehead first, a promise that this could be trusted. Nicholas almost believed.

❧

A few hours later, the younger Fisher was sprawled on the couch, his head tilted on the back of it so he could look at the night sky through the large windows behind him. His cheeks were starting to hurt from smiling. Their apartment was full, and he couldn't hear his own thoughts over the sound of everyone's joy. The food had been a success, although their guests were now wondering aloud how they were supposed to have space for desert whenever Nicholas found the strength to get up and serve it. Sloane was still at the table making eyes at one of Will's coworkers, while Leila was busy giggling at Ajay's outrageous stories and Matías and another of Will's guests were covertly fighting about which one of them knew Will best.

When Nicholas looked back down from the sky, he found his brother staring at him from across the room.

They both let out a small smile, and for a minute, Nicholas thought he was looking into a mirror.

They couldn't maintain eye contact for long, but it didn't take more than a second to say everything that needed to be said. They were surrounded by people who loved them, miles away from the cold home where they'd swallowed down meals without exchanging a word and disappeared again in the pockets of their museum of a house. They'd managed to leave their closed-off father and empty-eyed mother behind, and now they were in a room that was almost too warm, surrounded by friends who were thankful for them, the table littered with the remnants of a meal that had kept them busy for hours.

They had made it.

Nicholas couldn't be greedy enough to ask for more.

He knew Will had been anxious about the afternoon going smoothly, and when faced with the damning evidence that everyone was happy to be there, his brother had started drinking headily in relief. Nicholas's suspicion that Will was getting drunker than he was letting on was confirmed when his brother suddenly got up and came to join him on the couch.

"Hello, little brother." Nicholas's look of horror at the affectionate tone didn't seem to faze Will. "How are you doing?"

"I'm fine," Nicholas answered warily.

"Great. And how's my best friend doing these days?"

"How would I know?" he asked, looking over Will's head to find Matías, who was looking at them over the rim of his glass—water, Nicholas noted disappointedly.

"You seem to be spending more time with him than I do these days. Cooking together, eating together... Heard about these little soccer games of yours."

Nicholas tensed up. "Should we bring out dessert?"

His brother tried to turn toward the rest of the room, which only resulted in his drink sloshing around on the floor. He was clearly drunk. "I don't know, do you think Matías wants dessert?"

"I have no idea. He's your friend, not mine."

"You would think so, wouldn't you?"

Uninterested by his brother's attempts at discussing the one man he already couldn't stop thinking about, Nicholas rolled his eyes, grabbed Will's glass of wine before it finished its clumsy journey to his brother's mouth, and emptied it into his own.

"That's not even the same wine," Will said indignantly.

"Can't do as much damage as it will if you drink it. I didn't remember you being such a messy drunk."

This seemed to chasten his brother, who joined Nicholas in his quiet contemplation of their guests. He wondered if it tugged at Will's chest the same way it did his to see all of their friends mixing together with an ease they'd never reached themselves, methodically blending until no one could tell who was whose: Leila and Will's friend looking at the books and CDs on the shelves, Matías asking Sloane for advice on haircuts, Ajay and Will's coworker laughing by the kitchen sink together.

It soon became clear that it was Matías they were both staring at.

"Do you mind it?" Nicholas asked out of the blue. He wasn't sure what he meant.

William grimaced. His face looked like he'd stepped into something particularly slimy. "I'm not thrilled, that's for sure."

This was the answer Nicholas had expected, but so many things had gone differently than he was convinced they would lately, he'd caught himself hoping this would too. Disappointment seared at his insides, mostly at himself for being stupid enough to hope things would be different.

"But that's not the problem, is it?"

Nicholas frowned. "What's the problem?" he asked, unsure where William was headed but certain he wouldn't like it.

"You'll never let yourself be... around someone who would treat you half-right," Will hiccupped. "And he won't ever understand why."

William's tone wasn't kind, and alarm bells rang inside Nicholas's head. This was not a conversation they should have with the amount of wine they'd drank. Still, William went on.

"You're still punishing yourself for surviving that car accident. You're still stuck in the mindset that you don't deserve to be happy because Emma never got to be."

"That's not true."

"It is. Every choice you make feels like it's with the direct purpose of making yourself more miserable. So, I'm sorry, but as long as you're stuck doing penance for being alive, I can't be okay with you taking Matías down with you," he continued sternly.

Sloane and Matías were starting to throw furtive glances their way, probably aware that the Fisher brothers spending this long talking to each other was unlikely to bode well.

"I'm glad I got to meet your friends today," Will boomeranged too quickly for Nicholas to react. "They care about you very much. I don't know how they did it, but they're the first people you've let in your life in years that aren't trying to leave it all the worse for it."

Despite his quickly worsening mood, Nicholas let out a small smile at that. "I'm still not sure how I landed them either."

This seemed to annoy his brother. "I wish you could see yourself the way everyone here sees you."

Nicholas stayed silent for a long beat. When he spoke again, his voice sounded like that of the little boy he'd once been. "I suppose I still see myself the way you've always seen me."

Unkindly, William dismissed this. "I never saw you. I was too busy making sure you had food on the table."

Nicholas wanted to punch him for that. But then he saw that most of their guests were starting to argue about who should clean up while the rest enjoyed their evening, and he decided he had no time to rehash old fights with his brother.

"Funny how things work out, isn't it? What with you being so useless at cooking now," he added caustically, before getting up and telling his friends that he and Matías would take care of the dishes.

It worked like a charm, sending Sloane, Ajay, and Leila running back to the other side of the room with barely hidden smiles on their faces.

From: Brianna Ann Nelson

To: Nicholas Fisher

Subject: Feedback

November 23, 9:28 PM

Dear Nicholas,

I got my grade back and really good feedback from Miller-Reed. A!!!??? I'm super happy, especially as this is my first grade in this class and it's really setting things off just right.

Thank you so much for your help. You're going to make a great teacher one day. You really made me believe that this silly little passion of mine could be a job if I worked hard enough at it. I'm going to keep working on what I'm interested in, really try to give myself a good chance, and I'll take computer science classes on the side so if it doesn't work out with Swahili and poetry, I can still work in tech and make lots of cash.

I'm grateful for your help and guidance. Please let me know if you ever TA a class. I'd love to attend.

Bri

CHAPTER 20

EVEN THE DECLINING suburbia they'd grown up despising didn't seem so dreary when they got to the Fishers' house on Wednesday evening. November, this drab excuse of a month that usually made the emptiness of his parents' house feel even heavier, had rarely seemed so bearable.

It helped that they only had to stay for three days. Nicholas had never been so thankful for his brother's all-important corporate job. Will couldn't take any time off, or so he'd said, and Nicholas had been more than happy to stay—home—in Chicago until they could drive up together.

It wasn't often that Lisa Fisher was able to enjoy the presence of both of her sons under her roof at the same time. Perhaps it was the knowledge that these instances were growing rarer with every passing year, or maybe it was simply Matías's infectious joy and his ability to smooth conversations along with exuberant, captivating stories that said nothing at all of substance, but his mother managed to behave almost normally for most of their stay. She asked clueless questions and looked beatifically at Matías as he answered with a kindness Nicholas hadn't been able to muster toward her in years. She spent the weekend making too much food, all of it excellent, and when the three twenty-somethings ate it all, it brought on her face a smile brighter than he'd seen in a very long time. She took a lot of naps, which Nicholas used to breathe again, and when she became too talkative, he went for long, freezing walks instead of blowing up at everyone.

It was better than it had possibly ever been; yet everything that had characterized their childhood was still true. There were moments when their mother didn't seem to be there at all, and others where she was so present they could barely move. Their father was as lifeless and uninterested as usual, and seeing him sit at the dinner table was enough to spoil Nicholas's appetite. Will was such a different version of himself from the man Nicholas had gotten to know these past few months, tense and self-contained and hard at work being what everyone needed him to, that the empathy Nicholas felt for him was unbearable.

But in the middle of these four people who hadn't known how to talk to one another in two decades, there was Matías Romero.

Matías was facilitating dinner conversation like a trained war diplomat and doing such a good job that Nicholas almost forgot about the pain he was probably in, being away from his own family. In a now-familiar turn of events, Nicholas found himself thankful for his presence, but he couldn't help the uneasiness he felt when he caught Matías's eye and saw a glimpse of the boy whose dad had effectively told him he didn't want him home for Thanksgiving.

It was new, this ability to understand Matías's Dionysian laugh and follow-up questions for the sadness that it was. As always, his answers were easygoing and appropriate, expanding on busy classes and challenging professors, without forgetting to be gracious and thankful. Had there always been so much underneath?

"Well, that busy schedule of yours doesn't seem to be leaving much time for a girlfriend, does it? In fact," Lisa Fisher sat up at dinner with a look and a tone both brothers knew to fear, "are any of you planning on bringing a partner home before I meet my maker?"

In an instant, William and Nicholas Fisher were brothers again. They exchanged a look, and neither hesitated before they proceeded to stuff their mouths with food, effectively throwing Matías to the wolves now that he was the only one who could answer. For a moment, everything that had ever put William and Nicholas on opposite sides melted away; with one glance they were back to being two boys with parents who did not know them, and the only side to be on was the one that made this interrogation end as quickly as possible.

❧

"Where are we going?"

Will and Matías sat silently at the front of the car, lacking their usual cheer.

It was their second full day in Wisconsin, and for the first time in as long as he could remember, the two best friends had invited Nicholas to join them on one of their mysterious afternoon drives. Granted, this was the first time Nicholas had ever left his bedroom door open while they were in the house, but that hadn't made him any less shocked when William had slipped his head in and asked if he wanted to join.

He didn't know what he'd been expecting, but it certainly wasn't this: complete silence, Matías's face closed, not forcing himself to be generous with his laugh and body. Will not asking him to, his own shoulders relaxing as they lost the weight of being the only functioning member of the Fisher family.

It took ten minutes of them driving around before Nick spoke up. "Well, this is boring," he muttered, somehow the only person in the car acting normally.

When no one even chuckled, Nicholas winced. He wondered if Matías had gotten to talk to his mom at all this week—he'd always talked about her with love and reverence, so she was probably the one he missed the most. But Nicholas didn't know how to ask, so instead, he continued, "I'm hungry. Are you guys hungry? I know a place."

He gave Will the address to the only Mexican restaurant he knew, almost thirty minutes away, even though he knew half the menu tasted bland and it was, well, not Salvadorean, which was where Matías's parents were from. Maybe it was good enough, though, because Matías kept trying to find his eyes when they finally arrived.

"Their dessert menu is decent. Don't know about the rest, so don't get your hopes up," Nicholas said dismissively when he realized they were both looking at him.

By the time the three of them were sitting and starters had arrived, Matías was smiling again, clearly revived by the food, and with his joy came William's.

"What was this thing Mom said about tutoring over winter break?" his brother asked, his mouth still full of *tostadas*.

"Nothing. She has this friend who has a daughter who wants to get into Yale, and she was wondering if I could help with her essay... I told her to give her my email."

"You're going to help her?"

"Don't sound so surprised."

"I'm not. I just thought your semester might be full. With the..." Annoyingly, William glanced at Matías, who was too busy eyeing the untouched nachos on Nicholas's plate to catch on to his best friend's oddly careful tone. "You know, with all the extra credits you'll be taking and stuff."

Nicholas hadn't told Will anything else about his academic situation, but he knew his brother was right.

Then there was the teaching assistant spot he'd applied for, the real reason he'd spent the week obsessively checking his emails. He knew Miller-Reed's decision would come any minute now. It was almost comical, really—he'd first gotten in touch with her in the hopes of avoiding the teaching requirement, and now here he was, hoping to get a non-mandatory position, even if it left him overloaded with credits. Perhaps Kieran had done more for his education than he'd taken, in the end.

"I'll be fine. And I might not need extra credits, anyway. Maybe… I think the professor likes me enough, so perhaps I could convince him to read my essay and grade it himself… Or maybe not. I don't know, I'm probably being stupid." He chuckled, but it sounded hollow to his own ears.

"What's this?" Matías asked with a frown, finally looking up from his plate, where Nicholas had wordlessly dumped half of his nachos.

"Nothing," he dismissed. "Some TA is trying to make me fail one of my classes. But I just won't know until I see the grade, so I have to act like I'm not getting the credits and figure out extra ones for next semester."

He thought his tone was appropriately detached, but he still avoided Matías's gaze for the rest of the meal, trying hard to hold onto his good mood. His brother took over the conversation after that. By the time they ordered dessert, William was regaling them with the latest gossip from his office, and for a heartbeat, it felt like they were three friends having dinner and nothing between them had ever been complicated.

☙

That evening, Nicholas was headed to his bedroom when Matías grabbed his elbow and made him jump.

"Sorry, I didn't mean to startle you."

Nicholas thought it wiser not to answer until he got his heartbeat under control—standing alone with Matías in the dark hallway of his parents' house made every inch of his body ache with the restraint it took to stay still.

Why had he not bothered turning the light on?

"What was that thing with the TA? From dinner?" Matías's tone was demanding, and Nicholas was eighteen again.

He frowned and took a step back, putting some much-needed space between them. "Nothing. Did Will not tell you about it?"

Even with only the weak light coming from the living room casting shadows on Matías's face, Nicholas could see the way his jaw locked up, his chest rising more than it had to.

Nicholas kept walking to his bedroom, and Matías followed.

"He didn't tell me anything. What is there to tell?"

Nicholas rolled his eyes and walked ahead. "Nothing that's any of your business, that's for sure."

"Did you know him? Why would he try to make you fail? How can a TA even do that?"

Nicholas reached for the door of his childhood bedroom with a sigh, leaving it open behind him for Matías to follow. He didn't think Matías had ever been in there, and a part of him still childishly wondered if it would be good enough for his eye.

His was the bigger of the two bedrooms at the end of the hallway; for years it had housed two twin beds, one against each wall. That was until one random Wednesday afternoon when Nicholas was ten years old. He'd walked home from school to find the other side of the room empty. The smaller bedroom, on the other side of the hall-way, which had stayed vacant for two years, had been painted from pink to blue, the old princess bed had been dismantled, and Will had moved into it.

The wooden desk that stood by the window had always looked lonely to him, never quite large enough to fill the void left by William's bed after his departure. But things weren't so bad between the four walls that had now been his for so long. At least he had taken down the embarrassing posters that had once adorned his light blue walls. He'd taken care of that right after Matías's first ever visit, and the memory caused him to feel a grateful pang of appreciation for his fifteen-year-old self.

"It's complicated. But there was nothing I could do about it," he said over his shoulder as he headed toward his desk and turned around to lean against it. A voice in his head reminded Nicholas that he could have pretended to date Kieran until the grades were in, but he could feel his mood worsening even just thinking about it. "Nothing I was willing to do, anyway."

This was the wrong thing to say. The expression on Matías's face flew somewhere between anger and concern, and Nicholas got a nauseating feeling of déjà vu.

"It's not like that. Don't."

Matías nodded, taking a deep breath. "Okay, I won't. Unless I should?"

Nicholas scoffed dismissively. "No. If it helps, Will knows all about it, and no one's dead or injured. I think." He grimaced.

Matías seemed to be relieved by that. It was an ugly thing, the way Nicholas suddenly missed his anger, and the concern he would have hated coming from anyone else. Something young and fragile inside of him wanted Matías to want to protect him, which explained his next words but didn't justify the bait in them.

"Don't think I'd mind if he was, though."

He heard Matías's intake of breath and knew it had worked. He was so glad for the wrath he could glimpse in his eyes that he struggled to remain angry himself.

"Let's just say that what I'm calling an academic disagreement, others might call me dumping him and him… being unhappy about it."

A heady mix of shock, curiosity, and murderous rage painted itself on the canvas that was Matías's face, so Nicholas gave him time to process his words while he headed back toward the door and closed it.

"Were you… dating for long?" Matías asked in a strained voice.

Nicholas shrugged, finding that he didn't have to fake his nonchalance anymore.

"Not really. I suppose I had a crush on him because he was smart and everyone wanted him, but it didn't have time to turn into anything serious. Maybe I just liked feeling special even if I wasn't, like you once said. Old habits die hard, eh?"

Matías's face fell, and Nicholas wished he could take it back. He'd made enough mistakes in his own life to know how it felt to have someone repeatedly bring up the things you regretted after they'd said they had forgiven you.

He realized then that he really had forgiven him. He would always forgive Matías.

"I'm sorry," Matías said quietly. "I didn't believe that."

"Why would you say it, then?"

This was a stupid question to ask, considering Nicholas's own propensity to say things he didn't believe just to hurt people more than they were hurting him.

"I was scared."

"What were you scared of?" Nicholas asked with surprise, but Matías just shrugged and turned to the side to look out the window. It wasn't clear what he thought he was looking at, considering the thick cloak of darkness that surrounded their house at night. Nicholas's room overlooked their lightless backyard, but this didn't seem to stop Matías from staring intently in whatever direction his eyes wouldn't catch Nicholas's.

He'd given up on getting an answer by the time Matías spoke up, still facing his own reflection.

"I knew you liked me, back then," he said, low and stilted.

Despite the odds, there had always been a hope in Nicholas's mind that perhaps he'd managed to keep that secret to himself all his teenage years. Matías may have made his indifference obvious, but he had never mocked or acted repulsed by Nicholas, and the cruel voice in the younger man's head had always claimed this could only be the case because he didn't know about his feelings. Surely, if twenty-year-old heartthrob Matías Romero had known about his little crush, he would have made a terrible joke of him.

But suddenly, Matías's insistence on repeatedly calling him his best friend's little brother, constantly talking about how young he was, and generally just reminding him that he only saw him as a child every chance he got echoed very differently in his ears.

The question remained: what had changed?

"I thought I was doing the right thing by ignoring it. I thought you wouldn't want me to mention it, you'd be embarrassed if I did... I thought it'd go away when you met someone your own age, but then when I found out that while I was too busy looking the other way, someone had been..." His voice broke. "I'll always regret treating it like a big secret. If I hadn't, you wouldn't have thought you had to hide who you were, and he couldn't have..."

Nicholas sighed, walking across the room to sit on the edge of his bed. "I think it would have always ended up that way, even if you'd decided to acknowledge it, you know. I would've had to get over it in some way, and there he would've been, waiting for the first lost boy who walked through his classroom door."

Nicholas's tone was soft with the realization of the truth in his words. There was nothing Matías could have done differently or better. Nicholas was always going to arrive at university, eighteen years old and miserable, in dire need of someone to see him.

"And did you? Get over it?"

Nicholas scoffed, trying to duck his head so Matías wouldn't catch the heat that he could feel invading his neck. "Don't make me answer that."

He thought it was cruel when he saw Matías smile. But Matías wasn't usually a cruel person. The last time he had been, it had taken Nicholas years to recover from it.

He looked down at his bony hands and didn't look up at the sound of Matías walking toward him, didn't turn his head when the mattress shifted next to him under the man's weight or when Matías's knee appeared next to his.

The Texan grabbed his chin, forcing his head to turn so he was looking into his eyes. "I hope you haven't."

Those four words took his breath away. Matías's gaze dropped to his lips, and Nicholas knew he should just close his eyes and let himself enjoy it. But there was one last thing he needed to know. Even when Matías leaned closer, Nicholas swallowed hard and didn't meet him halfway.

"What changed?" he asked instead.

"Huh?" Matías asked, caught off guard.

"What changed? You knew I liked you then, but you didn't do anything about it. Now you're... well, here."

Matías leaned back, sighing as his eyes flicked to the ceiling like the answers might somehow be written there. He must have known this question was coming; surely it wasn't unreasonable for Nicholas to want to know when he'd gone from Will's annoying little brother to someone Matías wanted to kiss goodnight.

"I'm not sure," Matías admitted. He shifted on the bed, putting some distance between them.

Nicholas immediately regretted the space, but he stayed quiet.

"I was barely figuring myself out back then," he began. "I didn't know I liked guys—I didn't even know I *could*. It wasn't until after college that it all came together."

Nicholas frowned, but he let the silence stretch until Matías spoke again.

"But seeing you so much senior year, seeing how comfortable you were with your sexuality, how Will always treated it like it was perfectly fine... I started wondering. And just when I started to think, maybe—that was when I met Lucy. You remember her?"

Nicholas's jaw tightened at the mention of Matías's college girlfriend, but he nodded.

"Well, I genuinely liked her, so I thought, 'perfect—I'm not gay.' It wasn't until after the breakup that the questions came back."

Nicholas wanted more. He was hungry for every messy, conflicting thought Matías had ever had.

"And why me?" he asked instead, fiddling with his fingers, his voice barely above a whisper.

Matías chuckled. "I don't know the answer to that. I mean, you were so angry at me all the time. I definitely could have chosen an easier path."

Nicholas didn't laugh.

"I just missed you," Matías continued, softer. "I know you think I was just doing you a favor in college, but I genuinely liked being around you. You were so different from all my other friends. You're the funniest person I know, even though you never try to be. Always so angry, so uninterested in my bullshit." He smiled, almost fondly.

Nicholas stared at him like he'd lost his mind.

"I know," Matías answered with his usual laugh. "Maybe I should've put two and two together. But I just thought you were great, and I wanted to be around you all the time. And I used to think it was cute that you only ever softened when you talked to me."

Nicholas felt his neck heat, his chest tightening.

"I genuinely just thought that my friendship with you was... different than my other friendships," Matías added, a hint of embarrassment in his voice. "I only realized there was something else there when I moved in."

"But I was a dick to you."

Matías grinned at that, inexplicably pleased. "True."

A long silence fell between them. Nicholas let himself look at Matías, who was already looking back at him. He didn't know how to believe any of this.

"Can I kiss you now?" Matías asked finally, breaking the quiet.

Nicholas nodded. Matías came back, closer, and suddenly his lips were on him. Nicholas let himself be kissed, lightly, softly, unsure it was really happening. The only thought swimming around his brain was that this would hurt. When Matías got bored and moved on to someone shinier, Nicholas feared the state he would be left in.

But the more selfish part of him wanted it, whatever the cost. So he kissed him back, taking the lead this time, and he could feel Matías's mouth smiling against his, letting him. For a minute.

Then his touch, this brilliant thing, grew hungrier. Matías had one hand in Nicholas's hair, and his lips started swinging between slow and careful explorations and a biting hunger that did not help Nicholas's breathing problem. When Nicholas stopped thinking altogether, there were roaming hands and biting teeth, little noises and a sigh of satisfaction when he nibbled at Matías's jaw. He was kissing Matías, really kissing him, and the other man was asking for more.

It wasn't long after that before Matías's hand left his hair and settled on his shoulder, slowly but steadily pushing Nicholas until he was lying on his back. There was still a part of his brain screaming at him that surely this couldn't be happening. But then Matías looked at him like he was starving; he climbed over Nicholas and straddled him, his strong thighs holding onto Nicholas's shaking hips.

He took everything the other man had to give him, but Nicholas was still tense, scared that the spell would break the moment he put his own hands on Matías. This seemed to annoy the older boy, who grabbed Nicholas's hand and gruffly put it where he wanted it to be.

This wasn't a game anymore, Nicholas thought with alarm. This wasn't a fantasy or a self-indulgent daydream.

He closed his eyes and wove a hand into the dark curls above him, something he'd wanted to do since he had first learned to touch. Then, he showed him just how many things he'd learned in the five years they'd been apart.

They were both exerting themselves trying to keep things from moving too fast. Matías's hand under the hem of his shirt was gripping Nicholas's waist with such force he hoped it would leave a bruise. Nicholas tried to keep their hips apart, knowing a single graze would likely break him, but then Matías started kissing his neck and he stopped paying attention and their hips buckled into each other.

The air charged with enough electricity to power the entire town through Christmas.

The noises escaping both of their lips came from somewhere deep in their chests. There were hands grabbing at everything, and as swiftly as he'd climbed on top of him, Matías rolled off to lie down next to him with a grunt.

Matías laid there with his eyes closed, the side of his body touching Nicholas's from head to toe, breathing deeply. His chest was heaving, his cheeks were flushed, and he was visibly struggling to regain some self-control. Nicholas knew he'd never smile this wide again in his life, so he allowed it, still in disbelief that he was the one who had just put Matías Romero in this state.

"We're not doing this at your parents' house with your brother next door," he finally said.

Nicholas laughed quietly. "Okay."

This was enough for now. Anything was enough.

They stayed there a moment longer, the silence only broken by their uneven breaths. Matías tilted his head toward him, his expression softening into something Nicholas could barely look at without feeling his chest tighten. It was too much—the closeness, the intimacy, the weight of this moment happening here, in Nicholas's childhood home.

Nicholas shifted, breaking the contact between their bodies as he sat up. "You, uh… you should probably go before Will comes knocking. He's going to wonder where you've been."

Matías sat up too, leaning back on his elbows. "I wasn't planning on lying to him, if he asks."

Nicholas exhaled. "Well, good luck with that conversation. I know he likes you, but he's never been a fan of the guys I'm sleeping with."

"Sleeping with?"

"Well, put it however you want. He has this thing about guys' intentions when it comes to me."

"What do you think my intentions are?" Matías asked, his voice cooling.

"You know what I mean. He won't exactly... believe it if you tell him you're, like, planning to date me or something."

Matías stared at him, his frown deepening. "Why wouldn't he believe me?"

There was an edge to his voice that made Nicholas pause. "Come on, Matías, It's us. You're—you're you. And I'm me. No one's going to look at us and think we make sense."

"Why would I care what anyone else thinks?" Matías's voice was sharp enough to make Nicholas flinch.

He hesitated, his stomach twisting. "It's not just other people. I mean... We don't make sense—you can't seriously think this is—"

"What?" Matías cut in, his eyes narrowing. "Real? Worth it?"

Nicholas hesitated again, his mouth dry. "I just mean... I'm not asking for it to be this big, serious thing. We can just—"

"No." Matías's voice was flat.

Nicholas blinked at him. "No?"

"No," Matías repeated, his tone firmer. "I'm not doing this if it's just some casual thing to you. I want the whole thing. Going on dates, telling our friends, everything. I want... I want to introduce you to my mom one day. We've got years ahead of us, going to the same university every day. We can take our time, actually build something." There was something that looked oddly like longing in Matías's eyes. "I'm not fooling around in secret. I've struggled too much to get to this point to go back to that."

Nicholas stared at him, stunned into silence.

Matías shook his head, standing up. "If you can't see that this is worth it, then maybe you're right—we don't make sense." It was clear he didn't know what to do, standing in the middle of Nicholas's room. "I want to do this right or not at all."

Nicholas didn't know how to believe that—he could see the truth etched onto Matías's features, but something deep inside him screamed that surely this was a trap.

"I don't know what to say to that," he admitted in a small voice, the honesty of it cutting through his heart.

Matías walked to the door, his jaw tight. He paused as he grabbed the doorknob, glancing back at him. "Let me know when you figure it out."

His voice was devoid of anger, but Nicholas knew it was final. Even he had thought it would take him longer than a few minutes to ruin everything.

The door clicked shut behind him, leaving Nicholas alone in the silence, his chest aching.

From: Jasmine Miller-Reed
To: Nicholas Fisher
Subject: ENGL 22454
November 30, 4:15 PM

Dear Nicholas,

While I was hoping to tell you this in person, I did want you to hear it from me rather than Student Employment. I was really impressed by your application for the teaching assistant position, particularly the essay portion. After Brianna's convincing words on the pedagogy and dedication you showed her, I have decided to ask you to join me next semester.

I hope this will be an opportunity for you to expand your horizons, especially as you start thinking about what you want to do after you earn your doctorate.

I haven't attached any material to this email; enjoy your break, and let's schedule a meeting next week.

Best,

Jasmine Miller-Reed

CHAPTER 21

NICHOLAS DIDN'T ASK if anyone wanted to come to the cemetery with him.

He'd stopped asking at around twelve years old. By then, he was able to get through the hour-long walk there by himself, and he didn't have to hear the poorly rehearsed, stuttering excuses his family always found not to drive him.

He had only seen William there once, when they were both in high school, but he'd turned back around before his brother had noticed Nicholas's presence or could offer to drive him back home. It took the younger man years to admit that maybe his brother wasn't as heartless as he acted—maybe he just liked to deal with his grief on his own.

He'd never seen his parents there.

The fifteen-minute drive was oddly unfamiliar because he'd grown so used to walking the route, and he almost would have regretted not doing so if it wasn't thirty-five degrees outside. Everything was grey and wet and definitely not walk-friendly, and he reminded himself with a low chuckle that his teenage self would have actually reveled in these kinds of dramatics.

There were fresh flowers next to Emma's headstone. He wondered if they were from William, but he doubted it; people often left flowers on five-year-olds' graves, whether they knew them or not.

The grass was wetter than he had expected, the frost not having had time to harden it yet; still, he sat down, letting out a grimace as he sunk into the muddy ground. At least Thanksgiving was over; those were the only half-passable jeans he'd brought.

Soon enough he ran out of rambling observations, and all he had left to ponder was where he was sitting. He rarely talked out loud when he was here, had never found a word that didn't make him wince with guilt.

Emma had been five when they'd gotten into the accident that killed her. His father had just picked him up from soccer practice, back when he let himself enjoy the sport. For some reason, Emma had insisted on coming along. She had no reason to; it was a short drive, uneventful. His parents rarely ever needed to even get out of the car before Nicholas made a beeline for the backseat, asking about snacks. But it was Saturday, and she was bored, home alone with her parents while the boys were at practice. Will had just turned twelve, which meant he was allowed to stay behind and hang out with his friends for a few more hours. He was at that age where he'd started to be too busy for his little siblings, especially on the weekend, but Nicholas tried not to mind. He and Emma were just fine on their own, anyway.

So their father had let her come, probably out of laziness—laziness to engage with her or bother convincing her to stay behind. Nicholas had rolled his eyes when he'd walked up to the car and noticed Emma's toothless grin through the dirty window.

Everything had happened so fast after that.

One moment they were laughing, Emma bouncing in the backseat as she sang one of her made-up songs to annoy her brother, her small voice high and careless. Untouchable.

Then—the screech of tires. It was that sound that still haunted him—the sharp, shattering silence just before the brakes screamed. And then, the impact. A car slamming into theirs from the right side. Emma's side.

When Nicholas woke up, he was lying in the grass, the smell of gasoline thick in the air. His body ached, but it was nothing compared to the panic gripping him when he realized he couldn't hear what the faces hovering above him were trying to say. His ears were ringing, covering every sound. All he could see were their mouths moving and the flashing lights of emergency vehicles.

He couldn't see his dad or sister, something on his neck making it impossible to turn his head. He asked about Emma, screaming her name repeatedly until he saw someone nod. She was there. She was somewhere.

The ambulance ride was a blur. He tried pushing away the oxygen mask to tell them they needed to take care of Emma. His little sister, Emma, she was in the car too, he kept trying to say. Had anyone seen her?

Everything that happened between that moment and when he woke up in the hospital almost twelve hours later was recounted to him by nurses. Everything but the most important thing. It took hours before someone finally answered the one question he couldn't stop asking. In the end, it was the doctor who told him, because his mother couldn't stop sobbing.

Yes, they'd found Emma right away. She had still been in the car when they'd arrived. Yes, they'd taken her to the hospital. No, she hadn't made it.

It had been the internal injuries that had gotten her, not the impact. Her little body had been too fragile to survive the trauma. Nicholas made them tell him what happened exactly, and then he made them tell him again. But no answers could take away the weight pressing down on his chest. He kept thinking his sister would just walk through the door of his hospital room, teddy in hand, asking what he thought of her prank.

If only it had been his side of the car. If only they'd stopped for ice cream. If only his father hadn't let her come.

Nicholas had known he looked bad because his mother could barely look at him whenever she came to his room. When they moved Nicholas to another floor, Will was allowed to come too, and already, he was changed. Nicholas watched his brother listen to the doctors, bring their mom food, and go back and forth between Nicholas's and their dad's rooms. Nicholas let his brother take care of their family, pretending not to see his shaking hands, his paler-than-normal face.

Already, Will was trying to save them all, but Nicholas didn't want to be saved. He stopped talking, disappearing under the weight of losing something he could never get back.

By the time the Fishers made it home, four days after practice, it was without Emma. And without their parents too. Their mom, their dad, they were both gone.

William and Nicholas would never get their parents back.

So, yes, maybe Nicholas had changed, then. He'd become mean and caustic and had slowly isolated himself until there was no one left around him. He'd stopped playing soccer and going to friends' houses and started hating the world when it kept turning.

His brother kept living, though, and Will was right when he said that Nicholas had never forgiven him for that.

There was a small voice, shy and new, whispering in his ear that if William had stopped living too, then it would have killed them all: their mom who wasn't getting out of bed anymore, their dad who only did to drink, and Nicholas who refused to leave the house so no one would have to pick him up later.

William kept getting up in the morning, always feeding him waffles or donuts or muffins, coaxing their mom into opening the curtains and closing the living room door when their father was growing belligerent from the drink. Somehow, to a young and grief-stricken Nicholas, this had provided irrefutable proof that his brother was heartless and didn't care about his family.

He'd spent years fighting against thoughts of the contrary. He hated being wrong after all—there was also the tugging, painful realization that if he had been mistaken, he would never be able to make up for the years he'd thought of William as evil and treated him as such, leaving him to grieve on his own and refusing to see him as the child he also was.

It felt futile to keep fighting now, but admitting that he'd done wrong by both his siblings was a kind of agony he knew he couldn't face on his own.

And still, despite everything, William was telling him he deserved the good things he'd refused himself for years.

So what? Nicholas was just supposed to forgive himself for everything and be happy instead?

He was tearing off blades of grass around him, trying to speak. He felt silly talking to the stone, yet today he couldn't help but hope for an answer.

"How will you know?" he started. "How will you know I still think about you every day if every time you look down, I'm just… happy?" His voice broke.

This wasn't working. He would never be able to be sure—that his little sister wanted him to be happy, that she didn't mind, that she wasn't yelling at him from wherever she was.

"I'm sorry, I'm so sorry," he said through a gasp.

He got lost in a litany of senseless apologies, until his voice was hoarse and the light started dimming.

Did he deserve to keep on living while she couldn't? Maybe not.

But for the first time, he wanted to anyway.

❦

When he got home, Nicholas found his father on the porch, reading the paper. This wasn't an unusual sight so he ignored him, let his presence wash over him without looking up. He was almost at the door when the man spoke.

"Nicholas." He wondered when the last time was that he'd heard his dad say his name. He was the only person in his family who didn't call him Nick, and it annoyed him how much he preferred it.

When Nicholas looked over, his father hadn't moved, ever the stoic presence he'd grown up navigating around.

"Come sit with me for a minute."

For long seconds, Nicholas didn't move. Not because he didn't want to, but it was as if he'd forgotten how. No one, as far as he remembered, had ever sat next to his dad on the porch. What for? There was no conversation to be had that wouldn't result in a fight, none of the warmth they'd ever needed to be found by John Fisher's side. Yet, when Nicholas finally came closer, he noticed on the second rocking chair a cushion that he was sure hadn't been there before, clearly embroidered by his mother's hand. The chairs were angled toward each other, mirroring those of every other happy couple on their street.

He suddenly realized that their parents had kept living in his absence, just like they had after Emma had died and after William had left for college.

Nicholas sat down silently, looking out onto the quiet street. It was almost fully dark by now, and the suburban landscape was sleepier than he remembered it, which made sense considering the neighborhood's heart used to beat at the rhythm of its children's squeals. Almost everyone had grown up and left since then.

"I talked to your brother. He said school was going well."

"It is."

"Have you decided what you'll write your thesis on?"

Nicholas would have considered answering honestly, if it had been anyone else asking. "It's coming together."

"Good."

"Where is this coming from?" They both knew Nicholas was talking about his father's sudden desire to know anything about his son's life. His tone wasn't kind, but he was sure it was nothing John didn't deserve.

The man took a deep breath, and for a millisecond, he looked so human that Nicholas had to look away. "Your mother. She left me, for a while."

Nicholas looked at him in confusion. His father had never been a sharer, never been the kind of man who would tell his sons about this sort of embarrassment. Nicholas wondered how serious it had to be for this conversation to even happen. Had his parents been pretending for his sake all weekend? Were they going to sell the house? Even if it had just been two days, his mom and dad had seemed as well-oiled a team they always had. But he didn't know how to ask for more, so he waited.

"We're working it out now, I think."

After a long silence, even Nicholas, who was usually immune to the awkwardness of his family attempting to communicate, had to say something. "All right… Well, that's a good thing, isn't it?"

"It is. She… expects me to do better. By you boys, especially."

Nicholas almost wondered if an apology was coming. It wasn't. "She's doing well, then?"

"Yes. She's been… going out a lot. She has this talking group, and she made some friends there. She's doing her crafts too."

Nicholas was growing restless. So his mother had tried to leave his father, and then she'd come back on the condition that her husband start being a father again. That was great for them, but he needed to go home.

"You boys used to tell me everything about school. You used to come home and start screaming faster than I could understand. There wasn't a thing I didn't know about what you were up to or what you wanted to do next."

"I don't remember," Nicholas said.

It was only a half-lie; he didn't remember as much as William did, as much as everyone else did, but there were remnants. Remnants of a time when his parents were in love and proud of the family they'd built, when every one of their sons' differences was a thing to be celebrated. There was a time when everything was perfect, and everyone knew it had started with how much John and Lisa Fisher loved each other.

Even after the accident, when his father had grown silent and started drinking, when his mother wouldn't get out of bed, it hadn't surprised him that they had never even spoken of separating, that they had never turned their anger toward each other.

"What's the talking group Mom is in?"

"A grieving group, up in the city."

"Have you been?"

"No." There was a long silence. "I go to the drinking one."

Nicholas didn't know what to make of this entire conversation. His father had never so much as talked about his drinking, and they were both too old for hope. Every instinct inside him told him to tell his father just that.

He thought of William instead.

"I just got a job offer today. Well, it's not a job, strictly speaking. For next semester, TA-ing a class. I haven't told anyone yet, so don't say anything. Will's been hounding me about the answer. So I'll be pretty busy next semester, because it's on top of all the other classes I already have to take." He was rambling. When he looked up, his father was staring straight at him, listening aptly like he was trying to memorize every inch of Nicholas's plans. "Usually, these positions really aren't open to second years. It'll basically be a guarantee that I can teach for every year after that if I already have experience. And it's an interesting class, not exactly what I study, but not too far off either. It'll be good to have different perspectives. Maybe."

"That's excellent news, Nicholas." His tone wasn't excited or hopeful. It was grave, and when Nicholas turned his head, he found his father's eyes looking straight at him. Like he was trying to impress the weight of his words into his son's skin. "So teaching is something you're interested in?"

Nicholas shrugged. He was glad that no one had asked him this question lately, because now a lump rose in his throat, and he had to shake his head to force the words to come out.

"This isn't really teaching," he said, his voice quiet and brittle. "It's mostly paperwork. They'll still have a real teacher."

He couldn't meet his father's gaze, not when the memories pressed so close, the weight of them making it hard to breathe.

Because what if he couldn't take care of them? What if he couldn't protect his students, the way he hadn't been able to protect Emma? What if his father agreed? The thought coiled deep in his chest, the same gnawing fear that had driven him to Green's office half a year ago.

But beneath the fear, there was something else now, something fragile but insistent, trying to push through the fog of his certainty. He thought of the preschoolers at the library and their hesitant questions, of the spark of curiosity in Brianna's eyes when she asked about his own research. It had stirred something in him, a longing he hadn't dared to acknowledge before.

"Well, it's a start anyway," was all his father said.

༚

The drive back to Chicago was a lot livelier than he'd expected, after the muted afternoons of the past few days. Will drove, and Matías seemed to be on a mission to play the most obnoxious singalong songs he could find on the radio. Nicholas was sitting in the back with his headphones in, although it was hard to fight off a smile every time he could hear the boys' screams over the sound of his own music. When they weren't singing, they talked in circles about things they had discussed a million times before, and it was only sheer curiosity at how two adults could so instantly turn into teenagers in each other's presence that made Nicholas stop pretending he wasn't listening.

Even the slippery streets and the heavy traffic as they got into the city didn't alter their high spirits, and Nicholas felt something embarrassingly close to disappointment when they stopped on a narrow street corner and Matías announced that was where he got off.

Although he was trying his hardest to pretend nothing had changed, it was clear that Matías was guarded around him, tiptoeing the line between ignoring his presence and treating him as a friend rather unsuccessfully. The awkward edge to his movements whenever

Nicholas was involved was new, and so was the vague mumbling about seeing each other soon that served as goodbye.

Nicholas sighed heavily—one more thing he'd have to apologize for. But there was another conversation he needed to have first, so he let Matías go, heading home with his brother to put on an episode of *Golden Girls*.

"Did you talk to Dad?" Nicholas blurted out halfway through a laughing track, making it clear he hadn't been listening.

"Yeah. So weird," Will answered right away. He hadn't been paying attention either.

"Did he tell you about the group?" Nicholas asked warily.

"Mom did. She said they went to couple's therapy too. Sounds like it helped."

"Yeah. Never thought I'd see that."

Nicholas took a deep breath. He'd spent all night rehearsing what he wanted to say next. About how he was tired of being miserable and feeling guilty all the time. About how much he missed Emma. And football. But nothing came, and he exhaled in the silence.

Will spoke instead. "I was thinking I might try it too."

"Well, you need to get a girlfriend first to go to couple's therapy," Nicholas said, sounding every bit the little brother he was.

"Do I? Because I already have someone at home nagging me and leaving their shit everywhere," Will said. When Nicholas looked up in outrage, he was smiling.

"Fine." Nicholas grabbed the remote from where Will had put it down on the coffee table. He stayed silent for a long time, wondering if his brother had meant what he thought. "We can go after my paper is due. Together. If you want. But your insurance is paying."

"Fine," was all William said. "I think it'll be great."

Even with Nicholas's eyes screwed onto the TV in front of him, he could *feel* William's smile in the air around him. When the thought came that Emma would have been proud of them, it didn't hurt as much as Nicholas was used to.

"Whatever."

☙

Despite the life-altering decisions he was in the process of making regarding his healing and happiness, Nicholas still had to go to class and pretend like the future of his degree wasn't up for sabotage. On the first Monday back to school, he left home an hour earlier than he needed to, trudging through the snow and the crowds that still hadn't learned how to walk in a manner befitting a busy urban center. While he loved the poetic undertones of a white Christmas, his commute went from unpleasant to life-threatening, and he caught himself wondering if maybe it was time to look into what train lines stopped near the apartment.

Both the bus and campus were back to their pre-Thanksgiving effervescence. His friends asked that they get together as soon as possible, Sloane bursting with stories from New York while Ajay had clearly been bored out of their mind without either of them in the city. It was almost like no one else's world had imploded and rearranged itself over the holidays.

Thankfully, he was too distracted to dwell on the past few days much longer. There were other essays and other classes and December to get through, Miller-Reed's syllabus to work on, and his friends' questions about Matías to evade; there was also every evening with William, who was clearly making an effort to be home. Nicholas even found the time to email the health center on campus asking about the free therapy waiting list.

The tune of yet another, colder week came to a scratching halt the next Monday.

It started with a scathing look thrown his way across the classroom.

Nicholas had been prepared for it; he knew Michaelson was handing out their grades today. He'd braced himself for mockery and ridicule, perhaps even the mean kind of satisfaction he'd come to find out was one of the Kieran's specialties.

But when he looked up, Kieran just looked angry.

Somehow, the first thing in Nicholas's mind as his professor bid them to sit and quiet down was his older brother. More than whether or not he had passed, he wondered what he would tell William when he got home. Would he walk in with good news, see the quick flash of pride he'd caught both times Nicholas had been accepted into his first-choice schools? Would William be angry when he shook his head in defeat or just disappointed? His brother hadn't mentioned anything about the class since they'd come back home, but Nicholas knew Will was waiting for the grade just as much as he was.

Of course, because he was neither stupid nor optimistic, Michaelson made them sit through an entire class on a particularly boring piece of translation theory without mentioning the essays once, even though the haphazard pile of papers on the corner of his desk seemed to exert some sort of magnetic pull on everyone's eyes and minds. Kieran didn't speak for the whole class, and after about forty minutes, Nicholas stopped trying to decipher the back of his head for answers.

Finally, it was time for lunch, but not before almost thirty adults proceeded to run to the pile of essays. Everyone immediately proceeded to ignore the constructive comments on their hours of labor, instead hoping to catch a glimpse of the scribbled percentage and take it as an effective assessment of their worth. When it was Nicholas's turn to be handed his paper, Michaelson caught his eye.

"Come see me during office hours tomorrow," Michaelson said to him curtly, his tone hinting at nothing of his intentions.

Nicholas knew then.

One quick glance, his eyes moving fast enough that he hoped the glaze of wet wouldn't have time to settle, enough to confirm—but he couldn't find a grade anywhere, not at the top like every other paper, not at the end either. All he could see was red, so much red, crossed out words and circled ones, lengthy notes in the margins and what had perhaps been a percentage before it had been repeatedly scrawled over.

He was already in the corridor, almost running to the freezing exterior, hoping it could ease the sweaty panic threatening to overtake him, when he bothered reading the Post-It note that seemed to have been slapped at random on the last page.

Insightful and layered work—let's discuss your grade together. Good job!
                                        - Dr. M.

❧

There was something wildly dispossessing about Nicholas's inability to stop smiling, to keep himself from letting hope engulf him as he walked across campus. His eyes quickly scanned the rest of his paper: disparaging comments, entire arguments crossed out in Kieran's hand, and the resounding absence of a grade.

His phone was already in his hand, the force he was holding it with threatening to crack the screen. His thumb hovered over it, barely resisting the euphoric impulse to press a familiar name and share the news with whoever answered first. But no matter what he told himself, there was only one person he wanted to talk to right now; and it wasn't the one who cared the most about him getting an education, or either of the friends who had been ready to storm the university for him to get the grade he deserved.

No, it was Matías.

So, Nicholas did something stupid. Something very unlike him, with a decisiveness that was all Emma's.

He hadn't talked to Matías in the week they'd been back in town, finding excuse after excuse to delay the inevitable. But this felt like too big a sign that maybe things didn't have to be so hard. Nicholas was long past pretending he didn't know Matías's schedule inside and out, so he headed to one of the law buildings before he could change his mind.

Instead of turning around when he realized he'd have to loiter outside until Matías came out, Nicholas found a bench to sit on from which he could see the building's main entrance and sat down to give the comments on his paper a proper look. Maybe there was useful feedback among the bitterness and resentment. He didn't know what had made Michaelson decide to double check the work, but it was clear now: his paper was a battleground, and Nicholas had won.

As was to be expected, soon enough Matías came out in a sea of laughter and attention. He stood in the middle of a line of people, long enough that it couldn't possibly be comfortable to walk the corridors—but what would Matías know about that? He'd always stood at the center.

Nicholas had barely gotten up from the bench he'd been sitting on when Matías met his eye. Unlike every other time they'd caught a glimpse of each other on campus, Nicholas didn't look away or pretend like he'd missed him. When Matías realized this, staring at a Nicholas who was staring back, he looked almost comically shocked, his mouth left hanging, to the confusion and annoyance of his audience.

Nicholas thought he could handle all the snow in the world if he had the warmth that bloomed in his chest as Matías instantly waved goodbye to his assembly and started half-jogging toward him. He looked ridiculous, suspiciously underdressed as he was, and Nicholas forgot not to grin.

"Hey, there," Matías said when he caught up to him, uncharacteristically awkward.

Nicholas, aware that he was still smiling, didn't know what to do, so he just raised the hand still holding his paper and waved it around like it would mean anything.

It seemed like it did, because Matías's eyes grew round with a hesitant excitement.

"Is this what I think it is?" he asked tentatively, extending his hand for Nicholas to hand him the paper.

The younger man did with a proud hum and hurried to point out the Post-It, hoping to distract Matías from all the admittingly worrying red markings. The yellow square was already threatening to slip away from the page, the corners rolling up from all the times Nicholas had swiped an unbelieving thumb over it. But the words were still clear: *Good job. Insightful. Layered.* When Matías finally looked up, he was grinning too.

"I suppose the teacher took a look at it himself, then?"

"Seems that way."

"I knew it."

Still riding the high of his own success without immediately assuming the worst was just around the corner, Nicholas didn't want to ask what it was that Matías apparently knew. Instead, he jumped into his open arms. Matías wrapped his arms around Nicholas, pulling him close with a tenderness that quieted Nicholas's restlessness. With a shift, he pressed himself deeper into Matías's embrace, burying his face in the crook of the other man's neck. His skin was soft, and its warmth seeped into Nicholas's chilled body, anchoring him.

"I'm so proud of you," Matías murmured against Nicholas's temple.

Nicholas stayed still, savoring the words, his eyes shut as he took them in. The world outside the circle of their arms seemed to blur, shrinking into insignificance. For the first time in weeks, months, maybe years, the chaos usually swirling in his mind quieted. Nicholas didn't want to move, but in the quietness of the moment, he realized he owed it to Matías to feel as at peace as he did himself.

"I wanted to tell you first," he said, barely audible against Matías's skin. "I thought maybe that was part of 'the whole thing.'"

Then he felt it—a low chuckle from Matías, shaking them both until they had to disentangle their limbs. He knew the words weren't enough—he needed to explain, and apologize, and maybe make sense of it himself. But when he caught sight of the hopeful mirth in Matías's dark eyes, all he could do was tilt his head and kiss him.

It began softly, tentatively, a meeting of cold lips sending a shiver through Nicholas that had nothing to do with the winter air. Time seemed to stretch, the world quieting as if it, too, was holding its breath. The contrast of warm breath and cold skin was a new kind of divinity Nicholas was sure he hadn't come across yet in all his years of studying religious texts.

An enthusiastic whistle came from the group Matías had left behind, but it may as well had come from another world. Matías's attention was wholly on Nicholas, with a kind of focus that could only be called scientific.

Matías's hands came up, cupping Nicholas's face, the crumpled essay forgotten somewhere between their bodies. Matías pulled back just enough to kiss Nicholas's eyelids, soft and deliberate, then the ridge of his cheekbone, his temple, and finally his forehead, each touch as gentle as a brushstroke.

Nicholas stood still. For the first time in a long while, he allowed himself to believe that perhaps, just perhaps, he was deserving of it.

"Walk me to my next class?" Matías finally asked. He didn't seem self-conscious, didn't look like he'd just snapped back to reality after forgetting himself for a few minutes. No, disarmingly, he just looked like he wanted Nicholas to walk him to class.

Nicholas, of course, was probably red-faced and too embarrassed to be capable of saying another word, ever. But as they started walking side by side, Matías wrapped an arm around his shoulders and waved his friends goodbye in one single move, a simple smile on his tired—Nicholas realized then—face. Then, he did something with his shoulders, stood straighter, looking around like he was proud of walking with his ridiculous arm around Nicholas's neck.

"I knew he'd read it. No way this guy has had you in class for three months and doesn't know you'd smash that essay. We need to celebrate. Do you have plans tonight? You'll need to tell Will."

And just like that, Nicholas had too many questions to have time to feel self-conscious. "I'll tell him when I get home."

"Good, good. Tell him today. So he can call off the army he's probably gathered to kill that guy."

"I don't know the grade yet. Maybe Michaelson is planning on keeping Kieran's grade, whatever it was, but he just wants to see me to, like, make sure I don't jump from a roof or something."

Matías hummed. "We keep the army until the meeting, then."

They got to his next class early, and Matías decided to stay with him in the hallway until he had to go inside. He was leaning against the wall, looking much too content for someone who still hadn't gotten a proper apology. "Can I read it?"

Nicholas looked up in confusion.

"The paper that was so good it beat academic sabotage. Can I read it?"

The thought of Matías trying to decipher seventeen pages of self-important theorizing on conceptual relativism in translation made him laugh, and he told him just that.

"Whatever, I don't care. I'll read it with a dictionary next to me. I want to read it."

Nicholas shrugged. "Okay."

He would have shouted an enthusiastic yes if he'd known about the preening look it would get him.

But he was still wary of taking more than he was allowed. Matías deserved a proper conversation, not just this stolen moment.

"What are you thinking about?" Matías asked, cutting the thought short.

"I'm starting therapy soon," Nicholas answered, not knowing where else to begin. When he looked up, Matías's grin was morphing into confusion. Nicholas scrunched up his face trying to figure out what he was trying to say.

"Okay," the Texan continued, careful. "That's great."

Nicholas knew the kind thing to do was to wait. To take whatever time he needed to get his life together and become the man that Matías saw.

But I don't want to wait, he kept thinking.

Catching the blink of joy on Matías's face, he realized he'd said that out loud.

"I'm sorry about what happened in Milwaukee," he clarified, his voice wavering. "All the stuff you said... it wasn't true. Of course you're worth it," Nicholas said through a disbelieving laugh. "You're so worth it that I didn't even consider that's what you'd think. It's me, I'm—"

Matías opened his mouth, about to retort, but Nicholas shook his head. "No, really. This is real for me. It's so real that I wanted to do it right, but now... Maybe I'm being selfish, but I want to try now, right or not."

In his rush to get the words out, Nicholas had looked down, and it was Matías's fingers on his chin that forced him to look up. "It feels pretty right from where I'm standing," was all he said.

"Would you like to come for dinner tonight? We can tell Will. About the essay. And... the rest."

Matías was nodding before Nicholas had finished speaking.

"I don't want you to get your hopes up," he had to add. "I'm still going to be me."

"It's you I want, so I'm not worried."

Nicholas's stomach tightened. This was going to be torture, wasn't it?

When Nicholas couldn't muster the same lightness, Matías grew serious again. "Look, I know this isn't going to be easy. I *have* been around for years, in case you've forgotten. I know you, Nicholas, and I'm not expecting you to change. I wouldn't want you to change. I just want you to be all in before I risk my own heart."

Nicholas's breath stopped. Already, every bone in his body wanted to chuck the afternoon study plans out the window, ask Matías to do the same, and keep him close. Already, working on himself and his life and his relationship with his brother seemed like it really didn't matter, like everything was fine as it was as long as he had Matías.

"I do want some things to change, though. I don't want to be a walking time-bomb anymore. And it's probably going to take a while," Nicholas said instead.

Matías was about to answer when a group of guys turned the corner, heading toward them loudly. They had the self-important look of most first-year law students, but Nicholas didn't even comment. Matías's crinkled eyes made it clear he knew how much he wanted to.

"See? Easy. You're already making progress." Nicholas rolled his eyes, but he was interrupted by Matías draping a hand over his cheek. Unprompted, he leaned in and kissed Nicholas gently, a brief taste of what was to come. "I have to go. See you tonight?"

All Nicholas could do was nod, afraid if he made too much noise, someone would realize he wasn't supposed to be happy like this.

Nicholas took the fastest way home that afternoon, rode the train, boring and sleek and entirely soulless, all the way to the end of the line with a stupid smile on his face and the memory of warm skin still thrumming under his fingers.

℃

ACKNOWLEDGMENTS

When I first began writing *To the End of the Line*, I had no idea that so many people would become essential to shaping it into the story it is today. What I initially thought would be a solitary journey turned out to be one of connection, support, and gratitude.

My deepest thanks go to Jamie Ryu, my exceptional editor and the first person to believe in this story. Her thoughtful insights and genuine love for these characters have been instrumental in bringing this book to life. I am equally grateful to the team at Contrarian Publishing for their steadfast support of independent authors.

To the writing community I discovered along the way—thank you. To Cielo and Lacy, for reading early drafts with a kindness I won't forget, and to Amarie Wheeler, for being my very first author friend.

Much of this book was written in libraries across the world, and I owe an extraordinary debt to the public libraries of France, England, Hungary, Croatia, Spain, Mexico, El Salvador, and beyond. These spaces remain vital sanctuaries for those of us always searching for a sense of home.

To my brilliant and inspiring girlfriends—Charlotte, Laura, and Judith—thank you for your unwavering support, no matter where in the world I am. To every friend who forgave me for taking months to share I was writing a book and embraced it immediately—your support meant more than I can express. To Camille, thank you for turning our house into a home and making sure I went outside when things got hard.

Finally, to my little sister and baby brother—making you proud is the reason I do anything.

ABOUT THE AUTHOR

SAGE GREER has always been passionate about languages and the power of stories to bridge cultures. Born and raised in France, she holds a BA in Political Science and an MA in Sociology. She became a translator in the hopes of sharing diverse voices with French readers.

When she isn't traveling the world for inspiration, Sage writes stories that explore queerness, mental health, and the search for self in adulthood. *To The End of the Line* is her first novel.

Visit her online at sagegreer.com